Stickleback

Stickleback

John McCabe

Granta Books
London

Granta Publications, 2/3 Hanover Yard, London N1 8BE

First published in Great Britain by Granta Books 1998

A CIP catalogue record for this book is available from
the British Library

3 5 7 9 10 8 6 4 2

Typeset in Imprint by M Rules
Printed and bound in Great Britain by
Mackays of Chatham PLC

Routines

As with the stereotypical courtship behaviour of the stickle-back, human life can inevitably be reduced to a number of discrete actions which fulfil an overall aim. The overall aim may vary, as may the nature of the constituent actions, but generally each action serves to relieve the brain of the conscious effort of thought. We *can* think, evidently, but prefer not to, relying instead upon the safety net of involuntary patterns of behaviour. Stereotypical behaviours comprise a number of constituent actions, all of which can be performed without troubling the idling brain. Collectively, a number of such actions is termed a routine and, ultimately, many routines make an overall aim. The aim may be cloudy, at best, but without it none of the actions of any of the routines would make any sense. And routines must always make sense, even if the only sense is to hamper constructive thought.

Ian Gillick, for instance, had a breakfast routine. In fact, he had a number of routines, which could be divided into two categories: A, without girlfriend and B, with girlfriend. Routines of categories A and B encompassed two distinct and opposing aims. Routines of category A satisfied the general aim of sloth. They were, chronologically: Get up. Have breakfast. Go to work. Work. Come home, picking up a take-away *en route*. Watch television whilst eating take-away. Have a wank and then go to bed, or reverse order to suit. Repeat for five days. Omit work at weekends.

Routines of category B satisfied, superficially at least, the aim of persuading a potential or current girlfriend that he wasn't a category A man. Category B routines were as of A but appended with non-essentials such as showering, shaving, washing clothes, actually buying and cooking food, reading larger newspapers, visiting the cinema, theatre, opera, ballet and any other venue of performance torture, buying underwear, reading novels, eating out at the places he bought take-aways from, re-tuning the radio from One or Five to Four, ironing, discussing issues, giving to charity, shopping for presents, returning presents, tidying up and drying dishes. Subtractions from A mainly totalled wanking. Well, obvious signs of.

For Ian, routines were ingrained but not intransigent. New routines could always be found to replace old ones which, for one reason or another, became inappropriate and had to be abandoned. The most frequent reason for their impropriety was his girlfriend, now ex-girlfriend, who had suffered his routines with sighs that punctuated each constituent action of each routine. For the sake of camouflage, Ian occasionally switched routines, in order to appear more spontaneous. Even on holiday though, where old faithful routines such as breakfast could not be strictly adhered to, a new one would immediately take its place and the spontaneity would soon be lost. Moreover, routines of category B, drafted in to camouflage category A leanings, were by definition repetitive actions, and as such had the power to irritate. In Ian's experience, nothing irritated a woman more than habit, no matter how well-intentioned. But for Ian, routines avoided the need to think. Routines were cruise control journeys through mundanity.

When they were still together, they saw a film. The man in the film had constructed a series of routines through and around his life, which had become a well-oiled, stripped-down, dependable machine. He had things sorted. Everything was under control. To the woman the machine was an alien contrivance that dulled her senses and had to be destroyed. For the man, love meant sacrificing his routine existence for a life of spontaneity. Ian was appalled. It was one of a plethora of films where a man who has pared his life down to the bare essentials is changed for the better by falling in love with a woman who muddies his waters with trivialities. In real life and in terms of mediation, relationship counsellors maintain that the irritation provoked by habit and routine is just a barometer of deeper unfulfilment. But for Ian and Sue, routines were the cause and not the symptom of their unhappiness. Everything else was fine. Ian resented change and to some degree was afraid of it, and Sue resented his resentment. So Ian occasionally switched routines. But not at breakfast time.

Breakfast comprised one bowl of cornflakes and muesli, three slices of brown toast, each with margarine and marmalade, one cup of supermarket tea and one glass of orange juice. It wasn't so much the contents of the breakfast that were important but the order in which they were consumed. The cereal with semi-skimmed milk was first, accompanied by three quarters of a glass of orange juice. Then came the toast, and it was the toast that had driven her mad as she stood in the kitchen slowly drinking her coffee, silently daring him to enact his routine one more time. Ian filled the kettle to the one cup level and placed two slices of brown bread in the toaster. He selected a mug from the mug tree, put it next to the kettle and walked into the adjoining bathroom. One more time. Just one more time. That's all it's going to take. One more and I'm leaving you. In the bathroom, Ian washed his face and combed his hair and emerged with just enough time to remove the margarine and marmalade from the fridge and select a knife and a plate before the toast popped. He buttered and marmaladed pieces one and two of toast and slotted piece of bread three into the toaster. Sue continued to watch him as he stood in the kitchen consuming piece one. As he finished, piece three popped from the toaster and was then similarly buttered and marmaladed. After and partly during this, a tea bag, a splash of milk and some boiling water were thrown into a mug, and the tea bag fished out almost instantly. Conscious for the first time of the scrutiny he was receiving, Ian retreated to the living room with what remained of his breakfast and watched the news in the company of pieces two and three and his mug of tea. Down the hallway came the sound of a door gently closing.

Ian was more than aware of the effect his breakfast routine was having on her. In common with most men who cohabit, he understood sigh language. But breakfast was, nevertheless, the most important routine of the day, and to lose this would be to threaten the very fabric of his life.

Some weeks earlier, Ian sat opposite Mark in a greasy spoon and had consulted him on the matter. He described his girlfriend's symptoms and explained the mechanics of his breakfast routine in minute detail. Mark, whose advice Ian often sought on relationship matters, had a suggestion.

'Right. I think I've got a solution.'

Ian looked at him expectantly, over his bacon and eggs. 'Yeah?'

'Yeah.' Mark took a swig of tea, carefully keeping his top lip clear of the rim of a mug that had doubtless served several previous and less hygienic customers that day already.

'Go on, then.'

'Right. What you ought to do is put piece one in first, have your wash, and then put two and three in together – otherwise you'll always be eating cold toast.'

'Right,' Ian muttered, with half-expected resignation. He resumed his struggle to injure a particularly stubborn length of bacon rind with his teeth.

Although it wasn't quite the advice he was looking for, it was an improvement of sorts nonetheless. He tried it, occasionally switching back and forth between the two protocols when he felt the need to appear spontaneous, and initially it was a success, if only in terms of toast temperature. After a while though, he realized he had reverted entirely to his former, inferior technique. The established routine had consumed the new one, and that, for Ian, was the danger of routines – the cruise control was so permanently on that the accelerator would cease to function. Because of this she left him one day. Routines of category Λ switched automatically back into gear and Ian's life continued, undeterred.

Anoraks Now Rule The World

Archie was a wanker, as far as Ian could see which, characteristically, wasn't very far. Ian was more than capable of hating people he didn't know or had never met. He would take a deep loathing to someone's haircut and be unable to dissociate the person from the object. He would hate a particular brand of car, many brands in fact, and reasoned that if he hated the car it was more than likely he would hate the person who chose to drive it. In essence, anything which could be easily put into a box and classified could be easily despised. His hatred was, however, fickle at best. Except when it came to Archie. In this instance, it was hatred based purely on personality. Archie was a plodder, a painful one step at a time trudger from routine to routine. Sure, Ian was a big fan of routines, but to him they were protectors from mundanity. Archie, however, *was* a routine, and he was rapidly becoming a focus for all the things which were wrong with Ian's stickleback existence. This morning, though, Ian had a plan.

'Pass us the dNTP manual, Archie,' he said, trying to suppress any signs of his predatory disposition.

Archie looked up from his screen and squinted through

his glasses at Ian, his nose ruffling slightly as he did so. 'Mmm?'

'The manual.' Ian gestured towards a computer manual, which was clearly on his own desk.

'Which manual?'

'That one there,' he pointed, his finger only a matter of inches from it, '*your* manual, the only manual in the room.'

Ian and Archie shared an office. This had been the situation now for about eleven months. It wasn't what either of them would have wanted. Ideally, Ian would rather have shared with The Spice Girls, but would have settled for virtually anyone else on the planet. Archie, on the other hand, would have been happy by himself, and maybe a Sun workstation or two.

Ian was a Tractor, in stark contrast to Archie who was a Permie. This marked him out to Ian, before any other criteria were applied, as an inferior. Archie was relatively, though by no means absolutely, poorly paid for the same job. He was the nine to five man, the company boy, the annually salaried permanent member of staff. He resented, as did all Permies, the contractual, temporary and, most of all, highly paid nature of Ian and the other Tractors' work. All Tractors saw Permies as inferiors. All Permies longed to be Tractors. Permies knew that this was the way that employment was heading. Short-term, insecure, lucrative, contractual. Get someone good in there, get the job done, pay them off. No pension, no private health care, no dead weight in times of economic downturn, no unions, no training courses, no yearly appraisals, no politics, no increments, no complex management infrastructure, no gold watches or carriage clocks, no maternity leave, no sick pay. Just bait the trap with gold, get the right man in, pay him as a self-employed contractor, then get him the hell out. No more job for life. Just a job until the job is done.

'Er . . . the manual's on your desk,' countered Archie.

'It's on my desk, is it?'

'That's what I said.'

'It's not a case of what you did or didn't say I'm afraid, Archie.' Ian was going to reel him in. 'It's gone well beyond that.'

'It's gone well beyond what?' Archie tried to appear uninterested, but despite himself was forced to ask, 'And what is "*it*", anyway?'

Salary and conditions aside, essentially, Ian and Archie did similar jobs. They were DBAs, database administrators, labourers in the field of computer paranoia. They worked for a corporation called Intron UK, which administered the systems, the computer programmes and the networks which helped to keep track of the daily three-hundred billion pounds which passed through the hands of tradings and investment companies in the City. Intron had recently relocated from the City to Birmingham, where by the magic of fibre optics, satellite and telephone networks, they could do everything they had done in London, but for less than half the cost. Ian and Archie administered the periodic updating and re-programming which was necessary to ensure that the trading systems themselves ran without bugs. The trick was to update the colossal programmes whilst they continued to monitor stock market movements for the investment companies and allowed the banks' traders to trade. It was like working on a car while it was still being driven. It was pure paranoia. Should the programmes crash, City traders would be unable to trade and money would be lost. Or gained. The Unthinkable had happened recently, and trading had been interrupted by a software conflict. The investment company, however, made a killing by not being able to carry out the ill-advised transactions it had planned. But most of the contractors had still been sacked, just for good measure. So Ian and Archie dealt largely with the paranoia of the world's investments.

'*It* is a question of boundaries,' Ian explained, 'of personal space.'

'Meaning?'

'The manual,' Ian gestured, 'is on my desk, is it not?'

'Mmm.' Archie scratched his nose and feigned interest in a couple of printouts on his desk.

The fact that someone like Archie was responsible, at least in part, for decisions with enormous economic implication, is testament to the notion that anoraks are now running the world. The hooded playground loners who brought sandwiches in for lunch are the new gods – the gods of technology. Who could have imagined that the non-communicators would be the kings of communications, that the train spotters would be the new trend spotters, that the bedroom castaways would now be the boardroom castigators? Somehow the anorak had been shed gill-like during the ascendancy from the watery bedroom on to the solid land of the city, making way for Marks and Spencer suits and Hush Puppy brogues. Hackers had turned informant and become computer security consultants, guardians against hacking. Pent-up, acned authors of viruses had become innovators of virus protection. Bedroom players of games had become office designers of games. Producers of bedroom computer music had become dance music producers. And programmers like Archie had, well, remained programmers. But it was precisely the self-imposed solitary confinement that eighties anoraks had thrived on that predisposed them to the nineties computer workplace. Companies composed entirely of loners, so much so that the word 'company' became incongruous, and gave way to Corporation. No colleagues, comrades, cohorts, compatriots or work mates, just workers. Each worker with one job or one objective to achieve and to hand on to the next worker. Each hand-over accomplished not face to face but terminal to terminal. Database administrators, programmers, systems engineers, software designers – every worker had a different title to add to the overall effect of fragmentation. There were no social events, save a forced and awkward Christmas party, at which people retreated into their partners rather than face their fellow workers in a context where they weren't being paid to do so. This was the atmosphere into which Ian and Archie had been thrust more or less randomly and indifferently, respectively.

'And where exactly does my desk end and yours start?' Check. Ian had him this time, surely.

'What do you mean?' Archie looked up from his printouts.

'Well, our desks face each other, right?'

'Yes.' Archie looked back at his terminal, then at the print-out he was holding and then back at Ian. 'Look, I'm busy. Would you mind telling me where this is heading?'

Where Ian and Archie's jobs did differ was in the actual thought required for each to fulfil his role. Archie was a programmer and Ian an inspector of programming. Ian didn't check Archie's programming, specifically, but was responsible for ensuring that the code he received from various sources would run smoothly. Rarely, if ever, did it fail to run smoothly, written as it was with the pedantry that was the oxygen of Archie's ilk. Ian's job had long since exceeded the merely routine. Routine implied some sort of action. It was more of a constancy, a still, still river on a summer's day that went nowhere and accomplished nothing. It was static, uniform, invariant, perpetual, inevitable, constant and unchanging. And Ian had adapted, chameleon-like, by becoming more static, uniform, invariant, perpetual, inevitable, constant and unchanging than was natural even for him. Thought no longer came into it. It was beyond thinking, or rather, below thinking. It was opening your eyes and letting the screen project directly on to your brain and matching the code with a pattern. If the code matched, then fine and the next screen was checked. If it didn't, which happened rarely, he would pass it on to someone like Archie to fix.

There certainly wasn't much skill involved. What it required though was fastidiousness and paranoia. If a code with bugs or conflicts or glitches passed through your hands unnoticed, systems would fail, people would get angry and you would be fired. This was the edge that cut through the mundanity, for other people at least. But Ian had long since stopped caring whether the code worked or didn't work.

Ian ignored the question. 'And therefore, since our desks face each other, it would seem reasonable to assume that the boundaries of my desk are encompassed by my desk, and that yours begin where your desk starts.'

'Technically, yes,' Archie answered, looking out of the window with indifference.

'Well, since we've sorted the boundaries of our desks out, would you mind explaining what your *stuff* is doing on *my* desk?' Ian concentrated as much contempt as he could muster, which was fairly considerable, into 'stuff'.

'My *stuff*, as you call it, Ian, isn't on your desk.'

'What?' Ian looked at the manual, which was clearly on his desk, and then back at Archie, who was quite clearly blind, and stared at him with disbelief. 'Look at it, it's on my fucking desk. Just look at it, for fuck's sake.'

Unofficial Strike Action

It was Tuesday morning, day six of Ian's Unofficial Strike Action, and he was feeling antagonistic. He had started to notice some time ago that nothing he did really seemed to make any difference at all. The company was so fragmented that no one directly depended upon his work. What he did wasn't immediately relied upon by the next worker in line to pass on to the next worker and so on. The checking he did wasn't really checked by anyone else, least of all his supervisor who had her own targets and tasks to fulfil. No one seemed to be anyone else's boss, in the old-fashioned manner at least. Some people clearly out-ranked others, but no one appeared to have ultimate jurisdiction over anybody else. Some workers bravely clung to the fear and loathing that characterized the old-fashioned hierarchical systems, and this seemed to work quite well, if only in the short term. But you need a top- or bottom-heavy corporation to support a hierarchy; this was a middle-heavy one. All in all, the company was run by cogs, none of which seemed to turn or to be turned by anything that Ian did. His cog was a small and toothless one which just seemed to freewheel.

One morning, Ian had decided to put his theory to the test. He allowed small deliberate mistakes to pass through his monitoring. Nothing happened and there were no repercussions. Encouraged, he began to engineer larger and larger errors, until he fed through obvious, glaring howlers that no one could possibly overlook. They didn't so much creep through the system unnoticed as run through shouting and waving flags. But it was no good. The next logical step was to do no work. He was going to see just how long he could go without doing anything constructive at all. The five previous days had been a breeze. He had pretended to read manuals, tapped the word 'nonsense' repeatedly into the keyboard of his computer, which wasn't switched on, made and answered imaginary calls and calculated how much money he was making per week, per day, per hour, per minute and per second for doing nothing but calculate how much money he was earning. He had hit upon a winning system – being paid to calculate how much he was being paid to calculate how much he was being paid. It was beautiful.

Archie hadn't even noticed. They shared an office, their desks faced one another, and he had failed to notice that Ian had managed not to do a single thing of any use in six days. How could he have failed to notice? Could he not see anything beyond his terminal? It began to irritate Ian, and Archie's myopia became a new focus for Ian's frustration.

'It's not on your desk,' Archie repeated.

'What do you mean it's not on my desk? Look at it for Christ's sake!' Ian decided that maybe he should just kill him and be done with it.

'It's actually on my desk.' Archie looked squarely at him. 'That it abuts your side is immaterial. It starts on my desk and to all intents and purposes that's where I've put it.'

'Look, I don't care where it starts, it finishes on my desk.'

'OK, Ian, I think we need an analogy here.'

'No we fucking don't,' Ian breathed.

Archie carried on regardless, undoing the buttons on each cuff and folding his sleeves back to reveal pale, hairy wrists. 'If I plant a tree in my garden, and its branches overhang your garden, something like a sycamore or a willow . . .'

'Get to the point.' Ian was rapidly losing patience.

'OK . . .' Archie tightened his tie for dramatic effect. Ian knew that Archie gave a lot of thought to his clothes. This would have surprised people who saw him, because, from appearance alone, they could have been forgiven for assuming that Archie was still dressed by his mother. But, underwear aside, he wasn't, and he devoted time and attention to his clothes. Not the style of his garments, that much was obvious, or their cut, quality, design or material. What fascinated Archie about his clothes was their cost. He calculated the cost of outfits on the basis of the number of outings they made. The cost of a single garment was arbitrary. What really mattered was the number of times you wore it. A cheap shirt, for example, if only worn once or twice before finding its way to the bottom of the laundry basket never to emerge again, was an expensive garment. But an expensive pair of jeans worn day in day out, until their stitching finally surrendered a couple of years later, was a cheap item of clothing. In this way, Archie's wardrobe was made up of economical clothes which defied any fashion. Having pfaffed around with his clothing as much as he could pfaff, and having paused long enough to sufficiently irritate Ian, he continued, 'Well, whose garden is the tree in?'

Ian put this down as a rhetorical question and, with clenched molars, allowed Archie to answer his own question.

'It's in mine, isn't it?'

Ian stood up. He was on the verge of violence. 'Look, I don't care where the willowy fucking sycamore's planted, if it intrudes one fucking branch into my garden, I'll chop the fucker down. All right?'

Archie looked at him, then looked back at his terminal and

started typing. After a pause he said, 'You seem to be a bit on edge today, Ian.' And, after another pause, 'Maybe you're working too hard.'

'Oh, fuck this.' Ian exhaled. He must be fucking blind. Or stupid. No, he wasn't stupid. He settled for blind – he wore glasses after all – and that was as a good a sign as he knew. He was never going to win the argument, any argument in fact, against such odds. He grabbed the book, which was easily within his reach, slammed it down on Archie's desk and left the room.

It wasn't as if he despised Archie for a reason, it went beyond rational thought. It was somewhere less tangible but somehow more fundamental. What Archie brought out in Ian was instinctive and emotional and he acted like itching powder on Ian's consciousness. But it wasn't just genuine dislike that Ian felt for Archie. There was also good old-fashioned competition. They did similar jobs in the same office for very different wages and because of this they were unable to converse without scoring points over one another. Admittedly, this was more Ian's doing than Archie's. Ian suffered from an all-consuming competitiveness, not just with others, but with himself. He would compete as a matter of course with everyone he encountered and in every sphere in which he encountered them. Things he was truly uncompetitive in, by virtue of innate inability, and which couldn't be improved by practise, became subjects of feigned indifference which he then used to proclaim his lack of competitiveness. He competed when he drove, cycled, walked, ate, drank, slept, didn't eat, didn't drink, didn't sleep; when he worked, rested, played, particularly when he played; when he talked, told jokes, laughed, read; when he did *anything*, conscious or unconscious. He had to be faster, brighter, stronger, funnier, smarter, keener, nimbler, just *better* than anyone around him. There had been a time, as a youth, when he had to be drabber, lazier, crazier, drunker, duller, idler, dafter, just *worse* than everyone around him, but that was part of the anti-life which characterises adolescence. The nature of the competition didn't matter, as long as it was competition, and life, as Ian saw it, was nothing more and nothing less than just that. If there was no one else around to compete with, he would compete with himself, and usually win. Other people were merely a facility which enabled him to compete with the all-consuming boredom which tormented his consciousness.

Popularity

On his way down the interminable corridor of the low and objectionable building in which they worked, Ian had a mild panic attack as he stood in the queue for the coffee machine. He remembered a television documentary about interactions between people who live in cities. City dwellers, apparently, know two hundred people each. OK, don't panic. Two hundred. *Each.* He started to panic. Two hundred. He began to make a mental and finger list of everyone he knew. Mark, Clair, Martin, Rebecca, Chris, Tim, Tim's friend Rob . . . seven, second finger of right hand, Dave, eight, Marie, nine, Helen, right hand thumb . . . come on . . . friends from work . . . Nige . . . back to left little finger . . . OK, people from work. Russ, Justin, Paul, Sue, that cunt Jamie . . . new hand . . . Jesus . . . OK, friends of people from work . . . Dave's mate Paul, Ange, Clyde, Liam . . . oh fuck, how many's that? Two sets of both hands . . . twenty . . . shit, OK, people I've met that don't hate me . . . Jatinder, Dom, Margeret, Rueben, neighbour . . . what's her name . . . Edna, I think . . . twenty-five, keep going, that's 12.5 per cent, nearly there . . . milkman . . . paperboy . . . that sales rep . . . barmaid who sometimes smiles . . . parents, of course, that's two for a start . . .

He returned to the office with his powdery tea. One of the sadly inadequate number of people who made up his list, Rob, was a planning officer for the local council, and that had given him an idea for a new tack.

'OK, so you plant a tree in your garden, right?'

'Mmm?' Archie was concentrating on the manual that had been clogging Ian's desk, supporting it gently under its spine as if it was some sort of trophy.

'A tree, in your garden,' Ian persevered, 'and it hangs over my side, so much that it blocks the light from my house . . .'

'Are you still referring to your desk?'

'Yes, anyway, if that's the case, then I can call in a council adjudicator, and they can force you to chop your tree down.' He had him this time. 'It's called unreasonable obstruction, or something.'

Archie put the book down, carefully ensuring that at least part of it rested on Ian's desk. 'So, you're saying that we should get an adjudicator to assess whether your desk space is being unreasonably obstructed?'

'No, that's not the point. The point is,' the point was that he wanted to smack the pedantic twat, 'that if anything on your side of the garden fence trespasses on to my side, then the law is, I'm afraid, Archibald, on my side.' Checkmate, surely.

'What, anything?'

'Yes, anything.'

'So, what if roots from my tree enter your garden and deny your plants water?'

'Then I guess that if I could prove it was your roots that were damaging my garden, then I'd have grounds to dig them up.' Where the fuck was this heading?

'And so, if *your* roots protrude under *my* boundary fence then I can have them removed?'

'Yeah. Obviously.'

'Well, since you've brought up the concept of unreasonable obstruction, your legs are trespassing under my desk.'

'What?'

'Your legs, under my desk.' Archie looked back at the manual as though he was thinking about picking it up again. 'And you think *I'm* somehow committing a crime by resting some of *my* things on your desk. You should try having your legs to deal with all day.' He picked it up, glanced at it and then looked squarely at Ian. 'Now, would you kindly remove them from my side of the desk, or would you like me to have them dug up?'

Ian breathed in sharply and exhaled slowly, withdrawing his legs as he did so. Archie returned his gaze to the manual. Ian tried not to let it get to him. He changed tack and typed w-a-n-k-e-r repeatedly into the keyboard of his computer, followed by i-a-m-g-o-i-n-g-t-o-k-i-l-l-y-o-u, then c-u-n-t, c-u-n, c-u and finally, with his right middle finger, as if tapping out Morse code, over and over again, the letter c.

When his finger started to ache, he turned his computer on as a last resort and thought about ending his unofficial strike action, just to keep him from killing Archie.

Star Trek

After lunch, which Archie spent glued to his monitor and Ian spent desperately trying to antagonize other colleagues into some sort of argument that he could actually win, Ian returned reluctantly to his desk. But it wasn't his desk any more, it was an extension of Archie. Had there been another venue in which to stage his unofficial action then he would gladly have gone there. But no, this was where he sat, where he always sat and there was nothing he could do about it. He decided to try a different approach.

'So . . . anything good on TV tonight?'

'A couple of old episodes of Star Trek on BBC Two and . . .'

'. . . You don't still watch that shite do you? It's awful,' Ian encouraged, 'I mean, you must have seen enough episodes by now to realize that.'

Archie sighed but took the bait nonetheless. This was good. Ian would draw him in and then pounce. Star Trek was the single thing that he knew Archie had almost genuine feelings for. It was going to be a successful day's work. 'Why do you hate it, Ian?'

Largely because you like it so much. No, don't be too rude too soon. 'Give me one reason why I should like it.'

'Well . . . . well, there's lots of things which . . .'

He was edging it. 'You can't, can you? You're its biggest fan and you still can't. Not even one good reason.'

'What you don't understand, Ian, is that Star Trek was way ahead of its time, and that's what made it so great.'

'Yeah, it's set in the future, it's bound to be ahead of its time.'

'No, you know what I mean. It was ahead of its time in the sixties, Ian.'

It was Archie's turn to resort to tactics. He pronounced Ian's name as a long, drawn out 'Eee-un' and included it in every sentence he could when the chips were down. He said it with an overwhelming concrete confidence that his own belief was some sort of law of nature, and Eee-un's answers came from some vacuous child at the back of the class who hadn't been paying much attention. Ian recognized the strategy but was powerless to act. It was a well-worn path through any argument. First, annoy the opposition, through tone of voice, gesture, pronunciation or condescension. Second, lure them off the subject and on to your home ground by offering a loose statement on a barely related matter for them to leap upon. Third, when safely on your home territory, pounce. Archie's home ground was spotting tautology. Ian had suffered it time and time again, despite seeing it coming. Archie usually vexed him so thoroughly that it was impossible not to react. This time, though, he was holding on.

'Well it's the fucking nineties now.'

'So nothing in any other decade has been worthwhile, then?' Archie tempted.

Ian ignored the decoy. 'Look, any programme made in the sixties is bound to look dated sooner or later, usually sooner, right, and as soon as it looks dated, it becomes kitsch, and as soon as it's become kitsch it becomes cultish,' he stood up

and walked over to the window and continued as if address-
ing the car park below, 'which only encourages sad bastards
like you to believe you're a member of some special club, so
you huddle in anoraked groups and discuss the missing
episodes or whether Shatner wore a corset, or the physics of
travelling at the speed of light like you're doing something
secret and important because it's as close as you get to even
appearing to be doing anything remotely interesting or
furtive.'

'Oh, so what do you do that's especially interesting?'
Archie tempted a second time.

Ian turned round and faced him, falling for the diversion-
ary tactic as he did so. 'Well, for a start, I . . . I go out
occasionally.'

'So do I.'

'No, I mean properly out, you know, to nightclubs.'

'I've been to nightclubs.'

'Are you sure that's nightclubs in the plural sense?'

'Well given that I appended the consonant 's' to the word
'nightclub', which generally denotes plurality, then yes.'

'Oh yeah, where then?'

'Where when what?'

'Where are these alleged nightclubs that you've allegedly
been to more than once?'

'I didn't say I'd been to different nightclubs more than
once, I just said I'd been to nightclub*s*.' Archie's familiar
tactic was rearing its ugly head again. The correction of
grammar, when applied with the vigour that Archie was
inherently able to devote to it, always won in the end. Always.
A double negative, a split infinitive, an ambiguity, or even a
misquote and he would be in for the kill.

'Yes, whatever. But which alleged nightclubs . . .'

'No Ian, there's nothing alleged about them. They exist as
surely as my desk exists. You can't have an *alleged* building. It
either exists or it doesn't exist. There isn't a *supposed* Eiffel

Tower, or a *presumed* Tower of London or a *probable* Empire State building or a *possible* CN Tower.' Ian stared murderously at Archie.

'Look, which real, actual nightclubs have you been to a minimum of once?'

'I couldn't have gone to any less than once because in that case . . .'

'*Which ones?*' There was barely disguised hatred in the question. Ian wasn't remotely interested in the answer, he knew that Archie had never been to a nightclub, and if he had, he certainly hadn't been let inside by the bouncers. What mattered was winning some sort of conversational victory, no matter how trivial. He wasn't going home until he had accomplished this. Archie was forced into a minor climbdown.

'I can't remember now, I was a student and they've probably changed their names as they appear wont to do.'

This was beginning to appear a moral victory at least. Ian decided to capitalize.

'Well I'm going to a club tonight, should be a wild night. Why don't you join me? Should be just up your street what with all the clubs you've been to in your time.'

'I'm busy. Otherwise I would.'

'Baywatch on tonight, is it?'

'What?'

'Nothing.' Ian turned his computer off, rounded his things up and left the office. As he closed the door he held two imaginary score cards aloft, one with the number five on it and the other with nine, and announced to no one, 'And that's a five point nine for technical merit from the East German judge. Remarkable.'

Ian headed in the direction of his car. It had been a successful day's work and he congratulated himself by punching the air a couple of times as soon as he was sure no one could see him. His exuberance quickly waned as he struggled to recall which end of the car park he had dumped his car in that morning, or even whether he had actually driven to work at all. Often, inspired by a Mississippi-wide lazy streak, Ian would take the slow plodding bus to work, just to avoid steering, indicating, braking, changing gear, shouting, swearing, gesticulating and all the other necessary and sapping components of driving. He had even managed, on one now legendary and embarrassing occasion a few months before, to drive into work in the morning and obliviously take the bus home at night, calling the police the following morning to report that his car had been stolen. But today he was fairly sure that he hadn't taken the bus, largely because he had arrived on time, and guessed accurately that he'd parked at a defiant distance from the Intron building. As Ian left the car park and joined the misery of the five o'clock battle home, he swallowed a sharp breath in anticipation of the night ahead. Looking into his rear view mirror at the queue of traffic building up behind him he thought of Archie and tried, for the sake of comparison, to imagine the abject tedium of the night that Archie would doubtless be subjecting himself to.

Change

Ian changed from first to second and quickly back to first, achieving a peak speed of just over ten miles per hour before the traffic seized up once again. Archie would be rattled. There was no doubt about that. To have half conceded an argument was a heavy defeat for him. He pictured Archie sitting and staring into the blankness of the screen in front of him, occasionally pacing around the office and muttering. In the months they had cohabited the office Ian had come to know and not to love Archie's habits. His reluctance to lend change for the coffee machine, due to an obsessional fixation with spending the exact coinage he carried with him each day, his tendency to sniff repeatedly, whether he had a cold or not, the way he hummed and tutted and tsk-ed with almost every breath, the way he ruffled his nose and pushed his glasses back into their resting position when he was trying to make a point and, mostly, his remaining alive, were all constant sources of distress to Ian. When Archie wasn't happy, he paced and sat, muttered to himself and then paced and sat. Ian would then be unhappy too, but would have the good sense to swear rather than mutter, and remain seated rather than wear himself out pacing. But if anyone was an absolute creature of habit, and Ian knew the signs only too well, it was Archie.

Ian looked at his watch. Five-fifteen. He would probably be pacing further afield now, as far perhaps as his boss's office, in the vain hope of being spotted still at work an extravagant fifteen minutes outside his allotted hours. It would be a lost cause as Ian had noticed with some relief that his supervisor's office light was out when he had sneaked past at ten to five. Archie would then move on to his next irritating habit. He would return to the office and put a marker pen cross through Tuesday, 16 September 1997 on his MS Micros wall calendar. Ian had watched him do this day after day after day, and it pissed him off no end. Archie, well aware of this, continued to do it. Next, if convention was anything to go by and Archie was, if nothing else conventional, he would open his newspaper and begin to plan his evening. And this was how Ian had first come to appreciate the depth of Archie's love of science fiction. In the same way that normal people scour papers for sports results, personal columns, events to go to, advertisements, misprints or even, occasionally, news, Archie planned his evening's viewing from the TV listings. He would mutter and mumble, and scheme, all with the aid of his beloved transparent blue Bic biro, which seemed to be perpetually on the verge of running out of ink. Ian had asked him about it, and Archie told him that the pen was his pride and joy, because, in common with everybody else who has ever owned a Bic biro, he had never yet managed to hang on to one long enough without losing it to actually run it out of ink, and here at last was his big chance. Ian had been envious, momentarily at least, before regaining his composure, and wondering whether there was any way of filling it back up when Archie wasn't looking.

The car in front spluttered forwards and Ian was caught off

guard, allowing a lurid blue Escort to sneak into the queue from a side road. Ian swore and returned to speculating on the nature of Archie's evening. Chronologically, and again he had been unfortunate enough to witness this many times, Archie would unbutton the top pocket of the shirt his mother had recently bought him for his birthday and pull out the worn-looking creased black notebook into which he habitually diarized his evening's viewing. He would start a new page, which he would, with ruthless efficiency, entitle Tuesday the 16th and scan the TV listings. Ian knew this because he had once managed to get his hands on Archie's beloved notepad, and dull but organized reading it had made too. Recently, Archie let it be known that he had invested in cable TV, because of its seemingly endless coverage of science fiction. This made sense and was another good reason besides lethargy that Ian hadn't got cable himself. Science fiction was perfect cable fodder. Set in the future, its stories never dated and they encouraged the sort of anal-ity that welcomed rather than rejected repetition. It was perfect – show the same episode over and over again and a million Archies would tune in and learn the lines successively through each repetition. On a good night, Archie would be able to plan a seamless viewing itinerary of sci-fi from his estimated time of arrival home until the time he calculated he would be ready for bed. Often, Archie read his itinerary out loud for Ian's benefit.

'Good. Babylon Five, the second series. The Cybrex Mission. Seen it.' Archie would recite into the newspaper with a boyish excitement. '"Black holes may be the only thing between us and our other selves, Commander." X Files, yes, BBC One, nine-twenty. Hang on, that'll mean I'll miss the start of Deep Space Two on Sky One. Damn. Mmm . . . Maybe if I watch the Outer Limits and video the X Files, I'll be OK. Yes, that will work, I think.'

It was generally about this stage of the proceedings that

Ian would have to call it a day before violence got the better of him. On the rare occasions that he stayed later than Archie, he would watch him flip the notepad shut, replace it in his shirt pocket and button down the flap in one seamless, practised movement. He would then double check that he had already erased the day from his calendar, attempt a cursory 'Good night' and close the office door behind him.

The traffic was still heavy, but there was at least the chance of scraping into third gear from time to time. It was barely raining and the wipers spread an intermittent film of water droplets across the windscreen which dispersed just in time to be replaced by a fresh film. Through the occasional haze of his windscreen, Ian continued to picture Archie, who would now be on his way home also. From here on in it was largely conjecture, but knowing what he did of Archie's one-dimensional life, he tried to put himself in Archie's slip-on shoes.

One Pence in a Supermarket

As Archie left the office he suddenly worried that he might not have enough video space to cover his evening's viewing. He had some room left at the end of his Star Trek Volume VI tape. Maybe there would be enough to accommodate the X Files. He wondered whether it might be a bit sacrilegious to mix the two programmes on one tape, and slipped into a day-dream of Scully encountering the Clingons, and what the FBI might make of Spock and . . . this kept him more than amused while he walked out of the building towards the bus stop. A nagging doubt of change interrupted his sci-fi day-dreams. He really should be on the safe side and buy a videotape. If he bought a video, it would be bound to cost a sum of money ending in 99p. He checked his front trouser pockets for change and managed a curse skilfully untainted by swearing or blas-phemy. He had no change at all. He checked his wallet. One five-pound note. This presented a change-disposal problem. Archie judged purchases of lunch, newspapers and cups of tea not in terms of the needs they fulfilled so much as their merits of spare coinage disposal. He generally took five pound coins with him to work each morning and a five- or ten-pound note in case of unforeseen eventualities. Occasionally, if he was feeling adventurous, he would vary his coinage and leave the house with four-pounds fifty or five-pounds twenty or some other sum which prevented him simply buying the same items every day. In this way, Archie kept himself on his toes. Today had been a challenge. The sandwich shop he bought his lunch from every day had increased its prices without warning and he had been badly off balance ever since. It had been a struggle, but by the end of the day he had returned to equilibrium having legitimately spent every one of the five-hundred pence he had started the day with. The video, though, would doubtless result in a spare coin and it would be difficult to dispose of one pence in a supermarket. By his own rules, he wasn't allowed to lose, donate, throw away, deface beyond recognition or otherwise dispose of remaining coinage. He stood at the bus stop for some minutes trying to find a way around his predicament. Anonymous cars crawled by. There had to be some way. He pushed his glasses slowly upwards as far as they would travel on the bridge of his nose. This would take some careful planning.

Archie left the bus and walked towards the terraced row of shops which were vaguely on his way home. He knew they were vaguely and not directly on his way home because he had paced it out on his first two days at work, as he'd proudly told Ian, counting the number of strides required to walk from the nearest bus stop to his house via or not via the route which took him past the shops. It was sixty-one paces longer to walk via the road which carried the local convenience shops. To Archie this contradicted the description convenient. Nor was he particularly happy with the slogan which sought to entice jaded passers-by into what would have been called a Corner Shop if it had indeed been located on a corner. (Corner or no corner, it was almost ubiquitously referred to locally as the Corner Shop. The remainder of the almost was Archie.) The legend 'Kwik DisKount Supa Store', in orange letters which had lost most of their luminosity, pasted on a white plastic background which had gained most of the orange, particularly irked him. There was no danger of ever happening upon a discount within, no matter how quickly you shopped, and there was certainly nothing super about it. Store, he had no quibble about. He entered, for once with strident optimism. He had thought of a way around his dilemma. He walked over to the video section of the shop, picked up the blank video with the highest time to money ratio and took it to the counter.

'Four ninety-nine,' prompted the weary cashier.

'I don't think it's worth four ninety-nine,' countered Archie.

'What?'

'I think it's worth five pounds,' Archie persevered.

'So?'

'Well, if I want to give you five pounds for it, is that OK?'

'S'pose so.' The etiolated youth was beginning to have doubts about this transaction. 'I'd better call the manager over though.'

'No, look, just take five pounds for it, and we'll call that fair, OK?'

'But that'll put my till over and we're not allowed to be over — it won't balance when I cash up.' The youth looked round for his supervisor.

'Look,' Archie stabbed, 'take the fiver, I'm taking the tape.'

'Mr Jameson,' the youth called anxiously, but Archie was already on his way out. It was his understanding of the law, which was, at times, unnecessarily thorough, that he couldn't be prosecuted for paying too much for an item. He had solved his problem in that his rules didn't preclude bartering the price of a purchase upwards. He made a mental note, which would later become a notebook note, to raise his game by excluding anti-bartering from now on.

Birthday

This morning, things were different. The breakfast routine didn't work. The toast was burnt, his face unwashed, the cereal powdery. Sleep had been so scarce that Ian wondered whether the minutes he had spent with his eyes closed stretched to an hour. As the drug seeped away into the night, taking with it the transient warmth that had surged through his body, his stomach had welcomed the world with an open sphincter, encouraging the blackness of the room which surrounded him to permeate through his skin, swallowing his breath, and opening him up. In the darkness, he found his thoughts roaming lands they were usually barred from and was powerless to stop them. He wondered about mind control. The real problem with the brain was that you couldn't control your own, let alone anyone else's. It was free to trip you up, day-dream, cloud judgements, hallucinate, bedeck the world with pearls, strip a mountain of its beauty and replace it with fear, encourage you to believe what you feel to be untrue and worse, disbelieve what you know to be true. You could never reprimand it. It was without blame – who could ever question your motives when you hadn't even been consulted on them yourself? This was, given the events of last night, no time to rely on his brain. It was time instead to allow innate feeling to take over. He opened a can of beer. Today was his birthday. He was twenty-nine.

After his lager breakfast, Ian had a wash, a shave, wet his hair, dried it, put some gel in it, dried it again for good measure and had an unusually long look at himself in the mirror. He returned to his bedroom, hunted through a couple of drawers while swearing, and eventually dug out his old Polaroid camera. Then he delved into the depths of his underused vertical wardrobe (underused in comparison with his rarely out of action horizontal floordrobe) and disentangled a tripod from its adornment of clothes hangers. He set the tripod up as steadily as the clothes-littered floor would allow and screwed the camera into position. He looked through the view finder at a head-height space on the wall and focused, set the automatic timer and nipped around in front of the camera and tried to look young. This was a ritual he had enacted on every morning of his adult birthdays. In this way he had been able to chart a private running commentary on his life, with the lows and highs etched in the contour lines of his face. He held the young pose. The camera flashed and he relaxed his face. The undeveloped Polaroid popped out. This was the acid test. Anguished hours spent in front of various mirrors and at various angles trying to decide once and for all whether his hair was actually receding or not were irrelevant now. While he waved the maturing Polaroid in the air, he dug through another couple of drawers and retrieved his sacred Birthday Morning album. He opened it at 'Twenty-Eight'. If he looked balder and more haggard than he did on last year's photo, it would be official – he would be a year older. If not, he would have cheated the inexorable decline for another year, at least. The Polaroid was beginning to spring into life. He always used his Polaroid camera to fulfil this, and only this, function, because he had to know the answer instantly. The image came to life and the answer arrived. He looked worse, far worse, than last year. Even by holding both photos at different angles and in different lighting conditions, the conclusion was inescapable. Bugger. Bugger, bugger, bugger. Right, if he was going to look rough he may as well enjoy it. He opened another can and decided to start his birthday celebrations early.

After some morning TV, another can and a couple of records, it was nine am. He rang in sick, praying his boss wouldn't have arrived at work yet so he could leave a death's door message rather than faking it live. He was in luck.

'Er . . . Hullo Kate, this is Ian (disappointed sigh). Not going to be able to make it in today I'm afraid (throat clearance), I'm a bit bogged down with (cough) a head cold. Hope I'll be better tomorrow (sniff), cheers, bye (cough, for luck).'

It was pitiful, but it would do. He eased two tablets of Nurofen down with a mouthful of red wine from a bottle he had opened three or four days earlier and had optimistically attempted to re-cork. A few more loud records and a bit of morning TV and it was ten o'clock. As he left the house, taking the bottle with him, he noticed there was a message on his machine which must have recorded when the music was on. Could be his supervisor. Best not to find out. He needed a clear conscience. Today he was going to explore what it was really like to live in a city. Ian was going to take the Circular Route. He had a theory to test.

The Circular Route

The Number 11 bus was a circular bus, in that it toured a rough, and fairly arbitrary, circumference of the city. Ian's thoughts also toured rough and fairly arbitrary circumferences, stopping and starting with the progress of the bus, as a result of the excesses of the night before and the beer this morning. Stop. The gum-encrusted floor of the bus engrossed him. How did each piece of gum get there, from whose mouths had they been rejected, and why? Start. Were its previous occupants about to arrive somewhere where gum was not allowed, like work or school or the dentist's . . . Stop. Ian took another swig of wine, and interrupted a train of thought which was also going nowhere. Start. A middle-aged couple, who had clearly run out of things to say to each other and who were glad of the distraction from the tedium of each other's company, shot glaring looks of disapproval at Ian in a unison which belied their swallowed, mute feelings of unfulfilled need. Stop. Ian wished he was an ether that could float into the soul of each person on the bus. He wished he could choose to invade person A and then each subsequent person that A met when they got off the bus, and each subsequent person that they met and so on, and wondered whether he might return eventually to A. Start. If he did this every day for the rest of his life, he reasoned, he might know what it was really like to live. Stop.

Ian had also decided that he was going to visit the central library today. He had never been and thought it was about time that he did. He was going to look some things up. He didn't know what, exactly, but that wasn't the point. The point was that he would know more when he left the library than he did when he entered, and that was important. When he thought about the library he felt a sudden tightening of his bowels, as he always did when he thought about or entered libraries. As a student, he would enter a library with good intentions and sturdy bowels, but before he could even open a book he would be forced to make a rapid retreat to the toilet. He had never really thought it through but, as he sat on the bus with his buttocks clenched, he recalled an article he had read which said that burglars often defecate in houses they rob. Maybe that was it. In the library he was an impostor, a thief of knowledge, a charlatan, who, on the face of it, knew nothing, and the sheer weight of the wisdom contained within its walls bore down upon his bowels as if to emphasize his insignificance. He decided not to visit the library.

Ian remembered being told that it isn't the destination that's important, it's the journey you take to get there. Since the Circular Route didn't actually go anywhere as such, and would eventually deposit him at the place he had started out, he was going to put the theory to its ultimate test. As the bus lurched around Birmingham, the Circular Route began to assume new meaning in the half-opened doors of his mind. Generally, Ian's doors of perception were firmly shut to the hawkers, sellers and canvassers of new experiences but, in his state of recovery from last night's over-indulgences, his mind followed its own trajectory.

Night Club One

He and two friends had taken the drug precisely because of
the inevitable alcoholic numbness that occurs when you go to
nightclubs and drink away your senses one by one until you
are truly senseless. They had tried the drug, which suppos-
edly turns your senses on, the month before, and nothing
much had happened. Why they were trying again was unclear
to Ian, except that he didn't believe in the principle of once
bitten, twice shy. In fact, he didn't believe that anybody genuinely believed in the principle. It was just a falsehood, an
excuse people made, knowing that at some other juncture
they would be elbowing people out of the way to be bitten
again and again. If people genuinely adhered to the precept,
no one would drink alcohol after their first attempt, drive a
car after the fear and humiliation of their first lesson or have
any favourite albums after the first difficult listening.
Prisoners wouldn't return to prison and people would only
ever buy one house, and live there for ever with only one
child and one partner. So, they tried again.

Mark acquired the pills from someone who knew someone.

Ian and Chris didn't enquire more specifically, but handed Mark their fifteen pounds wondering just how you got to know someone who knew someone. They were sober and scared and made straight for the gents.

'This isn't going to kill me is it?' Chris asked Mark, hopefully.

'No. It's safe.' Chris surveyed the pill sitting in his perspiring palm with some uncertainty. Mark had told him that the indentation of a dove on its upper surface was a good sign but, as he examined the pill with ever closer scrutiny, he concluded that it could have been a vulture for all the detail the crumbly tablet would allow. He remained unconvinced. 'Really safe. As safe as houses,' Mark continued. 'Safer than drinking, probably – I mean, look at all the people who die from drinking.'

'What people?' Chris asked.

'You know, blokes on stag do's and eighteenth birthdays and stuff.'

'What, they die just from drinking?'

The conversation made Ian start sweating. A cold, clinging, guilty dampness which nearly made him shiver. He stared into the mesh of shiny white floor tiles beneath his shoes and felt himself sway a little, his unfocused reflection shifting its grid position slightly as he did so.

'Yeah, alcohol poisoning. Hundreds every year,' Mark continued, oblivious to Ian's suffering.

'Bollocks.'

'No, seriously. Why do you think people have their stomachs pumped?'

'I dunno. So that they never drink again?'

'It's because they'd die otherwise.'

Looking into the lattice of the floor tiles, Ian imagined them all melting into one dazzling, zealously scrubbed porcelain harshness. It became a screen, a solid, impenetrable veneer. Images appeared on its surface. He began to breathe more quickly. Mark's and Chris's voices were dissolving, bouncing off the cold unfocused hardness of the floor and intermingling with as yet unidentified sounds that he recognized from somewhere. He listened more intently. They were traffic noises. He stared through the floor into something darker, something which lay just under its gleaming surface. A road. He was watching from the pavement. There was movement and brightness. A car, many cars. Something imagined but still almost real. It was cold. Everything was blurred. A friend . . .

'Bollocks.'

Chris's reasoned debate brought Ian round. He lifted his head up and tried to speak. 'Look, just . . .' He put his hand between Mark and Chris. They stopped. 'This isn't really helping, you know.'

'Oh shit, sorry mate. I forgot.'

'Yeah, you know, we were just talking . . .' Mark looked a little sheepish, but also a little relieved that an argument he was clearly going to lose had ended, albeit under tactless circumstances.

'It's all right, really it's all right.' Ian pulled his fingers inwards to form clammy fists.

'You OK Ian?' Chris asked.

'Yeah. Fine.' Ian swallowed the foul-tasting guilt. 'Look, are we going to do this or what?' The sooner he was out of this frame of mind the better.

'I'm game.'

Ian had all the equipment that they would need – a ludicrously overpriced bottle of Britvic orange and a plastic glass. The trio looked doubtfully at the miniature bottle of orange.

'There's never enough there for all of us,' complained Chris.

'Yeah, why didn't you just get some water for fuck's sake?' The sympathy hadn't lasted long.

'Look, remember how bad that half a tab we had last time

tasted?' Ian replied in his defence, 'and besides, when I asked
for half an orange juice I was expecting, you know, half a *pint*
of orange juice, and not like half a fucking *segment* of orange
juice. It's not exactly my fault you can't get a decent measure
these days.'

'Ladies, ladies, this isn't exactly the stuff of brotherly love
now, is it? Are we going to get this down us or not?'

It was still relatively early and they were alone in the toilets. They faced each other and one by one took a barely
sufficient sip of the orange juice, said a silent prayer and
swallowed the tablet. This was the Real McCoy. The half-
tablet they had taken before lacked the ceremony and the
frightened, excited anticipation that a whole tablet engen-
dered. They looked at each other, checking for tell-tale signs
in each other's pupils. The last and only time, they had been
drinking, their expectations had been low and nothing much
had happened. This time they were prepared. Nothing happened. They walked around the echoey club as it slowly
filled. Ian looked at his watch.

'How long?' Mark asked.

'Thirty-five minutes. I reckon your mate's sold us some
duds.'

'I didn't say he was a mate,' countered Mark, aware for the
first time that the burden of their expectations rested with
him.

'Well, whoever, nothing's happening to me. What about
you two?'

Neither reported anything out of the ordinary. Ian, however, was starting to feel uncomfortable in their company and
mildly claustrophobic. He needed to be alone. 'I'm having a
look around.' The other two nodded. He walked into the
chill-out room. It was better but still didn't feel right. It was
too small and was showing a film with imposing, though
unrealistic, monsters. The camouflage drapes began to close
in around him. He left and decided to head back to the gents,

but bumped into Mark on his way. Mark looked uncertain and less than pleased to see him.

'Where's Chris?' Ian asked.

'Dunno. Look, I'm going to check out the other room.'

'I've been there. It's not very big.'

Mark looked intently into his eyes. Ian needed to get away from Mark and Mark felt much the same. Ian walked into the gents and into one of the two barely enclosed, toilet paper-free cubicles. He lowered the toilet seat and sat down, his thumbs supporting his head at the temples. Why did they make cubicles so small? He could just about touch both walls with his elbows. Ian wiped his index finger across his forehead and discovered that he was sweating. He took his top off and tried to decide whether he needed to be sick. His stomach seemed to be rising and falling of its own accord. As it fell, the walls seemed to recede, and as it rose they came back at him. He tried to figure out what was wrong. The eventual realization that this time was different and he was experiencing the initial effects of the tablet came to him almost by surprise. Someone banged on the chipboard-and formica door. Ian could see his shoes through the eighteen-inch gap between the wet tile floor and the bottom of the door.

'Come on mate, you gonna be in there all day?'

Ian stood up, put his top back on, awkwardly over his sweaty back, and opened the door. A youth some ten years younger and paler than Ian sheepishly let him through. He walked back into the main room. The club was still nowhere near full and he spotted Mark and Chris against a large metallic pillar. Mark looked intently into his eyes. Ian understood the significance this time.

'Jesus, your pupils are fucking *huge*.'

'You should see yours – like fucking saucers.'

'You all right?' Chris asked, seemingly unable to keep from moving as he did so.

'Yeah. Went a bit weird there for a while.' Ian joined him in his perpetual motion.

'Great. I was sick.'

'Yeah? Nice one.'

'Look, I just wanted to say that, you know, you two, you're just like, you're the best friends I've ever had.' Mark hadn't realized this until now, and indeed would have hotly disputed it an hour ago. From now on though, things were different.

'I'm never drinking again. Ever,' said Ian, feeling surge after surge of delicious warmth throughout his body.

'Yeah, nor me. I mean, don't take this the wrong way, like, but I love you two.' Chris was virtually jogging on the spot. An unearthly sound disrupted the inevitable announcement of the trio's engagement. Chris, Mark and Ian looked over towards the front of the room and Chris withdrew his arm from Mark's shoulder. Whatever it was it was coming from the dance floor. It entered them and made their chests vibrate with a deep and warm resonance. The DJ was cranking things up.

'Fuck this, let's dance,' Chris suggested. They were pulled on to the dance floor by the puppet strings of the subsonic bass. Anonymous records came and went unrecognized and seamless. They danced in ways they had never danced before. Their shoes had springs and they seemed to hover several inches off the dance floor. The strobe lights, which in last week's club had frozen Ian's thoughts like sudden snapshots, now focused his thoughts. He was a machine, a robot that chewed gum and danced maniacally in a language of movements that he hadn't realized he possessed. He sweated, grinned and gurned without apparent control, talked to everyone he met, got very huggy with an overtly homosexual man who misread his intentions, drank bottled water at two pounds a go because the toilet taps had been turned off and greeted each crescendo of beats with a genuine ecstatic love.

Ian made his way to the edge of the dancefloor and

thought about buying some more bottled water. As he looked up from the warm pound coins in his sweaty palm he thought he saw Jamie, a cunt from work, and was about to go over and declare undying love for him, which was a very recent phenomenon, when a fellow robot draped an arm around his shoulder.

'This is massive, innit?' the robot gurned, though this time Ian didn't speak the language.

'What is?'

The robot continued undeterred. 'You larging it big time or what?' Ian was beginning to have his first doubts about the drug. Despite his euphoria, he realized that this was just another way of switching senses off one by one, but different senses. As he felt the melting of his sense of inhibition, sense of discernment (musically and socially), sense of humour, sense of foreboding, sense of separateness, he wondered whether that was the definition of true happiness – to have no senses to offend. Maybe deaf, dumb and blind people are ecstatically happy. Or perhaps bad odours, foul tastes and sticky hand rails offend their remaining senses and condemn them to the misery that people with five senses suffer. He looked around for reinforcements but couldn't see Mark or Chris.

'Er, yeah,' he replied.

'You gotta give it up for the DJ though.'

'Yeah,' Ian agreed, though precisely what he was going to have to go without wasn't clear.

'Makes you think, though. I mean, here's us two, never met, right, and we're talking and communicating and that, I mean, lager's the real enemy, if you know what I mean.'

Ian realized the language difficulty – the bloke was a Cockney – and whereas it was against his general principles to encourage a Cockney in any matter whatsoever, he felt a growing feeling of love, understanding and warmth towards him.

'Yeah, mate, it's like I don't usually like Cockneys, but you, you're a great bloke.'

'Yeah, sorted, Brummie.' The Cockney looked into his eyes. 'You don't support the Villa though, do you?'

'Er, no mate,' Ian mumbled, suddenly feeling that the robot he was draping his arm round might not entirely be the brotherly love type.

'That's OK, mate, just askin'.' Ian shook his hand, feeling his methamphetamine-overdosing muscles clench his fingers. He was sure it *was* the living and moving rigor mortis-like effect of ecstasy upon his muscles, and not Cockney animosity that was doing this, as animosity is as difficult to maintain under such circumstances as an erection. He even felt that if that wanker from work Archie turned up (which he wouldn't because he'd no doubt be at home cataloguing his Star Trek video collection) he'd hug him and smother him in kisses and beg his forgiveness for never smiling in his presence in case he encouraged him in any way to believe that some sort of friendship might be possible and it was time to find his friends who he hadn't seen for hours but not before he'd what was it bigged it up largetime but only after a drink I need a drink I'm dehydrating where are they fuck it's Archie it can't be it is what the fuck's he doing here has he finished his Star Trek collection oh no he's seen me I'm dreaming where are Mark and Chris find the door my feet seem to be floating above the floor it can't be him got to get out of here . . .

The bus stuttered on. It must be every bus driver's dream to find a ten-mile straight with no bus stops and just drive with one foot on the accelerator and the other languishing to the left of the brake. Ian wondered whether any driver had ever made it the whole way round the Circular Route without even once stopping to pick up a passenger and, if so, whether a lap of honour would be an appropriate way to celebrate under the circumstances. He was starting to feel irritable.

Discomfort was slowly chipping away at his dreamy, inebriated detachment. Something in his mind seemed intent on
sobering him up by actively seeking out external cues capable
of disturbance. The seats vibrated whenever the bus stopped,
which was far too frequently now. Couldn't people walk further than the fifty yards which seemed to separate stops? He
was sitting over one of the rear wheels, which tried its best to
pierce his eardrums when the brakes were applied, and this
was almost permanently, as if the driver were simply holding
the bus back to lesser or greater degrees with the brakes,
rather than actively moving it forwards with the accelerator.
He needed a pub. The wine was gone, and, for a while, he
floated like the bits of cork that had remained on its surface
from his misguided attempts to re-cork the bottle. As the bus
circled Birmingham, fluid and discomforting memories
began to flow in and out of his spongy consciousness.

The Unbearable Shiteness of Being

Soon after Sue's departure had subsided so that it only tortured him on an hourly rather than a minute by minute basis, a new need became apparent to Ian. The need to be loved and to give love gave way to the need to shag and be shagged. In lieu of any foreseeable opportunities (though hope remained throughout; in the bathroom mirror, in the shop windows he passed on his way to a pub, in the barmaid's eyes, in the nearest attractive girl, in a friend of a friend introducing a hitherto unintroduced beauty – 'Ian, I'm not sure if you've ever met the gorgeous and single Sarah' – in the taxi queue on your way home, even in the few strides from the taxi to the front door and finally, and somewhat desperately, hope that a passing *femme fatale* has broken into your bedroom) Ian decided to invest in some erotic literature. Scared of visiting Adult Bookshops, he scoured the shelves of Waterstones' central Birmingham branch for anything which would satisfy his need. The shop, from the inside at least, was church-shaped, and worshipped a plethora of paper and hardbacks, organized with a librarian's zeal into every conceivable category.

He began at A and perused the shelves for books which suggested graphic descriptions of lurid acts. This was an easy task for Ian. In any page of single-spaced small font text, he could instantly locate words pertaining to sex. This was an obvious advantage while scouring the bookshelves in Waterstones, but would irritate him when he found himself skipping sections of important text to home in on Essex, Sussex, Middlesex, Roger, Fanny in American novels, beavers with tails, cocks which crowed, tits which chirped (great, blue or otherwise) and virtually every other word in the English language which held a sexual connotation for Ian, which was most of them.

Ian knew of several authors whose philosophical ramblings were allegedly no more than façades behind which vivid descriptions of sexual perversity lurked. In this category he placed Anaïs Nin, Milan Kundera and Henry Miller, largely because he had seen the films *Henry and June* and *The Unbearable Lightness of Being*, both of which he had enjoyed for more than their philosophical content. He decided upon Miller's *Tropic of Capricorn* and Kundera's *Unbearable Lightness of Being*.

At home, he began scanning. He started with *Tropic of Capricorn*. He had been led to believe that there was virtually nothing except sex in it, but this text seemed to contain little more than anecdotal descriptions of Miller's childhood. He fast forwarded – surely the author had to grow up at some point. More pre-pubescent ramblings. OK, don't panic, the lurid descriptions of depravity with Parisian prostitutes are at the back. They weren't. He broke his sacred rule and read the reviewers' comments. 'A vivid consideration of Miller's formative years', '. . . the prequel to the erotic adventures of the *Tropic of Cancer*'. Bugger, he never could remember which tropic was Cancer and which was Capricorn. OK, the reserve book. There could be no doubt here; no sequel, no prequel and the film had been a sensual treat throughout.

The scanning recommenced. This time sex was mentioned so often that he could have been reading an ornithological study of two great tits called Roger and Fanny set around the Essex-Sussex border. The descriptions of sex, however, were about as interesting as if this had been the case. Kundera, instead, seemed preoccupied with Nietzche's notion that life is roughly meaningless because it is only lived once per person – if, however, it was lived over and over, each decision, action, incident, would assume an epic proportion as it would have to be faced, endured, accepted every time. Because this is not the case, life is unbearably light and of little consequence. For Ian, were he to live many lives, getting off the circular bus at a particular stop would become an event to bear again and again. Because this is not the case, and Ian will never get off the bus at the same time on the same day and under the same conditions, Kundera would argue that, in terms of human experience it is meaningless. The experience he was about to have, however, as he at last spotted a pub and made his way to the front of the bus, was far from being unbearably light.

Pub

It wouldn't have been his first choice of pub certainly; it wouldn't have been the first choice of even the most bitter, vicious or stupid person passing with a raging thirst. But an overwhelming need to drown his serotonin-deficient brain in crisp, tasteless American beer consumed any reservations he may otherwise have had. He was in an unfamiliar district – it may have been called Brierly Hill or Brierly Green or something similarly misleading – and taking a quick glance up and down the street on his way into the pub, he realized why he wasn't familiar with it. It was crap. The whole area looked like it had been hurriedly slotted together in the sixties as some sort of nightmarish experiment in concrete.

The pub was called The Jug of Ale. That was all you needed to know. It was a pub and it sold ale. This was the sort of pub which was probably, in all fairness, OK at night. No better than OK, and, at times, probably a lot worse. In the day though, when seasoned all day drinkers sat in corners like funnel-web spiders and occasionally shouted at each other or nobody, it was not OK.

Ian ordered a bottle of Budweiser and sat down equidistant

from two lone nutters who were guarding their corners. He surveyed the bar. Sturdy, ornate, cast iron legged tables, presumably too heavy to throw, were decorated with equally unaerodynamic stools; a wooden, stained, black, butt-strewn floor, with what looked to be an ingrained glass effect which, on reflection, probably wasn't decoration; a dart board with concentric rings of alcohol-addled inaccuracy extending well beyond the bisected tyre which attempted to protect the surrounding wall from stray darts; the pretence of a juke-box, which was probably stocked with ageing ballads that would be mouthed inaccurately at the end of each night; the progressively yellower walls the further you looked towards the ceiling; a single, frosted window, tarnished with the logo of a brewery which had long ceased to be. Even on a good day, after an early night and a full term of sleep, the pub would have appeared dire. This morning, it was much, much worse. He needed another beer. He knew he was paying the price for too much fun in too little time. Alcohol, he reasoned, would level him out. He approached the bar, watched by the two funnel-web spiders.

'A bottle of Bud, please.'

The ageing thirty-year-old barman held out his hand. 'One-eighty.' The money was taken first, like the city centre petrol stations late at night, where you have to hand over your cash before you even think of approaching the pump.

A man came into the bar and stood uncomfortably close to Ian. He had tattoos. Ian was automatically afraid of anyone with tattoos, on the simple basis that they wanted you to be. They were advertising their contempt: contempt for the pain of repeated needle stabbings, contempt for what people might think of the not-so-golden eagles, index finger to thumb swallows and daggers with or without hearts or skulls which adorned their visible flesh. More pertinently, to Ian at least, they were advertising their contempt for white collar university-educated non-tattooed types.

This wasn't just forearm decoration though, there was

facial as well. This man had defeat tattooed all over him. A Borstall 'tear' below his right eye, an unconvincing tattoo earring on both lobes and what looked like an inverted crucifix, flanked on the left by 'B.C.' and on the right by 'F.C.', roughly in the middle of his forehead. Ian had never been able to meet the eye of the few men he had encountered in pubs with facial tattoos. Maybe that was the point. He turned to sit down. The tattoo stood in his way.

'You a student?'

'No.' Red Doc Martens with steel toecaps. Faded jeans. Royal blue Birmingham City shirt. Arm tattoos. Brief eye contact. Brown eyes. Angry brown eyes. Crew cut. Look away. Lone nutter's looking over. Brief eye contact again. Sticking out ears, tattooed lobes. Fists tighten.

A slight pause.

Tattoo looks into his eyes, head at slight angle. 'Well, you're still a cunt.'

I'm dead. The tattoo remains in the way. Knees weaken.

Another pause. Look somewhere, anywhere.

'I said you're a cunt.' More tortured eye contact. Immobile, incapable, mute. He was determined to insult him, it was whether he wanted to kill him that was the point. Think of something. Think of something.

'LEAVE HIM ALONE.' A man-mountain was suddenly standing behind Ian. The voice made him jump, physically, and seemed to make the room reverberate. The tattoo registered Ian's terror and, partially satisfied, slouched back to the bar. 'ME AN' HIM'S PALS.' Ian felt a wall of hand on his shoulder. 'We're going to have a drink together, jus' you an' me.'

'Fuck,' breathed Ian. He hoped that this was the reverse of the frying pan/fire situation. Maybe the colossus who had saved him was the lesser of the two evils. Ian observed him as much as possible without catching his eye. He was forty-five-fifty, but his body hadn't yet turned into the mockery of its former youth that usually occurs at around this age. On the contrary, he would still compare favourably with brick toilets. His face was dominated by a jaw which seemed to have abandoned all idea of conventionally tapering down to his chin and which, instead, distended to meet his bullish neck and then angled sharply upwards to form a reluctant reunion with his chin after all. Above cloudy, dark green eyes, his face was bisected by a unibrow – a solitary, thick, brown eyebrow with no apparent join, a bad sign in any book of tell-tale Neanderthal features. Unlike the first challenger, he had no tattoos, and this was probably a bad thing. The first wore his like an under-powered saloon car brandishes go-faster stripes, to camouflage the struggling one litre engine under the bonnet. For the Frying Pan, however, such mimicry would have been superfluous – it would have been like sellotaping a spoiler to the back of a Ferrari.

People You Want to be With

Within the seconds that counted out the bar room melo-
drama, Ian felt painfully alone. This was the inevitable
hangover of a drug which encourages unity, and momentarily it instilled in him an echo of the first true loneliness he
had experienced in his adult life, in the weeks and months
after Sue had left him. He had felt then, as he felt now, totally
unprepared for the crushing sense of isolation that circumstance had forced upon him. He wished someone would have
told him right from the outset what it would actually be like,
rather than being forced to sketch endless pictures of fallop-
ian tubes.

'It's like, you want to be with them all the time. Sure,
there are times when you can't actually stand to be with
them, but, all things considered, you want to be with them
and for them to be with you. Then she leaves you, and as
soon as you accept that it's permanent she becomes the
person you can't bear to be with. You will do anything to
make sure she won't be where you are. You'll ring your
friends and edge the conversation round to whether she's

going along to the place you're thinking of going that night. You'll do anything to avoid walking past her house. You'll stop going to shops she shops in, pubs she drinks in, streets she parks in, the houses of friends she likes visiting. You'll avoid mutual friends because you don't want to talk about how it still strangles your every positive thought a year later. Your friends, who you have been led to believe will always remain and will always be there, no matter what, start to be elsewhere, and you realize that the last three letters of friend spells '-end'. They will begin to drift through your life, ring you less often, until after an elapsed period of time, maybe only two or three weeks, when to ring feels awkward, and to lose touch seems by far the easier option. Once it's definitely over, your parents will tell you that they didn't like her anyway. You will find yourself wanting to be alone and with someone else at the same time, maybe because you felt alone when you were with her. You may find from time to time that you give in to the overwhelming temptation to speak to her, to find out how she is, why she left you, who she left you for, and why she is so happy now. You will then vow never to ring her again to be told exactly why you didn't make her happy, why she left you and why someone else makes her so happy now. You will watch the patience of your closest friends turn to dispassion, to irritation, to impatience, to 'You've got to sort yourself out and get over this'. You will lose confidence in your every move. You will see her everywhere, even abroad, as you begin to forget what she looks like and start moulding her fading features on to the face of every girl you meet. You will compare all new females you encounter with her, knowing that none will compare. You will bump into her parents, who will be in a rush to go somewhere, anywhere, away from someone they tolerated for their daughter's sake. You will meet her one day, and she will stop you and suggest a coffee, and she will apologize and say she was messed up and it wasn't you and she can't be happy without you and will hold you almost desperately like she used to and . . . but no, it never happens.

But worse, far worse, than all of this is leaving someone you love because you know you are making them unhappy. To tear yourself away from someone not because you have stopped loving them, but because you have too many feelings, too many unexplained, mute, tied, constricting feelings that possess you like some sort of fucked up person running randomly amok inside your head, this carries no anger, only puzzling and depressing defeat. To be left by someone, however, sticks a pin in your pride, you feel aggrieved and this anger turns out to be healing. And this is essentially what happened. Sue left Ian and soon afterwards left Birmingham. And months later, as Ian looked back and tried to recall the last words he said to her, her last expression, her last words to him, and realized that they were trite and irrelevant, something like, 'That's my taxi, then', and that he would never say one more word to that person or ever see her again, and that even her last expression was fading, he thought to himself that this was how most relationships end – as they started – with an irrelevance. And the girl disappears as if she never existed outside the closing vice of your brain, and there's so much you are desperate to know but never will, to say but never will, to do but never will, to ask forgiveness for but never will. So, in an instant, the person you had to be with becomes the person you have to be without.'

But no, all you get is, 'They're all the same, son.'

He did meet up with Sue, twice in fact. The first time was three or four months after she had left him, and they went for a coffee. She had changed – she was happy. He noticed her clothes had softened. She had, item by item, dropped strong clothes from her wardrobe. Leather jackets, tight denims, cumbersome black boots and wonderbras had been replaced by soft, shapeless garments, no longer designed to accentuate anything except pacificity. It was a sign of happiness, of a peacetime dismantling of barriers, of openness. She didn't wear baggy clothes in the way that other women might – to camouflage bodily imperfections – but the way that relaxed people tended to wear relaxed clothes, and uptight people to wear tight clothes. Hippies had worn flares, exaggeratedly wide at the wrists and ankles, inviting the world to look inside, in tie-dyed contrast to the tightly closed cuff-linked sleeves and drainpiped trousers of bankers, lawyers and city workers. Her hair had also softened from its peroxided harshness to a lazy yellowy brown tone, as the counterfeit blonde had grown out to be replaced by its organic counterpart. Her hair had grown long, in parallel with her tranquil state, in the way that the sixties' generation had foregone hairdressers and allowed tight, short, cropped haircuts to relax into flowing, wavy tendrils. It wasn't a protest as such – it was just the natural phenotype of progression from one state of being to another. But Ian couldn't help thinking that the sixties didn't last for ever and, one by one, the barber shops had become busy again, and cuff links and tight trousers had returned to fashion. He had watched many decades of change happen to her in the six or so years that he had known her, but now seemed to be the season of her content, and there was no reason to suspect that this shouldn't last for at least another of her decades, how ever long that might be.

The second time they met was very different.

People You Don't Want
to be With

'So . . . what d'you wanna drink?' Ian had a habit, which he knew to be transparent, of dropping as many consonants as he thought might seem natural whenever he found himself surrounded by people who scared him. It was a feeble attempt at burying the intonations he had somehow picked up at university under the sand of an assumed accent. It rarely fooled anyone, and, dangerously, was sometimes construed as taking the piss. It wasn't always conscious though – he would often find his voice dueting with other people's accents of its own accord.

'Don't you worry about that cunt. Thinks he's 'ard. Pint of barley wine and bitter.'

Shit, the guy's drinking tramp juice. Ian had experimented, during a short and very unsuccessful phase, with drinking Gold Label and bitter. It was scary stuff. The syrupy barley wine would enter your veins and flow thickly to your head, where it would coat every neurotransmitter with a barely penetrable cloak. It would be a rapid descent from there to lunacy. He was tempted to buy him a double, if there was such a thing, and, if there was, if it was legal.

'You sit y'self there,' the Frying Pan directed when Ian returned from the bar.

'Cheers mate,' Ian thanked him, with the most authentic accent he could muster.

Frying Pan leaned over towards Ian. 'You got a girlfriend then have you?'

'No . . . well I did have . . .'

He leaned even closer, until Ian could smell his tobacco breath. 'Married twelve year I was. Said I was no good for her, said I wasn't a proper husband. I said what's wrong with you, you know where I am if you want me, down the pub, that's more than most blokes, could be anywhere shagging anyone, but no, here's where you'll find me, I said.' He took a swig of his drink, thought briefly about returning the glass to the table, changed his mind and took another mouthful. 'Had the cops on me, said I smacked her one, even said I tried to rape her. Course they took one look at my missus an' they knew that couldn't be true. Who'd want to shag her? I said to the copper. Mind you they tried to do me. I said you lay one finger on me and I'll punch your fuckin' lights out. ABH they did me for. Two fuckin' year. If I see the cunt I went down for . . .' He looked reflectively into his pint, as if the thick cloudy drink contained the muddle of his life, and then looked back at Ian. 'You drive?'

'What? Er . . . yeah.'

'What car you got?' Frying Pan asked, staring at him with what appeared to Ian to be an unsettling mix of curiosity and predation.

'Oh just an old Peugeot.'

'Fast, is it?'

Since Ian had never known any male when asked this question to reply with anything other than 'Yes', if it was fast, or 'It's nippy', if it wasn't, he replied, 'Yes. Well, it's fairly nippy.'

'You got it here?' Ian had no idea where this was leading, and shook his head. A long fidgety lull ensued.

'See, the thing with women is, the better you treat them the worse they treat you. Is that right or what?' Ian agreed with him, voluntarily this time, without the encouragement of the fear that Frying Pan was instilling in him. 'You knock 'em about a bit, an' who do they go running to? The fuckin' cops.' He drained his glass. 'Right, I'll have another barley wine an' bitter.'

Ian was glad of the break. He was starting to feel better, despite his unease. Another bottle and it would be time to try and make a move, if he could still find his way home. He bought the drinks.

"There you go.' He couldn't think of a single safe topic for conversation (football, work and women, three mainstays of pub conversation, all seemed potentially disastrous ground) and so he watched the Frying Pan drain just enough volume from his pint to make way for the small bottle of Gold Label, which he then decanted slowly into the remaining beer until the yellow syrup had restored the fluid to its original volume. He lit a cigarette, a pre-rolled roll up which appeared to be lacking only in tobacco, and continued to stare alternately at his drink and at Ian. The juke-box sprang into life at regular intervals without any human assistance, launching unsolicited into Vienna. Ian had always hated the song. There were many reasons to dislike it, but, uncharacteristically, this dislike wasn't capricious – it was a deep seated resentment from his school days, since when the song always made him judder. He was fourteen and was nurturing, unbeknown to the friends, family and teachers who read his work, an incisive writing talent. Words would flow from his dreamy adolescence through his Parker cartridge pen, urged on by the encouragement of his English teacher who would garnish lessons with 'Experiment, be open to the world, capture mundanity and make it sing for you'. Ian had done just this, and had launched himself into three set essays, eschewing all other homework for two or three weeks while he tried to capture the essence of just about everything he could think of in as many long words as he could muster. The essays were returned with the simple appended comment 'Vienna'. He marvelled at the obscurity of the compliment, until his conceit could bear the suspense no more and led him to ask out loud in the middle of a lesson what it meant.

'What is the chorus of the song Vienna, Gillick?'

'Er . . . isn't it "The feeling has gone, only you and I, this means nothing to me, this means nothing to me, this means . . . nothing . . . to . . . ."' He lost interest in literature there and then, and went on to study science, where you weren't made to insult yourself in front of the class. At least not often.

'The feeling has gone, only you and I, this means nothing to me, this means nothing to me.' Ian found himself mouthing the words. He was most of the way towards being soundly drunk.

'Where d'you work?' The nasal Midge Ure was overwhelmed by the booming Frying Pan.

'In a shop,' he lied instinctively. He was becoming increasingly aware that Frying Pan was on edge. He had been scraping his empty bottle into the varnish of the table, and in-between surveying his handiwork looked at Ian with an intensity that bordered upon the carnivorous. The less he divulged the less chance there would be of encountering this man again.

'What sort of shop?'

'Hi-fi.' He knew a fair deal about stereos, and figured he could fend off questions about working in a stereo shop.

'Where'bouts?'

'Edgebaston.' This was easy. A few beers inside him and he could talk like this all day.

'What time's it shut?'

'It's shut now – it's a half day today.'

A long, uneasy silence.

'Right, we're off.'

'What? I've got to . . .'

'I've got a job for you.' Frying Pan stood up. 'We're going shopping.'

'But . . .'

'Now.'

He opened his jacket slightly. The handle of what looked like a knife protruded from Frying Pan's belt. Fuck. Fuck. Fuck. Ian stood up unsteadily and blurted, 'I've got to go to the toilet.'

'I'll come with you,' Frying Pan snarled. 'Keep you company.'

Ian staggered towards the gents, trying to look behind and in front of him at the same time. Images from the film *Deliverance* flitted through his consciousness. 'Squeal piggy squeal' in a Birmingham accent.

Shopping and Dating

Ian shopped and sought women in much the same way. It is almost impossible to perceive shopping as anything other than an activity which will make you happy. You fill your glossy carrier bag with eternal advert-inspired optimism, take it home and try it on for size where it never seems to fit quite as well as it did in the shop. The actual type of transient pleasure shopping brings is dependent not on the products purchased, but on the way in which they are purchased. Indeed, there are many kinds of shoppers. When Ian shopped, for example, he wasn't the archetypal compulsive shopper, for whom shopping is an instant, spontaneous fix. He would decide that there was a commodity he lacked and would set a date to go searching for it. Had he been able to sit at home and order said item at a cheap price by phone, he wouldn't have. For him, shopping provided the thrill of the hunt. The product was fairly secondary. The day, probably a Saturday, would arrive. He would get up early and head into town. Somewhere the article would be waiting for him at a cheap price with the features he calculated he would need.

But somewhere else the same item would be five pounds or even ten pounds cheaper, and that was his grail – the unshakeable belief that if he really tried, he would always be able to find a better deal than the best one he had found up to that point. It wasn't that he needed to save five pounds or ten pounds – if it had been he could simply have contented himself with finding the lowest price of an inferior model – the most pleasurable part of his shopping ritual was the post purchase follow through. Once the item had been bought, taken home, used, and the euphoria evaporated, he would return to town in the following weeks, visit the shops which had been his hunting ground, and check and recheck the prices of his purchase, to satisfy himself that he had indeed got a bargain. One of the most heartfelt disappointments in his life would ensue if this was not the case. Gradually, he would stop monitoring the price of his purchase, and another future item would take its place.

The way he sought women was much the same, though not quite as successful. Someone from work, a friend of a friend, someone at a bus stop, a shop assistant or just about anyone would arouse his interest. He would start to notice them, in the hope that they would notice him, and would become aware of their habits. If the occasion arose, he would talk to them and get to know as much as possible about them. But rarely would he ever complete. Some imperfection would insidiously present itself, some defect not previously apparent to him. The imperfection would consume everything in its sight. He would lose interest. It wasn't that he didn't like the girls he met and went out with, it was just that he held the unshakeable belief that there was always a better looking, more intelligent, more pleasant, and, secretly, larger breasted woman out there somewhere who he would be able to find if he just looked hard enough. After disinterest had set in and everything had ended, he would still follow through, fascinated by who she was seeing now, what she would be doing with her spare time and whether he had made the right decision. In the absence of any hard evidence, he generally gave himself the benefit of the doubt.

One new fad that Ian had seized upon as a potential way of meeting his perfect woman was supermarket shopping. It was alleged that certain supermarkets, no doubt more than aware of the frozen lasagne and bottled beer spending power of single twentysomethings, encouraged the idea, at least, of singles shopping nights. This may or may not have been true – he had never seen such episodes advertised, but had heard of them anecdotally or through friends. It may even have been an elaborate hoax, but he was not about to be put off – swimming with single females or not, he had to shop, occasionally, and the worst he could come out with was a frozen lasagne and some beer – much, much more than any other dating disaster could possibly furnish. Combining the search for females and food was therefore, he reasoned, a win win situation. One autumnal evening after work, when he was feeling particularly susceptible to thoughts of the inexorable decline of daylight and temperature which characterized the coming slide into winter, he headed for a supermarket a couple of miles less convenient than his local. When he arrived, feeling both jittery and hungry, he sat in his car and discussed tactics with the rear-view mirror. This was virgin territory.

Under normal circumstances, he had a shopping routine. Number One. Always shop in the same supermarket. This way, you know what you are getting and for about how much. More importantly, you know the locations of the items you habitually buy, and this was Number Two – always buy the same things. This negates the true enemy of supermarkets – thought. What did I buy last week? What *shape* of pasta is best with a cheese dish? Thread noodles or eggs noodles? Semi-skimmed or just skimmed? White or red? Emmental or Danish blue? One-fifty a pound – is that better or worse than two-fifty a kilo?

Maybe such thoughts didn't plague other people, he didn't know, but he certainly didn't want to risk finding out. So, he shopped once a week and bought the same things each time, and ate them in roughly the same order throughout the week. This routine only had two potential causes of disaster. First, that the supermarket decided, for some reason, that reorganization was necessary. The very thought appalled him. Months spent perfecting a jigsaw pattern of shopping in a particular supermarket would be ruined in a minute by some over-zealous unhealthy looking store manager who would scatter the pieces on the floor so that Ian would have to track them down one by one and construct a new pattern. Second was the inevitable intervention of a girlfriend, who, around the second week of knowing him, would see through his shopping by numbers.

During the first month of their protracted cohabitation, Sue encouraged him to broaden his culinary horizons. Hints were dropped in the form of cookery programmes, meals out, recipe books and references to other males who had clearly failed to perfect shopping routines and who relied instead upon the misguided concept of spontaneity, whatever that might be. He was weaned on to a regime of enforced spontaneity by being coerced into buying one new or different item each week, then two, and so on. Different brands of the same product weren't allowed, he found to his cost, neither were different flavours of the same product, or any other potential loophole he attempted to exploit. Two new items hadn't been too bad, three had been bearable, four had been difficult but five was causing problems as he navigated foreign aisles, looking for uncharted goods. He gave up. He had pushed himself to new levels of imagination and could go no further. He decided that drastic action was necessary. Dumping his basket and picking up a new one, he began a new search – a search for unsuitables. He filled his basket with lychees, horseraddish, pickled walnuts, glacé cherries, lard, cranberries, pomegranates, cocktail onions, kidneys, bayleafs and gnocchi, rounded off with a box of cornflour for good measure. He returned home triumphant and the subject wasn't broached again.

Looking in the rear-view mirror, Ian surveyed the faint lines which fanned out from the edges of his eyes. It was obvious that there were literally hordes of single females – the ones he never met in the rest of his life – just hanging about in the aisles, desperate to meet a lasagne and lager lover. Tactics. If he was going to be hunter-gathering he would have to find a niche, occupy some territory. Tactics. He ruffled his hair in the mirror hoping that it would look naturally ruffled. The chocolate dessert section. No, that'll be a magnet for fat girls. The ice-cream section. Better. You hardly need to look at a tub of the stuff before women launch themselves at you according to the adverts. But then what? Ian started to panic, his limited imagination struggling with the exact details of what you were actually supposed to do with the stuff when it came down to it, which it inevitably would do if you purchased a tub. OK, not the ice-cream section. Think. Think. What's the world's best aphrodisiac? Beer. All right, the beer section. No. Too sad, somehow. Think. Focus. Single females. The frozen meals for one section. Do girls eat frozen meals for one though? Christ knows. Oh fuck it. He started the car. He'd buy some chips and have a wank.

Pub Toilets

Ian tried to piss, to micturate, to urinate, to open his urethra and expel the voluminous watery urine which was straining his bladder. Frying Pan was standing menacingly close, elbow to elbow, and was pissing a waterfall. Ian had a bad case of stage fright. It often happened. He would be in a pub with friends of friends or with some dullard from work, and a piss would suggest itself as a good break from the tedium. He wouldn't have been receiving relentless messages from the stretch receptors of his bladder, but he would nonetheless be optimistic of a successful trip to the toilets. Frequently, he would then find himself standing uncomfortably close between two walls of men, desperately trying to bring forth the desired tributary, whilst Niagara Falls on his left and Victoria Falls on his right darted him disparaging sideways glances. He would squirm, whistle, fidget, look down at his member and tutt as if it were some sort of faulty piece of machinery, hum, sigh, shake it, count backwards like NASA hoping for a launch at pee minus three seconds, two, one, zero, nothing, look hopefully down into the urinal, read the 'MUFC' in marker pen on the wall with 'are shite' in biro beneath, look at the ceiling, at his watch, anywhere, anywhere, except sideways. But the impotence of such a moment was a positive joy compared with the nightmare he was experiencing now. Frying Pan rested his hand-vice on Ian's shoulder and continued to gaze at him while almost flooding the urinal. Come on. Please. Come on. He looked down at his penis and tutted. Then something unexpected and generally unwelcome rushed to the front of Ian's head. It was an impulse. A pure, decisive, clear, spontaneous thought of action. It contained no ambiguity to mull over, no finer points to discuss, no contradictions to debate, no moral dilemmas to weigh. As an habitual ditherer, this was alto-gether new, and startled him like a wasp sting. Frying Pan removed his grip to rehouse his member. Ian reeled around and dashed for the door. Frying Pan grabbed at him and par-tially caught him. He didn't get a good grip. Ian shook him off and lurched again towards the door. Suddenly he was hurtling forward, ahead of himself, almost, and off balance. The door, which opened outwards, rushed forward to meet him. Something jolted through his head and seemed to travel down his body. He kept moving. He was through the door and a little sense returned. He focused as he ran through the bar, his fly open, his penis still free, trying to sprint and tuck his member away, like some sort of bizarre reverse relay race. Where's the door? Past the Tattoo. Through the lounge. Where is it? He touches his head. It is slippery. Frying Pan is growling behind, running and frantically rehousing. A door marked Emergency Exit with a horizontal push bar. Daylight. Out on to metal stairs. Head throbbing. Frying Pan, now joined by Tattoo, is through the door. Stairs two at a time, two complete spirals down. Tackle finally away. On to tarmac behind the pub. An alley. Frying Pan and Tattoo screaming behind. The road, thank God, the road. Think 'left', hesitate, run right. A bus. A Number 11 bus. A circular, all protecting, mother earth of a bus, shuddering diesel at the stop. Engine note rises, indicator indicates, doors about to close. Jump on, just. Bus pulls off. The others are fifty, seventy-five, a hundred yards away and shouting. He is safe. His trousers are soaking. So that's the cure for stage fright.

'S-seventy-five,' he stammered. He searched his pockets and looking at his hand saw that it was covered in blood. Worse, he discovered that he only had a handful of coppers and a couple of silvers. Forty pence. Two stops, maybe three at the most. It wouldn't get him home. 'Make that forty.'

The driver surveyed him as he drove, which was unnerving. 'You OK?'

'Yeah. Oh that. It's just a . . . a . . .,' he didn't know what it was. He was all over the place. 'Forty, please.'

'Where're you going?'

'I dunno. Wherever forty pee will get me.'

'Stirchely.'

The bus vibrated and Ian felt cold and slow. He wasn't in shock so much as shocked. Three stops later, he was in the high street of another former town linked to others just like it by the all pervading suburbia which refused to get any closer to the city centre and formed a wall of frightened solidarity around it. It was late afternoon and school children were milling around in thin imitations of uniforms trying not to go home. He was aware that they appeared to be looking at him. He found a cashpoint machine and looked at his reflection in the perspex screen which was meant to protect the cashpoint machine from he didn't know what. There was a lot of blood, coming from somewhere around his right temple. His head was starting to hurt, not at the point from which he was bleeding, but from the back of his skull. Frying Pan must have forced him into the door. Thank fuck it opened outwards. He reached inside his jacket for his wallet. Except that he wasn't wearing a jacket.

'Fuck. Fuck. Fuck.' He'd left it in the pub. 'Fuck fuck fuck fuck fuck.' A couple of young school girls surveyed him suspiciously. He looked up and down the high street, trying to orientate himself. Home was two or three miles if he could get the direction right but he was less than sure that he could. He decided to follow the Circular Route on foot, using the bus stops as compass points to guide his way home.

He arrived home an hour and a half later, a great deal more sober, took twice the maximum suggested dose of Nurofen and checked the messages on his under-used answer machine.

'Er . . . Hi Ian, it's Archie here, you know, Archie from work.' As if Ian knew any other Archies. 'It's nine-thirty am. I've got to speak to you, it's important. Very important. I'll try you later. Goodbye.' What the fuck was Archie doing ringing him at home? Ian had been quite clear, when he gave him his phone number some months ago, that he was only to use it, and he had stressed this on several occasions, in case of a programming emergency. In fact, he had only surrendered his number to the boring bastard as part of a reciprocal exchange of telephone numbers instigated by Archie, which Ian had unsuccessfully tried to wriggle out of by insisting his phone was out of order, only to be caught out a few weeks later by ringing in sick from home one day.

Beep.

'Um . . . Hi Ian, it's Archie here . . . Archie, from . . . you know, from Intron.' There was a substantial pause in the fragmented announcement.

Ian answered him, as if he were talking to him live on the phone. 'Again? For fuck's sake!' The pause continued. 'What the hell's going on four-eyes?'

The message continued, oblivious. 'It's now . . . it's now ten-thirty, and I've rung you at work and you're not there. I . . . I seem to have . . .'

There was another pause, into which Ian inserted, 'I thought I told you never, ever to trouble me with the tedium of your company when I'm at home.' Despite everything, Ian was quite enjoying himself. It was a chance to insult Archie with absolutely no come back. In fact speaking to him in this way was remarkably similar to the one way traffic symptomatic of conversing with Archie in the flesh, but was much more pleasurable now that the pedantic bastard couldn't answer back. And if Ian couldn't think of a good put down, he could always rewind the tape and play it again, but this time with the benefit of rehearsal to improve the spontaneity of his abuse. On the tape, Archie cleared his throat, tried to say something and then paused again. Ian resumed the disrespect. 'I mean, why the fuck would I want to speak to you at home when I have to put up with you all day at work, you boring bastard?'

Archie's disjointed speech continued. He sounded nervous and unsure, and Ian made the most of it. 'Look Ian, the things is . . . I've, I've been arrested . . . .'

'Yesss!' Ian punched the air with his free hand.

'I went to a nightclub . . . and I got arrested, and this was last night, well, at about half-past three this morning, and they detained me, but I haven't been charged with anything.'

'Bugger!' Ian lowered his arm.

'The thing is the nightclub, I think it was called the Banana club, didn't have a licence to, er, to sell intoxicating liquor, and there was a bit of a mix up as regards who was in charge of the room I was showing my films in,' Archie began to pick up a bit of momentum and Ian found it hard to interject, 'you know, some early science-fiction classics that my friend Steve from university had asked me, well paid me, in fact, to show – *The Thing With No Name* and *The It Thing* and . . .' Archie rambled on in this vein for a long, long thirty seconds, while Ian worried his machine might run out of tape before he had time to abuse him again, and then rounded off with, 'Well, anyway, none of this is of much interest to you, I'm sure . . .'

'Damn right,' agreed Ian.

'. . . And, actually, now I come to think about it, I thought I saw you there . . .'

'Yep.'

'But look, I'm afraid that it . . . well, it will effect you, ultimately, or may effect you.'

Archie was quiet again, but Ian remained silent also, slightly confused. What the fuck was he talking about?

'Look, there's a lot of things I've got to tell you . . . .'

There was another considerable pause. 'Go on, Nylon Man,' Ian encouraged the answer machine.

'Anyway, I'll try you later. Bye.' The one and only time Ian had ever been genuinely interested in hearing more of what Archie had to say, and the fucker had clammed up on him. He swore at the phone, which beeped back, indicating that there was at least one more message.

Losing Yourself

Ian watched the flashing red LED of his answer machine expectantly. He was cold enough just to be uncomfortable, and the central heating, like the Nurofen he had just taken, was yet to kick in

Beep.

'Bit daft, running off like that.' He frowned, trying to place the voice, and scratched his scalp for good measure. Sharp, disabling pain spread across his skull as his fingernails disturbed the still bleeding wound. Recognition quickly followed. It was Frying Pan. 'Do that again and you won't have any legs to run with,' he snapped, before adding, 'We'll be in touch' and hanging up.

Beep beep beep.

Ian forgot all about Archie as his heart began to surge and his bowels clench. How the hell did Frying Pan get his number? He couldn't remember giving him his name. Ian rang 1-4-7-1. A monotone robot female announced, 'You were called . . . tonight at . . . eighteenosix . . . we do not have a record of the caller's number.'

Ian looked at his watch. Six-thirty. The 'we' was menacing.
We? An organization? A gang? What? Shit, it must be Frying
Pan and Tattoo. They must know each other. They could be
on their way over. It would only take fifteen minutes by car.
Shit. The wallet, of course. It had his driver's licence in it. If
they had his number, they must have his address – they must
have rung directory enquiries. When would they come?
Surely not now if they'd taken the trouble of ringing and
announcing their intention. Maybe that was it – they wanted
him out so they could ransack his place. He was insured – it
would be better than a couple of broken limbs and some
more head injuries. He tried to convince himself, but it
squeezed too tightly around his stomach. He thought about
ringing the police. Two large problems immediately made
themselves known to Ian's clouded brain. Number One,
Paul's dope plants. Two healthy six-footers he had gladly
offered to accommodate while his friend Paul went off round
the world to find himself in a place he had never been. It
seemed that everyone managed to find themselves in India
after some sort of trek around the world. Still, it's always the
last place you look. Ian decided, should he ever lose himself,
that he would start by looking in India first, just to narrow
the search down a bit. The housing of Paul's massive dope
plants had seemed like a fantastic bargain at the time, rather
like someone asking you to mind a beer tree that continually
spawns cans of beer which are replenished every few days
with fresh cans. Even the West Midlands Constabulary could
hardly fail to notice the thriving plantation in his back room.

Number Two, well, he didn't like to think about Number
Two.

He started to hunt around for things he would need. He
had a good look in the bathroom mirror. Probably, it looked
worse than it was. He washed his scalp. It wasn't. His eyes
watered involuntarily with the spiked pain of cleansing. He
stopped washing the blood out.

The worst that could happen would be some of his belongings being stolen. But the more he thought about losing individual possessions, the more indispensable they became. He tried to think of possessions he could happily live without. OK, there were belongings that he had to all intents and purposes already discarded, in that he rarely, if ever, used them, but he struggled to picture a single item which he could happily bear to do without. Even the most dusty, bored, tired, cheap, malfunctioning, unwanted belonging suddenly assumed enormous importance, for it is only when faced with losing something that its value becomes apparent. He thought about hiding some of his most valuable possessions. But when it came down to deciding which items to lose and which to keep, he was unable to put any in the former category.

Astronauts

There was only one thing to do. Clint Eastwood, in real life, would have done the same. Ian abandoned his house, after locking all the inner, middle and outer doors he could find the keys to (in truth, this totalled one door) and securing the ground floor windows. He was too tired to explain his last twenty-four hours and newly clotted scalp to anyone, and was also paranoid that, having tracked him down this far, Frying Pan and Tattoo would be able to locate him at a friend's house, so he decided to go into work and sleep there. Having been denied what could reasonably be described as anything near relaxation or restfulness for at least a day, the idea of getting his head down in his office was becoming appealing to the point of urgency. He threw some clothes and the last remaining cans of beer into the boot of his car. The sometimes trusty Peugeot started at the first expletive, which was the fifth or sixth attempt, and he drove, some-what unsteadily, the three miles to the office he shared with Archie. He was certain that, if stopped, he would light a breathalyser up like a firework, given the contents of his bloodstream. Having read somewhere that drunk-drivers usually over-compensate for the paranoia of alerting the police to their actions by driving excessively slowly, Ian decided to drive as exuberantly as his one litre car would allow, which wasn't particularly exuberantly, to throw the police off the scent. This logic propelled him fairly precipitously to work, where for once he found a parking space within, at least, bus distance of the soulless sixties building where he worked. The building was still well lit – a sure sign of the all pervading, insidious paranoia which coated its walls and whispered, 'Leave your light on, let them think you're still here, still working, that you haven't gone home, that you haven't got a life outside work'.

The headquarters of Intron was a squat, elongated two-storey structure. Each storey consisted of a single, long, straight corridor, decorated on either side with offices, so that any cross-section along its length would reveal an office, a corridor and an opposing office. Essentially, what you saw from the outside was exactly what you got on the inside. There were no attachments, extensions or outhouses. Its design was economical to the point of bankruptcy. The colour of the building was less straightforward. Certainly, it was browny grey, but whether it was a grey which had browned with time, or a brown which had greyed, was open to debate.

It was eerie arriving at work not to work, at night, not having been there during the day. In the same way that astronauts returning from long bouts in space feel for the first time the enormous weight the earth constantly exerts on us all, Ian felt the dull ache of inevitability that he usually experienced as he entered every morning, and realized that it wasn't work but the sense of loss that the building held for him that made him ache. The loss of hopes, ambitions, day-dreams and sunlight, of timelessness, openness, expression, invention and instinct. The building meant work; work meant the building. Ian couldn't distinguish the object from the action. So, as he approached, he experienced all his normal feelings of loss, despite being there partially of his own volition.

In the absence of a security guard, which was fortunate given that his i.d. had been lost with his wallet, Ian entered the building. He made his way to the office, suddenly aware of the long corridor's stillness, in contrast to its usual air of unease. The corridors were, during the day, elongated torture chambers of civility, with their own rules and laws to be obeyed by approaching colleagues. The first step was identification, which, given the length of the corridors, could occur at distances of up to fifty yards. Second came eye contact avoidance. Third was preoccupation. Something outside the window, or a sudden interest in the state of the walls or the cracks in the floor or some other engineered distraction. Fourth, and finally, was confirmation. A mute head-nodding recognition between the conspirators. The further the day wore on, the thinner this façade became. At the start of the day, colleagues would greet everyone they had not encountered so far that day, and tick them off under the heading of First and Only Civility of the Day. After this, each subsequent corridor passing of a previously registered colleague resulted in a lower form of acknowledgement until both parties conspired to ignore one another totally. A fresh page was started and crossed off each day. Corridor strategy became more tangled the longer the day wore on, and depended upon the number of times you had encountered a given person that day, whether you had crossed the threshold of mutual ignorance, whether the person was someone who you liked, hated, endured, looked up to, looked down upon, wanted to impress, wanted to undress, needed to talk to, or had been avoiding for some time. In the midst of such an environment, some had adopted tactics like ignoring everybody, which generally seemed to work well. Ian had tried, temporarily, another tack, which was to greet everyone from a great distance, waving and smiling the length of the corridor. In this way he had hoped people would give him a wide berth. Maintaining a friendly enthusiasm for his colleagues, however fake, even for a day, had proved soul destroying and he quickly abandoned the idea.

Spared such considerations for once, Ian made his way down the vast corridor which served his office and unlocked the door. Inside, he slumped in the comfiest chair he could find and opened the first of his cans of beer. He was still on edge and the pain in his head was doing its best to shine through the soft haze of Nurofen. He got up and nosed around the low-ceilinged room, stopping by Archie's desk. He wondered what the sad wanker kept in his drawers. If there was ever a time to find out, this was it. Ian began to investigate. The desk looked more dishevelled than usual, almost akin to the catastrophe of his own desk. Two of the three drawers were unlocked, and housed nothing more inter-esting than a TV guide, an old scarf and variously discarded paper clips, staples and drawing pins. Like everyone else who had joined Intron, Archie had obviously raided the paradise of the stationery cupboard on his first day, only to be at a subsequent loss as to what exactly to do with the amassed items from there on. Ian knew this because he too had a drawer similarly full of hoarded and useless treasure.

But what was happening to Archie? First, Ian was fairly sure that he had spotted him at the club last night. He could-n't be certain of a lot of things that had happened in the last twenty-four hours, but if Archie said he'd gone to the club, a once in a lifetime event for the dullard, it was a fair bet that it was actually him that he had seen. And what the fuck was he talking about on the phone? Arrested? Archie? Most of the police force was in more danger of arrest than Archie. And how the hell could that have anything to do with him? Ian moved to his own desk and started hunting rapidly around in the drawers and then swore. He then made another similar sweep of Archie's drawers, and, failing to find what he was looking for, swore once more for good measure. He had obviously lost Archie's phone number somewhere, probably in the bin, and perhaps understandably Archie didn't keep a copy of his own number in his desk. Defeated, Ian took a heavy swig of beer and tried to imagine just what the fuck was going on with Archie.

The World of Archie

When Archie entered his house, he was startled by the unfamiliar sound of the phone ringing. Generally, he received approximately one call per week, from his mother, at around 8.00 pm on a Monday. Two calls in a week from his mother would be an unwelcome intrusion, since he would only have half the news that he normally had when she rang, which was generally minimal anyway, and would have had no time to prepare a list of what that news was, or broadly, wasn't. He approached the phone with some trepidation and answered with an tentative, 'Yes?'

'At last! Where've you been you old codger? I've been trying you since five.'

'Hullo.' Archie had no idea who it was. He had successfully and systematically whittled the circle of friends who had endured him at university down to something which now resembled more of a full stop.

'It's Steve, you know, from Uni, Film Soc and all that, remember? Come on Archie it's only been, what one, two . . . Jesus . . . three years.'

'Hullo Steve.' It must have been a couple of years since they had spoken, and it was unlikely that they'd been good friends when they had known each other.

'Look, the reason I've rung you is, do you still have all those sci-fi films and videos and stuff?'

'Yes, I've got the complete first three . . .'

'Great.' Steve cut him off before he got a head of steam going. Given Archie's difficulty with almost any form of communication involving actual people, it was unlikely that he *would* get a head of steam going, but nonetheless was a scenario to be avoided if at all possible. 'Look, the thing is, I need to ask a favour. I mean, I'll pay you, and well. There's this club, right, nightclub, in town, and they've given my company i.e. yours truly the job of doing the lighting and showing films and stuff for this one-off thing tonight. It's like, they have this massive old room where they show films and stuff so cheesy quavers can, like, chill out, and they're really into sci-fi stuff, obviously, but the trouble is I've only got that sort of thing on video, not, you know, actual film.'

Star Trek was rapidly approaching. Archie had no idea why crisps should need to be refrigerated, but he had long harboured a desire to dust off the old sci-fi films he had accumulated during his spell in Film Soc. However, as he didn't possess a projector, he had been unable to do so. The chance to inflict some of his most obscure sci-fi B movies on people, to control what they watched, oh yes, this was power. After a long pause during which Steve thought he had blown it and Archie entertained another sci-fi related day-dream of bringing his secret knowledge to the masses, he replied, 'Steve, would I be able to show whatever films I wanted?'

'Yes, of course, I mean, it's up to you, you're the boss, just bring your films and we'll set them up, and away we go.' Thank God, the pedantic twat was going to save him. 'It's at the Banana Club on Digbeth High Street. It might look a bit, sort of permanently closed, but don't worry 'bout that, be there about eight to set everything up – I'll sort you out for the taxi.'

'All right. Bye.'

Archie put the phone down and sat on the stairs with a rising nervous excitement which started somewhere in the base of his stomach and squashed the air out of his lungs, until he realized with horror that Star Trek had started and he wasn't taping it. He would have to execute some elaborate video programming, as he wouldn't now have time to watch any of the items in his itinerary. Archie was, of course, fully conversant with his video recorder and had memorized key sections of the instruction manual, dubious grammar included, which he would occasionally regurgitate in front of Ian when planning his evening's complex viewing and video-ing itinerary. 'Set timer off to recall programme mode display,' he muttered, grappling with the impenetrable cello-phane cover of his newly bartered tape.

The taxi arrived four minutes later than the time he had booked it for and so, as was his habit, he told the taxi driver he would be out in a minute, sat down on the stairs and counted out four minutes on his watch. After about ninety seconds, however, he realized he was too excited to maintain his principle. He heaved the dusty box of sci-fi films up to his chest and tried to lock the front door while jamming the box between his chest and the front wall of his house. This would give him a chance to really show Ian. The Banana Club. He'd slip it casually into their ritual morning quarrel tomorrow.

In the taxi, he imagined a growing sense of expectation from people readying themselves to go to the club. In the same way that he heard of people flocking to see a renowned DJ, he envisaged friends ringing each other up to discuss who the projectionist would be tonight. Another day-dream was shattered when he arrived at the club only to be con-fronted by a dangerous looking bouncer who was adamant that he wasn't coming in dressed like that.

'But I'm the projectionist,' he insisted.

'This isn't a fucking cinema,' the bouncer countered.

'But I can assure you that Steve told me to be here.'

'Where you meet your boyfriend is up to you pal, but you're not meeting him in here.'

'No, but Steve works here.'

'Sorry sunshine, never heard of him.'

Some twenty minutes of unscientific reality later, Steve arrived to find Archie leaning against a pillar in front of the monstrous metal façade of the nightclub, scribbling furiously in a notebook. Having avoided contact with Archie for at least a couple of years made for a slightly clumsy reunion, though any social interaction with Archie was bound to involve some degree of awkwardness.

'Hi Archie.'

'Hullo Steve,' Archie replied, with a flatness that aspired to be monotone.

'What're you doing?'

'I'm trying to run my ball point out of ink.'

Steve didn't enquire any further. 'Won't they let you in?'

'It seems that I'm not dressed appropriately,' Archie explained, nodding his head in the direction of the bouncer.

Steve walked over to the main door, exchanged a few pleasantries with the same bouncer and indicated to Archie that it would now be OK for him to enter.

'Er, I'm not sure if I mentioned it on the phone, but the club might go on quite late, all things being well,' Steve mumbled half-heartedly as they walked through the entrance.

'Fine,' Archie replied, without wondering whether his and Steve's ideas of late might not coincide.

Inside, the club was an enormous, enclosed, tinny hangover from the night before. The carpeted floor was like a morning-after tongue, sticky and yet dry, and the walls echoed like a metallic headache. This was the aftertaste of several hundred people's good time. It was one of the most depressing places Archie had ever been. The building's air of hangover was accentuated by the bar staff, bouncers and cloak room attendants readying themselves and the nightclub to witness another conveyer belt of joy.

The cinema in which Archie was to show his films wasn't a cinema but a room smaller than the main one, and which had been designed to hold functions in or to stage small bands. It lacked the sterile plastic and metal nature of the rest of the club, draped as it was in parachute silk and large camouflage netting to give an enclosed, womb-like feeling. At one end was a screen which would have been dwarfed by proper cinema screens but was, nonetheless, large enough to dominate the room to his satisfaction. An archaic projector was housed at the opposite end, surrounded by other, newer gadgetry, which he assumed was used for controlling the ample banks of lights which poked through the various wall and ceiling coverings.

'Pop your box down there, Archie.'

'Steve, I'm not sure I quite followed your gist on the telephone earlier. If I understand you, you're being paid to refrigerate some crisps . . .'

'What?'

'I've written it down.' Archie opened his notebook. 'Here, apparently you are running a "chill out room for some cheesy quavers."'

Steve made a composite nasal snorting-laughing sound. 'Christ Archie, where have you been? It's a room where ravers, or cheesy quavers, come to calm down, or chill.'

'Oh,' said Archie, still less than clear.

55 % Real Orange

No one came into the room, except a couple of miserable bar staff and the DJ, who put on an album and retreated. Archie examined the contents of the box which housed his treasured celluloid. *The Thing With No Name* was the title on the first dust cover he opened. This had always irritated him. If the Thing did have a name, it wouldn't be a Thing. But he tried not to let the oxymoron distract him. There were a million films that no one would have gone to see on the title alone. *Jaws*, for instance. What did that title mean, exactly? It may as well have been called *Gums* or *Mandibles* or *Cheeks*. It didn't *sound* scary. It didn't mention teeth or fins or anything. What was so scary about jaws? It was hardly *Nightmare on Elm Street* or *Texas Chainsaw Massacre* or *Night of the Living Dead*. The beauty of sci-films, though, was that the title told you everything you needed to know about the film. Since the plot was always the same, as long as the title described the nature of the thing that was going to try to take over the earth, you knew what you were getting. *Invasion of the Bodysnatchers, Attack of the Flying Saucers, Plan K*

From Outer Space, They Came From Mars – yes, you knew where you stood with science fiction.

Archie fiddled with the mechanism of the projector, and some twenty minutes later (a time filled, in the place of expletives, with phrases such as 'counter intuitive', 'design inadequacy' and 'unfuzzy logic'), he succeeded in getting the projector to play his beloved B movie. He looked in his notebook. Under *The Thing With No Name* was written 'one hour and fourteen minutes'. That would give him plenty of time to root through the rest of his films, have a wander around the building and maybe buy an orange juice. Not that it would contain more than 55% of anything which could be accurately and legally described as the juice of oranges. This was another thing that offended Archie. Britvic 55, he had been led to believe from advertisements, contained 55% pure orange juice. He pondered what the rest of it might be made from? Was it Water 45? Was it unpure orange juice? Was it 55% so that it achieved the majority of the contents, and could therefore be called orange juice, and not an orange drink? Why not just extract the juice of oranges and put it in bottles? What was so difficult about that? It wasn't as if it would be prohibitively expensive since the bottles were minute, and could, at a guess, hold no more than around 50 millilitres of fluid. What really annoyed Archie were the adverts he had seen which proclaimed, '. . . and now with **real** orange juice'. What was so wrong with oranges? Why did manufacturers do all they possibly could to try to keep the things out of any product which had 'Orange' on the label? They weren't dangerous, as far as he knew. He decided instead to order a pint of shandy, and made a note subsequently to boycott all products which proclaimed to be any percentage less than 100% of what they should have been in the first place. You didn't buy pints of 55% beer, '. . . now made with **real** beer'. However, as his frothy shandy was topped up with lemonade, he realised he had already broken his new rule by ordering a pint of beer which had been diluted by 50% with lemonade which had been carefully and strictly kept clear of any potential contamination by real lemons. Archie looked sheepishly around the room and hoped he wouldn't encounter any of the members of the Real Ale society he had joined during his half-hearted drinking days at university.

The club was starting to fill up, very slowly. The twilight hour or so of nightclub limbo was passing. Painfully young girls and boys with pale cheeks and too little clothing blinked in the stroboscopic lights, still not sure that someone wouldn't come up and say 'We only let you in for a joke – we know you're too young – we're going to have to humiliate you by throwing you out'. Archie was certain that most of them were yet to achieve the legal age of nightclub entry. The building's echo slowly receded and people started to file into Archie's room, and then, seeing it empty, file rapidly out again. Logic told him that, if people wouldn't enter a room because it was empty, it would always remain empty. He returned to *The Thing With No Name* to find that a DJ had installed himself and was leafing through his records.

'All right,' ventured the DJ, taking his headphones off in the way that men in the olden days used to doff their hats when introducing themselves.

'Yes, thank you.'

'Monster film, that,' the DJ motioned towards the screen. This rather seemed to be stating the obvious to Archie, but he had to agree, it did contain one monster, at least.

'Yes, that's correct. There are rather a lot of monsters in it actually.'

Undeterred, he tried again. 'Sorted.'

'Oh yes, they're all in order now,' Archie testified.

'No, I mean, you know, B movies and all that, they're safe.'

Archie regarded him quizzically. 'I'd say the Thing looks anything but safe, if you ask me.'

The DJ looked back at him and quickly replaced his headphones.

When Archie surveyed the room again, it was crowded. He felt a sudden surge of adrenaline of the kind he rarely experienced when he wasn't programming or thinking about change disposal. Here was his public. He couldn't quite sum up what it was about his public, but they seemed very excitable. They were big sci-fi fans, that much was obvious, though it puzzled him that they should find it necessary to dance while watching the film.

The Thing With No Name came to an obvious and sticky end. By the unwritten rule of sci-fi films, any invading monster cannot be dispatched simply by conventional weapons technology, whatever that might have been at the time. Shooting it, setting it alight or blowing it up would only encourage it. No, what had to happen was that a totally inappropriate method of dispatching the monster would be discovered accidentally. The more unlikely this procedure was to harm anything, the better. Luckily, every tentacled invader had an Achilles' heel which could be mercilessly exploited – like cold temperatures, hot temperatures, carbon dioxide, water, electric fields or any other relatively inert matter. *The Thing With No Name*, no exception, was slowly and painfully eliminated by magnetic fields. Archie set about cueing up the next film, *The It Thing*. Archie wasn't particularly happy with this title either.

One hour and forty-eight minutes later, as his notebook indicated, *The It Thing* ended, and the next film was dusted off, wound around the projector mechanism, and juddered into some sort of life. The room was, by now, full. On the whole, most of the young people were enjoying his films. Some even seemed transfixed by the images, watching in wide-pupilled awe, no doubt, at the quality of the direction. Others seemed almost too transfixed, and he had seen at least two or three run out of the room or scream during particularly vivid scenes. Yes, Archie was undoubtedly in charge, and his public were revelling in his films. He walked to the bar, suddenly self-conscious as he picked his way through the throng, and decided to toast his success with a pint of 100% beer. It was 12.30 am, two hours after his usual bedtime, but he wasn't tired. He was experiencing, or thought he was, something new – popularity. People were friendly towards him, warm even. Strangers said hello to him. Some so relished his films that they tried to hug him and had to be shrugged off. He decided to wander around the club.

He walked into the main room. What he saw and heard raped his senses after the womb-like atmosphere of his section. Blinding stroboscopes attacked the discordant, satanic sub-bass thump thump thump of industrial techno. There was an all-encompassing atmosphere of mania. Everywhere he looked, youths danced with a strange language of rapid movement, all facing forwards in unquestioning worship of a pulpitted figure with headphones on, who looked as if he had seen better days. So, this must be a rave. Then suddenly Archie spotted someone on the opposite side of the room who looked remarkably like Ian, and who seemed in an overwhelming hurry to leave the room. Archie made his way through the celebrating throng and back towards the relative calm of his own room, pondering as he did so the generally irregular behaviour he had witnessed that night.

The fourth film ended and Archie looked at his digital, plastic-strapped watch. 2.45 am. He was beginning to feel tired. He wound the fifth film on to the spool and leant over to the DJ booth.

'Excuse me, but do you know what time I have to stop showing my films?'

'As long as it goes on, I s'pose.' The DJ replaced his headphones and looked intently at a record sleeve.

'Yes but, well, do you know what time this event itself

stops?' Irritably, the DJ took his headphones off and said, 'What?'

'What time does this end?'

'What?'

'This night.'

'It's an all-nighter.'

'But it's morning now.'

'So?'

'Well, if it's meant to last all night, then it has already. I mean, technically, it's the morning now.'

'No, I mean, when I say it's an all-nighter, right, it ends in the morning. About six usually.'

'Six? Six am? Why is it so late? Why don't they just start earlier? If they started at teatime, say, it could be finished by midnight, and everybody could get a good night's sleep.' Archie made a mental note to suggest this to Steve, when he saw him. If his public turned up to see his films at midnight, there was no reason why they wouldn't do so at teatime – he would, after all, be showing the same films.

'I think you're missing the point, mate.' The DJ took welcome relief in a pale girl who had come up to make a request. Even if she'd come up to order a couple of pints of lager, an ego-crushing occupational hazard of DJing, it still would have been an escape.

Archie crossed the room to the bar and bought himself another pint of taste-free nightclub beer. He never usually drank more than a couple of pints, even in his Real Ale Society days, but it looked like being a long night since he couldn't very well abandon his cherished films and go home. He returned to the projection booth and slumped in a corner with his beer. The current film – *Space Zombies* – had at least another hour and ten minutes to run by his calculations, so he made himself comfortable and ducked out of public view.

There was a large commotion. Archie lurched awkwardly to his feet and looked around. People were leaving *en masse* and the lights were on. The DJ and bar staff had gone. He looked at his watch. 3.40 am. He must have slept. There were about ten police officers encouraging people out of the room. Some people seemed more eager than others to leave. Loiterers were being threatened with being searched. A couple of policemen were looking at Archie. They were separated by a man Archie had observed entering the club while he had been locked outside. He pointed over at Archie and then left the room. The policemen made their way through the throng towards him.

Special Offer

Having drunk and mused and muttered, Ian picked up the office phone and dialled his answer machine, which kicked in after two rings, signifying that he had at least one new message. That he had managed to amass another phone call in the hour or so since he had left his house would, by normal standards, have been a very healthy comment on his popularity, but judging by today it could only be a comment on the catastrophic state of affairs in which he seemed to be entangled. He mined the inside of his telephone-free ear with his little finger as he listened to his greeting, hoping it wasn't more bad news.

He had sworn to himself on his way home from the shop he purchased his answer machine from that he wouldn't record a comedy greeting. He got straight home and sampled Elvis Presley singing 'One more time, just one more' from This Time the Girl is Going to Stay. He looped it over and over again and, on top of it, drawled, 'Ian has now left the building'. The joke, slim as it was, was looking dangerously anorexic, and if he could have been bothered to change it he would have done so. When Elvis had finished, he entered the two digit code necessary to remotely access his message or messages.

'Um, hi Ian, it's me, Archie, again.' Archie sounded a little shaken. 'Look, something bad has happened. I didn't want to worry you earlier,' Ian prepared himself for a new round of insulting Archie on tape, 'But you may be in trouble. Look, I'll come straight to the point . . .'

'It's only taken three fucking messages . . .'

'. . . but I've given your name and address to someone I shouldn't have. Someone who might be dangerous.' And with that, Archie blurted it all out in unpunctuated monotone. 'There was this man, when I was in the police station, who I shared a cell with, and we were conversing and he had been arrested for attempting to break into somewhere and I asked him where and Ian, it was Intron, and I asked him what he wanted there and he said he was just interested and then I asked him specifically what he was interested in and he said why did I want to know and I told him it was because that was where I worked, and he said he'd been wanting to meet someone like me for a while and then became very interested in me, unpleasantly interested to tell the truth, and he was very threatening and I was scared and it was going to be a long night alone with him in the cell, and all he wanted to know was where I lived and I told him that I wasn't going to tell him and then he turned violent and asked me again and so I told him . . .' Archie went silent for a couple of seconds. 'Well . . . I told him where *you* lived. Look, I don't know why Ian, I just panicked, and I didn't want him coming around to my house, and after that he left me alone and I've been trying to warn you ever since and I think he may well be interested in breaking and entering.'

Jesus, what a day. Yesterday no enemies. Today, two lunatics in a pub and now a potential burglar in possession of his name and address. Just when his life seemed shit, Archie turned up and made it worse for him. A net of psychopaths was closing in around him, and for no other reason than taking a day off work and having an imbecile for a colleague.

Archie continued, 'So I don't know what to do, but maybe you should phone the police and explain that a burglar has your address and knows where you work, so knows you won't be there during the day, or maybe you should just lock all the doors and windows and stay at home in case he tries to break in.'

'Great idea,' Ian derided. There was little chance that he would be hanging around at home with Frying Pan coming to visit as well.

'I mean, I think I'm pretty safe in the meantime . . .'

'Great.'

'So don't worry too much about me . . .'

'Fat chance.'

'But I'm going to go to work tomorrow, and if you do talk to the police, then I don't mind if they want to talk to me or get a description or whatever. And you've got my phone number should you want to talk more about it.'

'Shit . . .'

'Right,' Archie sounded like he was going to apologize, but simply ended with, 'Bye'.

'Stupid wanker.' The machine, having fulfilled its end of the bargain by playing its one and only message, beeped four times, almost in unison with Ian's continued swearing as if he was being censored on pre-watershed television. 'Stupid, bastard (beep), trainspotting, shit dull (beep), four-eyed, (beep) fuck faced, acrylic wanker (beep).' The tape began to rewind and he continued uncensored. 'Brainless, arse faced, fucking twat wanker cunt.' Ian ran out of words and the line went dead. He opened a fresh can of beer and looked mournfully at his spider plant which was in its death throes and then swore again. He took a deep breath and then a deep swig and thought about playing some soothing music on his radio cassette, but it had a habit nowadays of playing tapes at bizarrely different speeds and often erasing them as it did so. He made a mental note that if his house was still standing, and if he could visit it without the threat of any one of a number of local villains popping in and helping themselves to his possessions, he would dig out the receipt for his cassette player and take it back to Dixons and club the sweaty bastard who had persuaded him to buy it as an alleged Special Offer around the head with the useless piece of plastic. Unable to think of anything to do in the meantime, Ian manoeuvred three chairs together so that they faced in the same direction and lay down on them with his can of beer. It was Wednesday, Wednesday evening. His most important routine was being disrupted.

The Reluctant Goalkeeper

Ian always played football on a Wednesday evening. There were two teams, neither with any particular name or direction and they played each other every Wednesday of the year. In the seven or so years that Ian had been playing, no one had once suggested changing the teams around. The lines had been drawn, some time before Ian started playing, and once you joined one of the teams it was your destiny always to be on that team. No one kept count of who had won more of the three hundred-odd games. It didn't matter. It wasn't an all-consuming competitiveness that kept the two teams separate, it was just convention. To change things would be to destroy them. Players on both sides were friends, except on Wednesday evenings.

There were generally seven or eight a side, all of them in-their-minds-strikers who would take grudging goes at playing goalie for ten minutes or so each. The shout of 'Whosnotbinin?' would come from the last goal keeper, and it would be your turn. You didn't like being in goal – it was an experience that you could only lose from. But fair's fair so you took your turn and stood there and willed your team on. Only it was frustrating when your team were doing well. When your team had the ball, you didn't. Obviously you wanted them to win and everything, but the more proficiently your team attacked, the less chance there was that you would see anything resembling action. So secretly you started willing your team to lose the ball so that you might have something to do. Then worse. You would actually start willing the other team on. You would no longer be opposing the opposition – you would be actively, but silently, cheering them.

Winning is abstract. Always, to win is to lose something. Winning is of the moment. It does not matter if you win or lose the game. Victory is in the second that you score. At that moment there is no sense of loss, only of gain. If someone else scores and your team wins, you have lost because you didn't score the winning goal. A team can therefore win nothing. Only lone people during isolated seconds can experience true victory.

'Nice goal, that second one.'

'Cheers.' Not that it matters now. The moment has passed. You won't relive it, it is empty, over, it might as well not have happened. Sure, you'd have been upset if it didn't, but only at the time. The moment was everything, and then disappeared into irrelevance.

'You coming for a drink Gillick?'

You never go drinking with them. You just think of excuses not to, excuses for yourself, not for them, and slope off quietly while they head for the changing rooms. This is the first time the subject has been broached for as long as you can remember. You thought they'd stopped asking.

'Oh, you know, there's this bird . . .'

'Crafty bugger.'

There is no one. But if you've got to use an excuse, at least in dealing with men, a woman will always suffice in some form or other. Either sympathy or envy will distract them from matters at hand. You cycle home.

Last February, on a freezing Wednesday evening, things were different. The game had finished, and for a short moment the all-pervading cold was forgotten. The house was cold. The building you worked in was cold. The dressing rooms were cold. You had half felt like getting off your bike and lying down by the side of the road, surrendering to the cold, welcoming the last pleasant stages of hypothermic delusion like the first day of summer, watching the stars turn into icicles.

'You coming for a drink?' They were trying again, for some reason. 'Y'got to, it's Neil's birthday. Curry and a few beers.'

Maybe they felt you were missing out. On what, exactly, no one would have been able to tell you. But you knew from the last time how it was, and how it would be, which is why you never usually went.

The routine began. The dressing room. Huddling in groups, cold but sweating, three or four to a bench. The banter.

'You were shit tonight.'

'I may be shit, but at least I'm not an ugly cunt like you.'

Even perhaps the odd song. No one feels comfortable, at least not entirely. It's a conspiracy of *bonhomie*. A gentlemen's agreement to deny the fear, envy, mistrust, love, indifference, hate, loyalty, companionship and brutality that men feel when alone and naked together. Except there aren't many gentlemen here tonight. Let's get this over with.

The bar is a works bar, staffed half-heartedly by two ageing women whose faces bear the trials of ten thousand nights spent witnessing other peoples' enjoyment. How insufficient enjoyment must look from behind the barrier of the bar, and how it must haunt the nights you spend searching for fun on the other side. There are, of course, bar workers who enjoy themselves, or at least appear to. But not these two.

'Two pints of bitter and a Guinness, please.' And give us a fucking smile, for Christ's sake.

'Five-forty.'

'Cheers.'

The Guinness takes for ever. Adverts seek to suggest that it is this very fact that makes it such a good drink, that it is the wait which makes it worthwhile. Make something appear unobtainable, or, better still, make something obviously unobtainable appear to be accessible. You are in goal and the ball becomes unobtainable, so you want it, at any cost, even at the cost of losing the game. It is evolution – man strives to possess the unpossessable, to achieve what was previously unobtainable, and to destroy it. To destroy the unobtainable, that is the ultimate quest of man. The barmaid makes a lacklustre attempt at a clover leaf in the foam of the beer.

'Fuck me, a rare outing for the boy Gillick.' Neil is racing his first beer, buoyant in the company of his team-mates and on his birthday.

'Not as rare as a pass from you, you old fucker.' And so begins the banter.

'What? What about that beauty in the first half?'

'That was a fucking shot!' The routine analysis of a game little resembling the one just played starts in vain. It is empty and pointless – the moment has passed – but it is common ground, and that is, at least, one thing to be thankful for.

The Poisoning

They had begun the inevitable discussion about the game. He was trying to drink slowly, to pace himself. But the dehydration and the gradual erosion of the foul mood that had possessed him for some reason during the game meant that he began to catch up, and began to feel good. He could sense himself getting sucked into the beckoning engine that the barmaids witness every night, the all-enveloping, throbbing, myopic tunnel with no light at the end, lined with your friends or team-mates laughing with you, their voices echoing into infinity with yours, an inevitable chasm which only ends when your poisoned body refuses to travel any further.

'Jesus, I'm pissed.'

'Yeah. What about this curry?'

'What about it?'

'Well, who's up for it?' It's time to quit. To peddle home and hope some speeding metal box doesn't run you over. It's excuse time. There has to be one. Shit, anything will do.

'I'm not really that hungry. And there's this bird . . .'

'Oh fuck off Ian, you're coming with us for once.'

'Yeah, I want to, it's . . .'

'Come on, we're off. And so are you.' OK, he'd dump his bike, have a couple of starters, then make his excuses. Maybe the Indian wouldn't be licensed.

They set off, about twelve of them, towards the Bristol Road, a region populated alternately by the pubs, Balti houses and launderettes which provide their own brick commentary upon student activities in the area. A suitable venue presents itself. The waiters almost look grateful. There is a bar, crudely fashioned in a material designed to resemble mahogany, housing several leaden fish in an integral tank, the cloudiness of which suggests that the fish are swimming in Real Ale. Drinks are ordered without any noticeable consent, and Ian has a cold weak beer in front of him which has probably come from a large brown plastic bottle with Sainsbury's on the front. But he's not complaining that it's weak. Neil is eyeing his drink suspiciously. He has a pint, but by the look of it it's never been anywhere near Sainsbury's.

'What the fuck's this?' he asks.

'We thought we'd treat you, birthday boy,' says Mike. The word 'treat' is unfortunate. Not only is it clearly not a treat, it conjures up images of treatment, as a farmer might treat an outbreak of scrapie or foot and mouth. Treatment. How you treat your fellow beings. People you are in the same team with.

'Go on, get it down you.' A chant of 'Down in one' ensues. Don't drink it, for Christ's sake. It represents a generous contribution from all the optics, with a bonus of cider, lager, bitter, and anything else from once-opened, now crusty or cloudy bottles lying around enjoying the general mahogany effect.

He drank it.

Neil started to enjoy himself again. The cocktail kicked in with a spurt which was much more noticeable to the others than to himself. A nod of expectation went around the table as Neil's volume quickly exceeded that of his friends'. For a moment he was alight. He blazed, his eyes shone, his movements were rapid. It was as if he had snorted some stimulant rather than consumed a depressant. He was allowed to become the focus. He wasn't slurring or losing co-ordination – he was in full flight and there, waiting for him to touch the sun, were his team-mates. They weren't disappointed. His flight ended as quickly as it had begun. His features became quiet and pensive and then melted to give the impression of mildly clouded confusion, like those of an old man who has forgotten what he came upstairs for. He stood up uneasily, looking at his surrounding team as though he had finally understood what this was all about, before lurching towards the car park. Ian would often recall that exact expression, even though at other moments he had difficulty in picturing Neil's face or the clothes he wore. They carried on with their meal, and, despite the food, Ian felt empty. They had punished someone they liked. They were saying if we didn't like you we wouldn't dream of doing this to you. If you didn't like us you would have grounds for complaint. But, by this logic, you have no reason to question our motives. We poisoned you because we liked you, and you drank the poison knowing this, and, for an instant at least, you understood why this had to be. And then, according to several witnesses, you spent three quarters of an hour being sick in the car park.

Night Club Two

Bubbles struggled to the surface of the murky fish tank water which harboured half a dozen unhappy fish. Tropical fish often appear to be almost smiling, basking in their heated, clean, airy water, in stark contrast to cold water fish, which jut their lower lips out like pouting children in silent protest at the misery of their icy environment. These fish, though, in spite of their tropical origin, aped the misery of their cold water counterparts. A club was proposed and passed. Ian went out to give Neil the joyous news. Neil was none too enthusiastic.

'You coming then?'

Neil looked long and unsteadily into Ian's face. 'No.'

'Right. You'll find your way home OK?'

Another long, unsteady look. 'Yeah.'

'See you later then.' This was a conversation Ian would relive and relive.

They caught the bus to town, butterflies struggling through the curry and depositing their wing powder in their veins.

Just the word 'nightclub' occasionally made Ian catch his breath, not that anything exciting ever happened there. On the way it would always be full of beautiful, dangerous girls who by the time you arrived had turned into men and women who lived shitty lives and packed all their dreams into their ironed shirts and short skirts and carried them into a factory for good times with sticky floors and ultraviolet lights which highlighted the bobbles on your shirt like dandruff and made the tar-stained teeth of the girl you talked to because you didn't want to go home alone appear milk white when you could see them when the strobes weren't saying you are enjoying yourself and you like this woman so you go to the bar and pay two pounds fifty for a bottle of beer with a clean sharp feeling on your tongue and no unpleasant aftertaste and one for her and you can't hear a word she says so you still want to take her home though you feel like it's all an elaborate way of turning off your senses one by one until you are truly senseless and they even have to persuade you to leave in the end packed into speeding metal boxes like some sort of product with the batteries removed home to your square brick box and you realize you left your dreams somewhere maybe on the bus there or in the club itself and you wish that the beer hadn't had all its flavour removed because the only aftertaste you have now is one of defeat.

It was like taking a jar of the Mediterranean home with you from your holidays. When you bottled it, the water held the same transparent radiant blueness you had immersed yourself in. Now, as you unpack it from your suitcase, pleased that it survived the baggage handlers' delicate touch, and hold it up to the light, you notice that its radiance and its blueness have disappeared and you are left with a jar of tap water. Somewhere, maybe over the Mediterranean, it lost its blueness.

But, just as Neil had knowingly drunk the poison they offered him, they entered the club and fully expected the

time of their lives. They bought clean, crisp beer and hud-
dled like sheep dogs contemplating which sheep to pen, and
Ian began to be thankful for the strobe lights and volume.
Since she left, he had been unable to face intimacy. He
wanted it, craved it, and now more than ever, even though the
thought of such familiarity made him shiver. And so, like a
spayed tom that still sprays and arches and serenades female
cats because it can't think of anything better to do, Ian joined
in with the group assessment of form.

'What about her there with the tits?' Justin was getting
descriptive.

'That's narrowed it down to the women.'

'Well, some of them,' Mike interjected.

Justin persevered. 'No, her there,' he said, nodding in the
direction of the dance floor, 'the one with the S'maritans
Shag.'

'The what?' Ian tried to focus.

'Every great-looking bird has an ugly friend, yeah? And
that's the one ugly buggers like you always get palmed off
with. But, just when you think, oh well, it's a shag, she gets
suicidal and starts cutting her wrists up that it's always her
mate that everyone chats up, and how no one decent is ever
interested in her, so you spend the night being a S'maritan
and telling her it was her you were interested in in the first
place, and basically not even getting to shag her.'

'That happen often then?'

'Oh yeah, all the time,' Justin said. And then, for the sake
of accuracy, added 'Probably'.

'Well, do you feel like crossing the road, then?' Ian asked.
'Eh?'

'D'you feel like being a Good Samaritan?'

'Oh. Go on then.'

So Ian and Justin sidle over. Luckily, Justin knows what to
do. All Ian catches is 'Me and my mate were having a bet . . .'
The strobes freeze his cringe as he tries not to stare at the

grimy wooden floor while attempting not to appear too keen to the Samaritans Shag, and wondering all the time whether she has any razor blades in her handbag. Ian attempts a cursory introduction.

'Hi, I'm Ian.'

'All right.' A name isn't proffered. He isn't disappointed. Ian tries to catch Justin's eye. He wants to abandon the mission, but Justin is off and running and won't be distracted.

'So . . .' Think of something, anything. A joke. Think of a joke. 'There's a job going for a check-out girl at Tesco . . .'

'What do you mean?' Samaritans Shag regards him suspiciously. 'I've got a job, thanks very much.'

'No, I mean it's a joke.'

'What is?'

'This is. Look, there's a job going for a check-out girl at Tesco, right, and they shortlist three applicants, and decide to ask all three candidates a trick question at the end of their interview.' Samaritans Shag looks a little unsure. 'Right, so they ask number one "You're fifty pee over when you cash up – what would you do?" and she says, "Well, I'd pop it in the charity box". Same question to number two and she says, "I'd put it in my pocket – no one's going to miss fifty pence". Number three's up, great interview like the other two, and she says, "I'd have a look through the cheque stubs and visa slips and see if I could work out who over-paid".'

'Yeah?'

'Yeah. So which one gets the job?'

'Don't know. The charity one?'

'No. The one with the biggest tits!' Samaritans Shag is not impressed. 'You know, the one . . . it's a feminist gag really, if you think about it.' Samaritans Shag looks like she's thinking about it. They look over to see how their respective friends are doing.

'Your mate's wasting his time – she's going out with the DJ – mind you she always gets chatted up, drives him mad, it's always happening, still, he's stuck up there, I mean, what's she supposed to do if he's doing his deejaying all night, it's not as if . . .' She continues in this vein, a vein clearly visible at the skin surface and now she won't shut up, and the Samaritan scenario, Ian is sure, is about to rear it's ugly head. He tells her he's going to the toilet but skirts around the outside of the club and rejoins the herd, who have returned to discussing the match.

'Ian, where's Justin?' asks Mike.

He explains and the situation is discussed with interest.

'Does the DJ look hard, then?'

'Dunno, just looks like some skinny geezer with big head-phones on.'

'My money's on the DJ.'

Whether or not Justin will get his head kicked in becomes the main topic of interest. A sweepstake is proposed but abandoned when no one will bet against Justin talking him-self into some conflict or other. Some people seek trouble, some attract it, some are oblivious to it, and the normal majority maintain a healthy distance from it. Justin fell into all of the first three categories. On the occasions when he hadn't sought trouble, he had attracted it largely through his appearance and, under such circumstances, was unaware of its lurking presence to the point of personal negligence. Justin sneered as a matter of course. In his most humble, sincere or forgiving moments he conveyed arrogance, deceit or revenge. It was an affliction, like having a permanent lunatic grin on your face. The fact that he naturally attracted antagonism often led Justin to seek trouble to allay his frus-tration. So no one would bet against Justin and some sort of affray.

On the way home from town, they sat upstairs on the night bus and decided the time was right to play Bus Rollercoaster. All twelve inebriates sat on the twin seats on one side of the top deck. Simon and Rick at the front raised their arms above their heads as if riding the coaster none-handed. The rest followed suit, and soon they were leaning into every bend with arms aloft, pressing their faces against the windows around roundabouts and screaming whenever the bus trundled downhill. Someone suggested a loop the loop, so they put their heads on their seats and waved their legs in the air, as much as not kicking any of the other passengers in the face would allow. This all went well until the bus hit a mile-long straight which seemed to take the fun out of it. Justin was ebullient.

'So this skinny geezer marches over and asks me do you know who I am, so I say no, and he says well I'm the DJ, and this is my girlfriend. So I say if you're the DJ who's that bloke up there fiddling with your records, and he goes kind of pale and dashes off somewhere up a ladder as fast as his fuck skinny legs will go, and this bird says sorry about that, he's a bit of a prick, give me your phone number. Get in!'

Some of the team are rueing not cleaning up in the sweepstake, the others not clearing up in the birds stake. He could, of course be lying. Then again, his sneer has, for once, turned unpleasantly smug.

Coffee Break

After a surprisingly satisfying night's sleep, which was so deep that it didn't even involve the usual fumbled trip to the toilet (this was a good job as the nearest toilet to Ian and Archie's office was a long, bladder challenging and disorientating corridor journey away), Ian lurched back into life. It may have been a pale imitation of life, but it was life, nonetheless. His head hurt, but it wasn't alcohol related. He touched his scalp and it stung. It was 7.30 am, probably earlier than even the keenest or most paranoid employees arrived at work. Ian couldn't know this for sure as he had always endeavoured, as a matter of principle, to be at work no earlier than nine o'clock. Some ill-fated mornings, school holidays and traffic permitting, he would reach the car park ten or fifteen minutes early, and would sit in his car squeezing the last few precious drops of freedom from his stereo until it was close enough to nine to enter the building. But the morning larks, who paced up and down at home impatiently waiting for the sun to rise and the building to be begrudgingly opened by a lacklustre security guard, seized every opportunity to announce the precise hour of their dawn arrival, and this is how Ian knew that they entered work at a ridiculously early hour. It may have been an elaborate scam, but Ian suspected not. These people seemed almost grateful to get to work. Scary, he shuddered, unfolding his prone form and heading down the interminable corridor in search of somewhere that might sell breakfast of some sort. The first routine of the day had already been disrupted, but he was more than willing on this occasion to sacrifice cereal and toast normality in favour of something fried.

By coffee break Ian had begun to feel better. He was still jittery about the state his house might or might not be in, but there was nothing he could do about that now. He had managed a full English breakfast and things were looking up. His head wasn't too clever but he wouldn't need it much today as he was preparing himself for another day of unofficial strike action. He washed out the remaining blood that had matted his hair in a toilet sink and took two tablets of the emergency ration of Nurofen that he kept in his desk.

Archie, however, was nowhere to be seen, and had not, as far as he was aware, made it into work the previous day, or even rung in sick. He suddenly felt in need of good company, but he was at work, so had to make do with a communal coffee break. Morning coffee was normally taken between 10.30 and 11.00 am, but would spill over to around 11.02 if a rich seam of conversation was tapped, which wasn't particularly often.

'Anyone seen Archie?' he asked. The only contribution which exceeded a half-hearted monosyllabic response to the negative was from Jamie.

'How come you're so concerned? I thought you hated Dr Spock.' Jamie was a new and fairly unwelcome addition to the catalogue of human behavioural abnormalities that was the Intron workforce. There was an edge to him which made his presence, at times, intolerable, and at other times just uncomfortable. The phrase 'you never know where you are with X' could have been coined just for him. It wasn't that he was one step ahead of you or was necessarily devious in his way, it was, well, just an edge.

'He's just been trying to get hold of me that's all.' Ian returned his stare. 'And anyway, it's *mister* Spock, not *doctor*.'

'Fucking hell, you *have* been hanging round with him – it's rubbing off.'

Several weeks ago Ian had been forced to go out drinking with Jamie as part of a transparent and unconvincing attempt by the personnel department to introduce new temporary members of staff to older disinterested temporary members of staff, and it was a nightmare. It is well-worn territory to suggest that the eyes are the window to the soul. But for Jamie, it was lager that was the window to his soul. Beer seemed to uncover in him a bottomless pit of loathing which manifested itself in a snarling unpleasantness, as if sobriety served to close the shutters on his repellence.

Ian returned the unpleasantness. 'Bollocks.'

'He wasn't in yesterday, I don't think, well, I didn't see him,' one of the anonymous beards piped up over his mug of coffee, before returning his attention to the Terry Pratchet volume he was hopelessly trying to immerse himself in.

Ian decided that solitude would be preferable to the company of his fellow workers and stood up to leave the coffee room.

'Fucking hell, who's had a pop at you?' Jamie spotted Ian's wounded scalp and was genuinely pleased to have done so.

'A pub door,' Ian replied, feeling somehow that he had lied and yet told the truth at the same time. Still, his explanation encouraged a nod of understanding and sympathy from the bearded Real Ale contingency of the coffee room, and even Jamie was unable to fault the logic of a drinking related injury. Fairly pleased with himself, Ian returned to his office, picked up the office phone and rang his home number. It was engaged. He tried again. It was engaged again. Someone must be leaving a message. He pressed redial. The phone rang through, and, unexpectedly, was answered.

'Hello.'

'Er, who's that?' Ian demanded, surprised and indignant.

'Who are *you*?' The respondent matched his indignation.

'Never mind that. Who the hell are you, and, more to the point, what the fuck are you doing in my house?' The cheeky cunt. Not only was he in Ian's house, he was answering his phone. He inhaled sharply. Frying Pan and an ever growing list of local villains knew where he lived and could have broken in. For all he knew, there could be a free-for-all jumble sale of his possessions going on.

'What do you mean your house? I'm in the street. And who the fuck are you?'

'I'm the fucker who's phone you're using, that's who I am. And what are you doing taking my phone outside? You'd better not damage my fucking cable.'

'What cable? This is a mobile. *My* fucking mobile.'

'A mobile? But I don't have a . . .' Ian's mistake began to dawn on him.

'Look, I don't know who the fuck you are but don't ring this number again, all right, or there'll be trouble. Real trouble.' There was a sobriety in the threat that encouraged Ian to apologize. Jesus, he was a magnet for nutters at the moment.

'Sorry, I think there's been a mix . . .' The mobile was shut off. Fuck. The redial facility of his phone was pissing about again. It was back to its old trick of storing the penultimate, rather than ultimate, number dialled. Christ knows who he had rung, but it was a fair chance that he had just insulted one of Archie's mates, and he couldn't, Ian supposed, have that many to insult.

He tried his own number again, carefully and manually this time.

'Right mate, it's Jon, Thursday, give us a call.' It was his brother, who only rang when he knew Ian wasn't in. In this way he had saved himself a small fortune over the years by relying on Ian to return his calls. Ian admired its simplicity as a scheme, and would have adopted it himself if his brother had an answering machine which, precisely for this reason, he didn't.

Beep beep beep.

He didn't know exactly what he was expecting, maybe something from the two lunatics from yesterday. At least they hadn't stolen his answer machine. He had hoped, maybe hoped wasn't the right word, thought, that Archie might have left another message. He obviously hadn't been at work yesterday but said he'd be here today and had, in the intervening time, taken the unusual and generally unwelcome approach of ringing him at home and leaving a series of successively more bizarre and perplexing messages. Added to this, he had begun to sound slightly more than monotonous. Not quite duotonous, more mono-and-a-bit-tonous, but certainly less unperturbed than normal.

The building started to empty at around 5.14 pm and was vacant by 5.16 pm. Ian sat at his desk and tried to think of the least dangerous thing to do. He needed beer, underpants, socks, food and television, in no particular order, although socks were probably further down the list than most of the other items. He decided a drive past his house in at least third gear would be a safe option. He left the office and headed down one of the endless corridors in the direction of the car park. Usually, at this time of night, he would be spared the awkward corridor rigmarole of identification, categorization, decision, assumed preoccupation and, finally, salutation or ignorance. Tonight, however, he was appalled to discover that a couple of colleagues were still at work and were approaching dot-like from the far end of the corridor. He enacted the compulsory feigned preoccupation with something outside the window, and they did likewise. He started the process of recognition through his peripheral vision. It had been a long couple of days and he was having trouble remembering whether he had encountered them that day, and whether some sort of conspiratorial nod of the head would be called for. It was getting too close to call from peripheral vision alone, so he turned his head and faced them as they approached some twenty yards away. He froze. Every muscle seemed to contract. It was Frying Pan and Tattoo and they were sprinting towards him. They were roaring and the awful noise he remembered from the pub yesterday echoed past him. He hesitated, then turned and ran. He sprinted with his head facing almost sideways. Tattoo was close behind. There was no one around. The security guards had not yet started their shifts. Tattoo was screaming. Ian slammed through a double set of fire doors towards the stairs. He heard the second set swing back and crash into Tattoo. He took the stairs three at a time. He was on the first floor. There was no easy way out of the building, now that they had blocked the ground floor passageway, without going up a floor, along another infinite corridor and back down through the unmanned security doors at the other end. He reached the end of the corridor. The growling and shouting had grown deeper. He whipped his head round. Frying Pan was now leading the chase, filling the corridor as he did so. Tattoo was nowhere. Ian panicked. He might have doubled back and headed towards the exit Ian had originally been making his way towards. This was presumably the way they had got in, though they would have had to breach the security doors to do so. He reached the top of the second staircase and plummeted down, jumping the last six or seven steps of each flight. Behind him, it sounded as if Frying Pan was simply jumping each flight without bothering the stairs with his enormous bulk. He saw the door, which fortunately opened outwards and didn't need a security code on departure. Ian lunged and went through it with an outstretched foot to guide the door open, just as Tattoo hurled himself at him from the connecting ground floor corridor. He opened and closed the hefty door almost in one action, slamming it shut behind him with a backwards kick, and it seemed to slow them down. Once outside he sprinted with renewed panic. There were few people about on the relatively leafy industrial park in which the unsightly buildings of Intron UK attempted to nestle. Ian looked around and realized that his assailants had given up the chase. He kept running until he reached his car. The thought had crossed his mind that, since they now knew where he lived and where he worked, they may well know which was his car, and might have disabled it. But no, his fairly trusty Peugeot was there, in all its dull red glory. He got in and turned the key. Nothing. This was not unusual. He cursed. Nor was this. He tried again. Nothing. It often needed coaxing. Ian screamed, 'Start you fucker, start.' He tried three or four more times, to no avail.

He couldn't remember when he'd last checked the battery, not that he was entirely sure what that involved nowadays. As a child, he had watched his dad top up the water and check the crocodile clips on cold Sunday mornings, but it seemed to have made no difference that Ian had barely bothered to look under the bonnet of his car since he'd bought it. Modern cars just seemed to run themselves. A component would fail, periodically, and you would pay someone to slot a new one in. Simple. It wasn't even worth peering under the bonnet if you broke down. Engines had become a meeting place for cables, tubes and reservoirs of various liquids. Nothing visibly seemed to move. The parts which did rotate or twist or fire evidently did so beneath the camouflage of wires and tubes and cables. Ian had looked under the bonnet of his car approximately twice since he bought it and attempted routine maintenance about once, and it hadn't seemed to matter, until now. He swore once more, for luck, tried the ignition, swore again and decided to cut his losses. He had a cautious look around the car park. Frying Pan and Tattoo weren't visible. He locked his car, resisted the filmic cliché temptation to kick it, and began a surreptitious walk towards the bus stop. There was a menacing surreality about the last couple of days. It was like the long extended after-effects of the drug, but far more drawn out and painful than even he had expected the come-down to be. Ian wondered how much lower he could fall. He stood behind the bus shelter where he couldn't easily be seen from the road but could spot any approaching buses. He was shivering. After fifteen anxious and uncomfortable minutes hiding at the bus stop Ian walked on to the solid dependable Number 11 circular bus. He stood in front of the driver's perspex garrison and looked at him with blank uncertainty.

'Where to?' demanded the driver.

'Um . . . seventy-five.'

'Yeah, but where to?'

'Just . . . away from here.' The driver continued to eye him through his perspex cage. 'Kings Heath. Yes, Kings Heath.'

He slid a pound coin into the change-free repository and sat down in the nearest seat which wasn't occupied. This wasn't easy, as all the seats, bar one uncomfortably close to an intimidating youth at the back, housed single occupants who used their bags or bulk or both to suggest that their seats were too small to be occupied by two people. This splendid isolation was further enhanced by walkmen or newspapers. Ian took the spare seat. He had no idea where he was heading, except on a circuitous journey around the city, as he could hardly drive by his house in a bus which didn't encompass his street on its tour. Neither could he return to work. No, he would have to stay on the bus until he decided which of his friends would least balk at the idea of putting him up for the night.

The bus eventually approached the area of Birmingham he

lived in. Kings Heath was a good area, people often said when Ian told them where he lived. Ian thought it was a good area too, though quite what set it apart from others with the same terraced houses, the same shops, the same street signs and probably even the same people he didn't know. The bus rattled down the street which ran parallel to his own. He sat forward and rested his chin momentarily and uncomfortably on the metal handrail which formed the top part of the seat in front, and then sat back again. The bus continued its relentless circle, threading its way through the adjoining dots of what were formerly small towns and villages but which now made up the Birmingham suburbs. People got on, variously grateful or frustrated, depending on how long they had waited in the graffiti of the bus shelters. Roads became streets, then avenues and drives and then back again. Old people in seats became young people who became middle-aged a few stops later. The intimidating youth became an old black woman, who became an unshaven drunk who became a pale youth with painfully short hair. It was a documentary of life seen through an unsteady camera. Ian was held, fascinated. He couldn't get off the bus. Three-quarters of an hour later, it approached the nearest point to his house once again, but he still couldn't bring himself to leave the human transformation which was occurring before his eyes. Maybe this was what they had meant in the old days when conductors had announced 'All change!'. Ian and the bus entered a third lap together. Each time, the circle seemed to be getting smaller. It was an ever-decreasing circle with his house at the centre, and for one all-enveloping moment, he saw his life as an inevitable spiral of insularity.

Self-Destruction

Although Ian had never felt suicidal, he had also never felt as low as this. He was, temporarily at least, homeless. True, he had a home, but he couldn't go there. He couldn't even seek shelter at work. He was on a bus that was describing a circumference of the places that he could no longer go, taking him close and then circling past them. He touched his head as a subconscious reminder of the more tangible pain that the last forty-eight hours had caused him. It had taken just two days for Ian to feel like a refugee. He was scared, but it was a numb fear. For a moment at least the thought of finishing it all off with a bottle of spirits and a handful of pills held him fixed in its welcoming headlights. Life was a balancing act, as far as he could see, between the world trying to destroy you from the outside by a multitude of various means and your very own being trying to destroy you from inside. Externally, the world had invented a million ways of destruction. Nothing was good for you. Nothing, not one single thing, was actually wholly and truly good for you. Food could poison you, breathing could choke you, the sun could burn you and exercise could strain you. Brushing your teeth could remove your enamel, taking vitamins could prove toxic for you, making love could infect you, sports could injure you, medicines could have side-effects and relaxation, the only activity he could think of which didn't seem directly dangerous, could harm you, if you relaxed too much. He had tried relaxing, in moderate doses. But he couldn't. His body could be attacking itself from within at any moment. He recalled a character in Julius Caesar who, shortly before running on to his sword, marvelled that the body never lacked the ability to dismiss itself. But Romans, their friends and even countrymen knew nothing of autoimmune disease – the ultimate self-destruction – destruction from within. Rogue immune cells, traitors in the midst, police attacking the very public that relies on them for protection. And just to make sure, biological material is built to self-destruct anyway, with each and every cell embodying a host of suicidal enzymes, just a switch away from lighting the blueprint paper and retreating to the safety of the cytoplasm. And worse. Even when you accept that your cells are built to self-destruct after a finite period, that the body is programmed only to see so many days, you find out that if they don't self destruct, you're in real trouble. If your cells decide to ignore the apoptotic order to fall on their swords, they achieve immortality, become malignant and kill the very tissues which ensure their and your survival. So, what sort of a chance do you stand? If the world doesn't get you, you will get you. If part of you does escape the innate mortality of biology, it will only serve to enhance the mortality of the rest of you. And if all this worries you, the anxiety will lower the efficacy of your immune system, and some new, and otherwise innocuous, pathogen waltzes into your unguarded body. There is nothing you can do against such odds. It's a miracle that people scraped from one day to another.

Ian surveyed the tired bus information posters. A West

Midlands Travel Co. Announcement, in the place where posters lingered for months, advertising re-start college courses, social security benefits or driving lessons, advised, 'We'll get there quicker if you have the correct change'. It annoyed him because he didn't have the correct change and had to sacrifice a pound coin in place of the seventy-five pence fare. What struck him though was the use of 'we'. It jarred. The bus was made up of 'I's. 'We' seemed to belong to another decade, another age. We had become I a long time ago, Ian didn't know when, maybe in the eighties. In common with the well documented fragmentation of the population from we to I, Ian's life had followed a similar theme. He had almost excluded the word 'we' from his spoken vocabulary since Sue had left.

Shelter

Ian began to suspect that the driver was taking more interest than usual in him by his third lap of Birmingham. It was getting late and the number of passengers was dwindling. The metamorphoses he had witnessed earlier were now slower and less spectacular. As they approached Kings Heath for the third time he decided to get off near his house. The bus driver continued to eye him with suspicion as he waited in the door-well for the doors to open.

'Student, are you?' the weary driver asked.

'No.' He had been down this avenue before and waited for the inevitable follow-through.

'Oh.'

The driver indicated and stopped the bus as close to the bus stop as he could while still blocking the road. Ian waited until the bus was fully stationary and alighted, as the bus etiquette poster advised. He didn't know whether the bus driver had been trying in some way to insult him. It seemed, particularly in the light of recent evidence, that if you were intent on insulting someone, but couldn't quite put your finger on one specific term of defamation, a multitude of abuse could be covered simply by insinuating student status. Why this should be such a slur on one's character is particularly well understood by ex-students, as they step out into the bright sunshine clasping a rolled up 2:2 in political history, which is already looking a bit worse for wear around the edges, wondering how hard the world outside the red-brick womb will slap them when they arrive. In reality, the driver had assumed that Ian was a student who had lost his way and, for the most part, this was the truth.

The street that adjoined his was quiet, as it usually was at this time, its predominantly working masses beginning to surrender to the day's fatigue. He turned into his street and surveyed the parked cars which decorated both sides of the tarmac. Nothing appeared untoward. Using the cars as partial cover, he walked apprehensively towards his house on the opposite pavement. There were no lights on and everything appeared normal. The front door didn't look as if it had been breached and all the visible windows were intact. He could just make out, through the open curtains, a small red flashing light, indicating his answer machine had been busy again. For the first time in its underused life it was earning its money. Ian scrutinized the parked cars. They were all empty. He thought about going in. There were many things he needed, like a shower, a toothbrush, clean clothes and some sort of balanced meal. The awful paranoia of the phrase that Frying Pan had used, the paramilitary cliché of 'We know where you live', seemed to surround the house. He hesitated, then turned around and walked back the way he had come. He would go and disrupt the domesticity of the nearest friends he could think of. Quite what he would tell them he didn't know. Two apparent psychopaths have attached themselves to me and are trying to kill me for no obvious reason, so I've been sleeping rough at work, only I can't stay there tonight because they know where I work and where I live and

I can't call the police round for a number of reasons, one of them being the room full of dope plants that they might not take kindly to, and which could get me sacked if I get a criminal prosecution for possession with intent to supply. He reached Mark and Clair's house and knocked on the door. Clair answered the door.

'Hi Clair.'

'Ian.'

'Look, the thing is, I've locked myself out. D'you mind if I stay at your place?'

Mark and Clair lived a few streets away from Ian, owned a small but comfortable house and had somehow become middle class in the few months since they started living together. Apart, as single people, this hadn't been the case. But, somehow, purely through cohabitation, they had risen in social standing. Class puzzled Ian. It seemed to be something that people could only gain from. It was a one-way escalator. People could social climb, but social abseiling couldn't, didn't, shouldn't happen. Sons and daughters of working-class parents could be educated, become aware, achieve success and responsibility, and suddenly, in a dinner party conversation on the topic of class realize that they had become middle-class. Of course, they would deny it, unless their ambition had been fuelled by a conscious desire to escape their upbringing, but they would go home in the car with their born and raised middle-class partner, to the house they owned in an area where their car would be safe overnight and where the street corners weren't populated by youths who scared them, and it might begin to dawn that they, through their occupation, friends and thoughts, had crossed a bridge which did not exist in the opposite direction. For when did people who were born to wealthy middle-class parents ever live out the reciprocal scenario? When did they leave a dinner party at their well-to-do friends and head back to the tower block on the estate where they felt scared of the young and realize on the bus that, somehow, they had become working class? If the escalator *did* go in one direction only, Ian reasoned, eventually, everyone in the country would be middle class.

Another thing that Ian was less than happy about as he stood on Mark and Clair's doorstep was the order in which people described a couple who cohabited. When Ian and Sue had lived together it had invariably been Sue and Ian's place. Not Ian and Sue's. Ian owned it, the mortgage was in his name and still it was Sue and Ian's place. It wasn't alphabetically correct either. He had made a list of all his friends who cohabited, and it seemed generally that the male was referred to first. Dave and Marie. Martin and Rebecca. Mark and Clair. Paul and Helen. Clyde and Tracy. Chris and Jo. Graham and Helen. Mike and Jane. The list went on. He agonized that his male friends got their own way at home and were rewarded with first name status in the partnership. Certainly, he didn't seem to get his own way, and had to make do with 'and Ian'. He decided to try and start a revolution by deliberately referring to his friends' houses in reverse order of partners, hoping that it would catch on and he wouldn't feel so oppressed. 'Have you been round to Marie and Dave's recently?' and 'Tracy and Clyde are buying a house.' Inevitably, though, it didn't catch on, at all. Couple name order was a living and breathing testimony to who was the more important or popular of the couple. 'Sue . . . oh yes, and Ian.' Fucking great. The final insult was that since she had moved out, Ian still occasionally heard his house referred to as 'Sue's old place'.

Clair let him in. 'Ian's here,' she shouted after him as he walked into their hallway, with an enthusiasm that suggested that she had strangled 'unfortunately' from the end of the sentence.

'All right mate? Look, d'you mind if I kip here? I've lost my keys,' he asked Mark, who nodded then shook his head,

but generally tried to indicate that yes it was OK. He continued to gaze intently at the television.

'Have you seen this, it's fucking incredible.'

'What is it?'

'The male seahorse, right, gets pregnant by the female,
incubates the eggs, then out pop all these baby seahorses, or
seafoals or whatever, I mean, how do they know that that's
not just the female – maybe they've just got it wrong, I mean,
what constitutes a female nowadays?'

'I dunno. Hasn't a male got to have a Y chromosome?'

'No, I don't think so. I seem to remember from biology
that fish and butterflies and some birds, in the ornithological
sense of course,' he said, as Clair frowned, 'have females with
Y chromosomes.'

'Fatima Whitbread, now there's a bird with a Y chromosome. Two probably.' Clair frowned again, and Mark felt the
need to pursue a more erudite line.

'The point is though, if it's fairly arbitrary that the male of
a species has the Y chromosome, why don't they just swap
them round and call the one that gives birth the female, and
the one that fucks off after sex the male? It'd make it a lot
simpler all round, really. I mean, male seahorses must be
really fucking confused for starters.'

'Yeah.'

Mark and Clair retired early, mainly at Clair's insistence,
and left Ian to pad around. He explored the foreign territory
of their bathroom. He desperately needed to brush his teeth.
They were so covered in filth that they had almost started to
itch. He surveyed their toothbrushes. One red one, well
worn, one green one, hardly out of the box. He wondered
who belonged to which brush. Clair was a messy sod. Hers
had to be the red one. And she had once said that her
favourite colour was red. Did people necessarily buy tooth-
brushes in their favourite colours though? Mind you, who
was to say that she bought her own toothbrush? Maybe Mark

bought them, and had just bought Clair a new one. He had already decided that if it came down to it he would rather use Clair's toothbrush than Mark's. It just seemed more hygienic somehow to use a female friend's toothbrush than a male's. He reasoned that he would rather kiss Clair than Mark, and this felt much the same.

He had, when he shared a house as a student, noticed that one of his flatmates had exactly the same taste in tooth-brushes as himself. They had even discussed the coincidence. Then, one morning, when he had been running late for a midday lecture, he entered the bathroom while the same flat-mate was brushing his teeth. He looked around for his toothbrush.

'You seen my toothbrush, Sam?'

'What does it look like?' Sam stopped brushing.

'You know, the one that's the same as yours.'

'No.'

'You must have.'

'No. This one's mine.'

'Where the hell is it? It's not in here.' A nasty thought occurred to him. 'Oh . . . fuck.'

'What?'

'If I can't find mine . . .'

'Jesus.' Sam spat out a mouthful of toothpaste foam.

'We've been sharing a fucking brush! Fuck. Fuck. Eugh. Well, what the fuck have you done with yours?'

'What d'you mean? This *is* mine.'

'How do you know?'

'What makes you think it's yours?'

'Well, I've never taken it out of the bathroom.'

'What, even when you go away for the weekend?'

'Fuck. Fuck. Fuck.'

He chose the newer looking brush. It could well be Mark's, or maybe they had given up the ghost of indepen-dence and shared the brush, or there was still the faint glimmer of hope that it could be Clair's, but whichever, he reasoned that it would have seen less action than the gnarled, older one. Just to be on the safe side, he balanced as much toothpaste as was humanly possible on the bristles and began the unpleasant task, pulling his lips away from his teeth with the fingers of his unbrushing hand and slowly skimming the surface of his exposed teeth with the paste-laden brush. With this finished and a quick nose around the bathroom for interesting toiletries accomplished, Ian returned to the sitting room and thought about unfolding the sofa into its bed alter ego. He was restless and the thought of preparing a bed where he would lie peacefully for the night seemed alien. What the fuck was going on? It was an affront to Ian that his routines, the very routines that protected him from the banality of his life, had been so easily destroyed by the appearance of a couple of lunatics. Then he remembered the flashing light on his answer machine. He picked up the phone and dialled his number. After Elvis, he entered one one, his two-digit remote access code, and listened to his messages.

'Hello Ian, this is Archie from work.' What the fuck was Archie pestering him again for? And where was he? He said he was going to turn up to work but hadn't. Although this wasn't the worst state of affairs that Ian could imagine, he was at least mildly concerned with what the hell Archie was up to, and this in spite of his own catastrophic, fear-ridden couple of days. Archie sounded as if his usual monotone had somehow compressed to make it flatter still. 'This is all very difficult to explain, I'm afraid. I seem to have got you and me into a bit of a mess.' Surely there couldn't be much more mess in his life at the moment. Unless he was in some other sort of trouble he didn't know about as well. Jesus, this was getting worse. 'Give me that bloody phone.' It was the snarl of Frying Pan. Christ, what was Archie doing with Frying Pan? Or rather, what was Frying Pan doing with Archie?

'We're here with your mate Archibald. Aren't we Archibald?'
A monotone 'yes' in the background. 'Right you little twat,
we're getting a bit fed up of chasing around after you.
Tomorrow morning, be at that bus stop just off your street,
nine o'clock. Right? We've got a few things we're gonna talk
to you about.'

Beep beep beep.

What the fuck was going on? Why the hell had they got
Archie? What could they possibly want with that boring bastard? What could anyone want with him? Ian guessed that
they were using Archie to get to him. So far so good, but
why then had Archie said that he had got *both* of them into
some sort of trouble? He paced around Mark and Clair's
living-room until it got too small to pad around. This made
no sense at all. He went to the kitchen. He needed a drink.
They had nothing, except a bottle of champagne. Side-step-
ping the impropriety, he opened the bottle as quietly as
possible, persuading himself that he would replace it in the
morning and hoping that it wasn't some sacred bottle from or
for some special occasion. He proceeded to drink and mutter
and wonder until he could do so no more, eventually slumping on the settee and pulling the duvet over him.

He and Sue had sex on this very settee, a year or so ago.
They were going through the death throes of splitting up
and, as a consequence, were having the best sex they had ever
had, as if to remind each other of what they were about to
lose. He touched her face with his hand and stroked her softly
with the tips and nails of his fingers, from her cheek to her
chin. It was soothing and she relaxed. She would say, 'Stroke
me' and he would, making her feel calm, placid and spoilt.
His parents were staying, the spare room was being decorated and hence they were enjoying the hospitality of their
friends' sofa bed. With barely perceptible changes in the slow
traces of his stroking, he began to bring his fingers closer and

closer to her mouth on their downward sweep. Successively, his fingers described an arc which ended on her chin, on the upper slope of her chin, beneath her lower lip. He felt her head move down to meet him. She understood what he was doing and what he was asking of her. Clair and Mark were feet away in their bedroom. He ran his fingers slowly and deliberately from just below her ear, over her cheek and across her mouth. She opened her mouth and took his fingers inside, sucking and licking them. He became hard almost instantly. Clair and Mark were going through the motions of getting into bed. He felt her pressing against him, everywhere. She took his fingers out of her mouth and stared into his eyes, and as slowly as he had been with his movements guided his hand down, between her breasts, down to her belly button, down under her jeans, down under her knickers, and pushed them fully inside her. She was already wet enough to be penetrated with ease by his index and middle fingers. As he did so, she inhaled sharply, allowing the air out in small, punctuated breaths as he began to rub her clitoris with his thumb. She opened his trousers and held him hard in her hand. They pulled their own clothes off, for speed. She stood in front of him as he sat on the edge of the sofa and lowered herself, slowly, teasingly on to him, fucking him slowly, leaning back, resting her palms on his knees, behind her. He was mesmerized by her breasts. Her nipples were hard. She started to come. He reached for her breasts and squeezed them. She told him to bite her and he clamped his teeth around her nipple. Harder, she implored. She was coming. Her breathing assumed a rhythm of its own. Deeper and deeper inhalations followed by short, rapid exhalations. As he felt her begin to come he felt the tip of his penis engorge even further. She came, pulling him to the edge with her. He withdrew, as they never used contraception, and came violently, shudderingly, almost dislodging her from the seat of his legs. She told him off for coming over Mark and Clair's sofa. The moment and his erection receded as quickly as they had begun.

As Ian tossed and turned, he thought how strange it felt to be afraid of a big thing like Frying Pan. It was as if we have ceased to be afraid of big things we can see, like bombs that shake cities and earthquakes that swallow streets. Now, instead, we are scared of everything we can't see, small things like viruses and bacteria, pesticides and free radicals. Bacteria in your food, in the air, on kitchen work surfaces, lurking under the rim, on the breath of a stranger, under your finger nails, waiting, dividing, conquering, waiting. Viruses everywhere. Cold, dead and deadly, needing to use you, their asexual organ, to multiply. Most menacingly, though, we have become afraid of our insides, afraid of the very matter which keeps us alive. The very stuff of life – blood – is now the very essence of death. Don't touch that needle, don't resuscitate that bleeding mouth, don't share my razor, because the thing that keeps *me* alive could kill *you* – the logical conclusion of 'one man's meat is another man's poison'.

Eventually, he slept and dreamt about Sue. He used to dream about her when they first met and even when they first started living together, but he stopped dreaming about her after they had cohabited long enough to take each other's unconscious presence in bed for granted. Now, she appeared in his dreams at times of stress. He dreamt that they were in a park. He was unhappy about something intangible. She bent down to kiss him from behind as he sat on the park bench, his arms folded and head slumped forwards. He observed the scene from some yards away. To any other observer, or if they were in a photograph, she could have been consoling him over a tragedy. This was partly the truth. No one had died as such – there was just a feeling of loss between them. Her hair fell in front of his right cheek with a rainbow of scent. He didn't want her there, invading him with her scent and her hair and her lips. He ignored her and continued to stare at the weed-etched paving slab in front of his shoes. She continued to try to drag him from his blackness with her strip-light sunniness. Having made him miserable she was at last happy. But she knew of no other way to cheer him up than leading by example. And so they had reached a sticking point. Rarely were they both happy, and if they were, rarely was it for the same reason. She gave up and slumped down on the bench next to him in silent resignation. Having been made unhappy, he couldn't be happy again until he could see that she was unhappy too. The dream dissolved, unresolved. He awoke alone. Clair was standing over him.

'Sleep OK?'

'No,' Ian grunted. He felt like shit, traced it back to its source, and remembered the champagne. 'Clair, you know that champagne in the fridge? I'm really sorry about this but I sort of drank it last night.'

'So I see.'

'Shit. Was it for something special?'

'No, I thought I'd buy a twenty-quid bottle instead of my usual four-pound pack of lager.'

Ian thought for a while. 'You're being sarcastic, right?'

'What the fuck do you think?'

'I think you're being sarcastic.'

'Well done.'

'Look, I'll buy you another bottle, I mean, exactly the same and everything.'

'It's OK.'

'What was it for, if you don't mind me asking.'

'It's a bit late for manners now.' Clair glared down at him, and then looked away. 'Oh, I'm sorry Ian, things have been a bit shit recently. Mark got me the bottle to celebrate a new job I didn't get, so it was only hanging around reminding me of fucking the interview up and having to stay put. In fact, and you might find this hard to believe, I'm glad you drank it.'

He rubbed his face. 'I'm not.'

Ian was spared the problem of having to decide where to go and what to do. This had haunted him on his way round to Mark and Clair's sofa. Work and home were out, his car was abandoned in a car park and he could only lose his keys for so long. Even thinking about going to the police squeezed his diaphragm, and now that they had Archie Ian realized that he no longer had any control over the situation. Frying Pan had provided an alternative. The loathing that Ian had nurtured for Archie over the months that he had known him was rapidly being gnawed away by an infuriating feeling of solidarity. They were in this together and Ian felt a common bond of humanity stretching between them. Archie was in trouble and, dislike him as he may, Ian realized that he was the only one who could help him. He cursed himself for it, but it was there nonetheless. Ian had never experienced anything approaching altruism before, but it was there, as clear as day, and he was unable to shrug it off. His philanthropy was however shaky at best, and was periodically punctured by the reality of the violence that might result from another confrontation with Frying Pan and Tattoo.

Ian began to fret. He would visit a cash machine and get a hundred, no, two hundred pounds out. Maybe some sort of payment would suffice, Archie would be released and he could get back to normality and resume his stickleback life. Then he realized he didn't have his wallet any more and swore. He thought instead about protection, or, more accurately, a weapon. Something like a kitchen knife, a baseball bat or a pool cue. Even with a weapon though he would be no match for the two of them, so he abandoned the idea. And they'd still have Archie. Mind you, as his solidarity again wilted, Ian began to feel that they were welcome to him. He was probably boring them rigid with obsessive descriptions of aliens and infuriating them by correcting their grammar. They would probably be desperate to get away from the sad wanker. He would have started a long, miserable and extensive run down of the compound interest payments on his mortgage by now, if his behaviour at work was anything to go by. He'd be monotoning the delights of dNTP programming as compared with Java script, or some other such delight.

Two simultaneous and opposing solutions rattled around in the thick of Ian's hangover. Philanthropy or self-preservation. Maybe he should leave them all to it. Frying Pan and Tattoo had caused him more than enough fear and inconvenience over the last couple of days, which would no doubt be more than repaid by the sheer tedium of having to spend time with the lacklustre Archie, who had, in turn, inflicted more than his fair share of misery upon Ian in the ten months that they had worked together. So, as it stood, the equation balanced. Everyone was unhappy. To disrupt the equilibrium by involving himself again with Frying Pan and Tattoo would mean that one or more parties would be happier and one or more would be less happy, and it seemed unlikely that Ian would be the one who would gain by meeting them. Sod it. He would leave them all to it. Self-preservation one, philanthropy nil. He would hang around at Mark and Clair's and watch some soothing daytime TV, maybe have a bit more of a nose around, and generally congratulate himself on making the right decision. Clair reappeared and Mark emerged from the bathroom.

'Right, we're off. What are you doing?'

'D'you mind if I just hang around here for a bit, just till the locksmith's due at mine.'

'What time's he due?'

'Er . . . ten-ish.'

'Right. Look, here are my keys, lock up and post them back through when you leave.'

'OK. Cheers. And thanks.'

'See you.'

'Yeah.'

Boxes

Ian relaxed back on the reassembled sofa and turned the TV on. He might even have a bath, Christ knows he needed one. He immersed himself in the soporific trivia of morning television.

'Today we'll be looking at dating for forty-somethings, and Simon Jeffries our resident vet will be here later to answer your questions on canine dental hygiene. First, meeting your *ideal* man from an advert in a newspaper may not sound the *ideal* way to go about finding someone, but, increasingly, in our culture of failed marriage and rising divorce, more and more women are turning to this medium . . .' Ian had been fascinated by personal columns since . . . he couldn't remember when it had started. What particularly intrigued him was the idea of classification, the idea of putting yourself into boxes. Not necessarily correct or especially accurate boxes, but boxes none the less. There were boxes which were ambiguous, suggestive, euphemistic, vague, solicitous and persuasive, all of which could be used in place of the truth. There were boxes you could use, such as lonely, single parent, widower, desperate to meet, and married, which were perhaps too truthful. There were boxes to be taken with a pinch of salt, like company director, understanding wife, with husband's approval and first time advert. There were a plethora of euphemisms for female build; curvy, curvaceous, cuddly, Rubenesque, buxom, rounded, womanly and medium build which all suggested the more accurate box of overweight.

In common with almost everyone he had ever met, Ian believed himself to be a good judge of character, especially when it came to other people. He was however a minimalist, rarely seeing or even looking for the whole picture. As a matter of routine he deconstructed the people he met into their constituent boxes, and this is why personal adverts so occupied him. It was not the thrill of a secret afternoon arrangement with a Rubenesque married business woman who lived in the M6 corridor and had the full approval of her husband, but the idea of meeting each person who advertised and seeing whether he could put them into the same boxes they had put themselves into. He knew, of course, that most adverts would carry a good deal of, at best, half-truths, but this would be the ultimate test of his minimalist abilities – assigning people to the boxes *they* thought they should be in. This would involve dragging people from their initial text through two translations and back again, to see how much of the original meaning was left.

'Now onto the very difficult problem of canine hygiene. What we often fail to appreciate as humans is that our pets have dental needs as well . . .' A snarling, squat, pit bull-shaped dog, but meaner, was toying with a canine hygienist who was struggling to brush its teeth without losing a finger. The cold brown eyes were hungry for fingers. It was waiting. An unprotected, ringless finger would get too close and the dog would ensnare it with its shark teeth. It was simply a matter of picking its moment. It was a canine Frying Pan. Ian looked sharply at his watch. Nearly eight forty-five.

Fifteen minutes to get to the bus stop, if he chose. He decided to let logic decide. He composed a list of all the favours Archie had done him recently. He'd bought him a cup of coffee the other day. He had lent him his newspaper one lunchtime. He'd been off sick a couple of weeks ago. That was it – he was struggling. OK, what had Archie done to annoy him recently, excluding just being around and breathing. He had refused to lend him some of the change he had patently been carrying in his rattling pocket, mumbling about his coinage rules. He corrected his grammar daily. His desk had started to expand and to overrun Ian's. He had bored him to tedium and back again every day with his monochrome existence. He had refused to change his floppy-fringed, pudding bowl hair style at Ian's request. He continued to drape himself in ill-fitting nylon. He refused to swear, to spit, to fart or to display any of the other vital signs of vigorous health. He . . . shit, ten to nine. Ian summed up. On the plus side, not being around occasionally, and a cup of coffee and a newspaper. On the minus side was Archie. The dog still hadn't bit his handler. Maybe it wouldn't.

'Oh fuck it,' he said out loud, turning the TV off and picking his coat up. He locked up and headed for the bus stop.

Cold

February 9th 1997

Legs won't work. Pavement like the deck of a ship in a storm.
Something is wrong. Something is very wrong. Lights come
and go, one becomes two, becomes one again, come and go.
Red and white. Try to focus. Eyes more closed than open.
Heavy, lazy lids. Where am I? Car park. Where the fuck am I?
Where have the football team gone? Pub car park. Home. Get
home. Bus. Taxi. Anything. Money. Three maybe four
pounds in coins, no notes. This cold, shivering, moving street
looks familiar. This way. Maybe. Find a phone. Ring Louise.
She'll know what to do. Find a phone. Ring Louise. She'll
know where I am. Don't feel well. Shivering. Stomach moving
like the pavement. Lights come and go. A phone. Two phones
maybe. A hundred yards, other side of road. Point body in
right direction, hope rest of me will follow. Left to right and
right to left across the pavement and back again. One step
forwards one step sideways. Don't feel well. God, it's cold.
Keep walking. Phone box/ boxes. Keep walking. Need to

cross. Going to be sick. Keep walking. Need to cross. Lights come and go, coming white and going red. Need to cross. Phone Louise, she'll know what to do. Always knows what to do. Wait for a gap. Wait. Wait. Steady. Wait. Something is wrong. Something is very wrong. I'm on the tarmac. Everything is still. No lights any more. Noises, somewhere. Oh Jesus. Are you all right? Just stepped into the road. No chance of stopping. Can you hear me? Stay with him while I call an ambulance. Just stepped into the road. Are you all right? You'll be all right, won't you? Who are they talking to? Louise will know. Ring Louise. Louise. Louise. Louise . . .

Traffic

The morning conveyer belt ground past, its wheels screeching, its drivers swearing. An endless stream of inevitability and misery. Each individual piece of traffic complaining about the traffic. Each individual component of congestion complaining about the congestion. Tributaries of driver-only cars feeding into slow-running rivers of movement, punctuated by the driftwood of buses and lorries. Cars passed at a pace which pedestrians would be ashamed of. None of the traffic was stationary long enough to be described as being at a complete stop, but it was a close call. Ian checked his watch. About five past nine. Maybe this was all an elaborate and unfathomable hoax. He would give them ten more minutes. Still nothing. The traffic eased momentarily, like a trickle out of the end of a hosepipe, then seized up again.

From time to time, buses approached him as he stood at the stop and so he adopted a range of complicated body signals to advertise his disinterest to approaching drivers. He wondered whether he should stand away from the stop but they had been explicit about his presence there, so he looked

at his feet, shuffled, looked away, shook his head and generally fidgeted his indifference in case passing bus drivers
pulled up expecting him to board. Like water finding leaks,
traffic searches out virgin tarmac which is free from speed
bumps and other cars, and establishes new short cuts through
the city maze until the tail-light word spreads and the virgin
tarmac disappears, fucked by the sheer weight of the rubber
wheels which burden it, and new leaks are exploited and the
watery traffic overflows in a different direction. In this way,
but in no other, traffic ebbs, through housing estates, up No
Through Roads, past schools and anywhere else it can save
seconds. It is an amorphous mass, bound loosely at the edges
sometimes by etiquette, and most of the time by the law. It
doesn't move so much as spread, down sideroads and up
roadsides. If it all moved on the same day and at the same
time it would freeze – it relies not upon space but upon time.
Unfortunately, time cannot be built into tarmac, otherwise it
would have been, in the interest of movement. For we still
believe that to be stationary is to die. Like sharks which sink
if they don't keep moving, to stay where you are leaves you
open and vulnerable. Move, and stay one step ahead of your
predators, whatever or whoever they may be. Just to be *trying*
to move is better than remaining hopelessly stationary – you
may be stuck in a tailback, but the possibility of movement is
still there, if not the actuality. This necessity for movement
fascinated Ian. He understood its flaws, as did everybody,
but he too found it irresistible. People, himself included,
actually drove for fun, not to get anywhere, as you invariably
ended up at the point you had started, but just to experience
motion and to shrug off the static. Everyone, even environ-
mentalists, knew that the car was the best invention in the
world ever. Nothing else came remotely close. He doubted
whether anything would ever be better and wanted to be
around to see it if it was. After all, we didn't so much design
it, as it evolved to meet our needs. We needed speed and it

gave it to us. We needed movement and it provided it. We needed warmth, security and protection and it gave them to us. We needed to be invincible and it caged us in steel. It was a god, except that whatever we wanted was granted. And all it asked for was a refined and explosive drink now and then, which we were more than happy to measure out in litres and gallons.

Maybe they were stranded in the queue of traffic extending in front of him and they could see him from where they were. He strained to see as far as he could. Maybe he should pre-empt the inevitable and walk down the line of cars and just give himself up. Maybe he should just lie down and accept an inevitable beating. He was jittery. He wondered what sort of car they'd have. It had to be a Sierra. Had to be. Or a Granada. He'd never met a Granada driver who didn't deserve to have some sort of shooting, at least, inflicted upon them. It may have sounded harsh, but it was the only language Granada drivers understood, and Ian should know, because he had once been in one. It is the archetypal better-than-you car for people who plainly aren't better than you. It adheres to the principle that people who drive Fords will drive a bigger one if they can afford it, purely because they can afford it and because it is bigger. It isn't a better car than, say, the Sierra or the Mondeo, both of which lived at the bottom of Ian's all time list of great cars. It's just larger, heavier, more cumbersome and has a bigger horn. Bigger cars have bigger horns, that is an indisputable law of cars. Big car, big horn, big get out of my way, I'm someone big. It doesn't work with the Granada though. Big horn, big wanker, small cock, that is the indisputable law of Ford Granadas.

Ten past, in a couple of minutes. Maybe his watch was slow. Maybe he had fulfilled his end of the bargain already. Then he saw Frying Pan and Tattoo. His legs felt shaky and his stomach gripped tightly around a central but indistinct kernel of dread. They were in the cab of a smart-looking

Mercedes van. Fuck. He thought about running. There seemed little point. He would take what they threw at him. If they wanted to beat him up or stab him it would be worth it just to get this week over with, one way or the other. The van crawled towards him. Frying Pan was in the passenger side. He didn't look particularly calm, but nor did he seem to be overwhelmed with the violence of the pub. Tattoo, as ever, looked nasty. Frying Pan wound down the window, said, 'Get in,' with a fair amount of contempt and thumbed Ian in the direction of the side door. He slid it back hesitantly and stepped into the gloom. The van rejoined the indefatigable vehicular conveyer belt.

Ian surveyed the inside of the van. It had a wooden floor which hadn't seen much in the way of action. There was no cement, sand, soil, paint, sawdust, nuts, bolts or any other residue of the work with which vans are usually associated. The van appeared both from the outside and the inside to be fairly new and it didn't appear to be rented. Ian hadn't noticed a trade name or any other markings on the side of the van which might furnish a clue to Frying Pan and Tattoo's occupations. He sat down and decided to accept his lot. There wasn't much else he could do – he couldn't go anywhere. He might as well get this sorted out one way or the other. He wondered where they were heading. It didn't seem as though they were travelling towards Ian's house, and even if they had taken a circuitous route there they would have arrived by now. By the speed of the van, it seemed that the traffic was either subsiding, or they were heading away from areas of congestion. He squinted through the sliver of space between the two back doors. He couldn't tell exactly where they were or where they were heading, but it certainly appeared to be out of town and into a more rural landscape. Ian started to panic. Country lanes could mean only one thing – a violent end, a barely beneath the surface grave in some undergrowth and, the final indignity, a belated appearance on Crime Watch. He tried the side door. It was teutonically solid. The back doors too. He continued to monitor their progress through the limited aperture of the rear doors. The roadsides were definitely becoming greener. Walls were becoming hedges and verges becoming fields. Other vehicles were rarer. The van slowed and stopped. They seemed to have turned into a country lane which had been chopped like a worm with a spade by a new motorway. The engine died in a reluctant diesel fashion, both cab doors opened and closed and the side door slid back abruptly. Frying Pan and Tattoo filled the doorway. Ian edged back into the van. Frying Pan climbed in. He had passed through fear and into a depressed state of acceptance. Frying Pan bent his mammoth structure almost in two, squatted down in front of Ian and began to tell him just what he wanted from him.

'There's something we want you to do for us.' Frying Pan actually smiled, obsequiously. 'Something that will make us all happy. Something that we could all enjoy.' Ian remained frozen. Christ. They were perverts. He wished again that he hadn't seen *Deliverance* recently. The instinctive fear he felt when Frying Pan accompanied him to the toilets of the nasty pub where they first encountered each other had been justified. Frying Pan continued, looking intently into Ian's eyes. 'We want you to do a little something for us.' A police photograph album of sexual atrocity burst through Ian's permanently vivid imagination. 'We've got your friend Archie as well.' Christ, no. The foursome of his darkest fears. 'I want us all to be on the same side.' Ian tried to picture the grotesque position. At least it sounded better than from behind.

Country Lanes

Frying Pan began a mono and occasionally disyllabic explanation of what he wanted Ian to do for him.

'So d'you know what I'm saying?

Ian thought he did know, and blurted, 'Look, I've got money, I'm not like that, I mean I've never been, you know, like that, and I don't think I ever will, but what you do, I mean between yourselves, is fine by me, but I'm just not . . . you know . . . I even went on a march about it once . . . I mean its not my . . . er . . . look, do what you like to each other in the privacy of your own home, just leave me out of it.'

'What the fuck are you on about?' Frying Pan was suddenly no longer unctuous.

'Look, I'm just not like that. Have you tried Archie? Maybe he is.' Ian edged further towards the back of the van. 'Come to think of it, I'm sure he is.'

A faint glimmer of understanding spread slowly across Frying Pan's leathery features. Ian recognized it and felt a simultaneous wave of relief and panic. Maybe he'd got the wrong end of the stick. Thank God. Oh fuck. He'd just accused Frying Pan and Tattoo of the most heinous crime two heterosexual psychopaths could have bestowed upon them – homosexuality. If he wasn't dead before, he was now.

'Fuck me, you think we're . . .' He turned his massive head away from Ian and shouted to Tattoo, 'This 'un thinks we're a couple of fucking player managers!' Tattoo scowled, relocating facial markings as he did so, and then managed something approximating a grin. Very approximating. 'Cocoa shunters!' he continued. 'Fucking mattress munchers!' Tattoo scowled again. 'Starfish stabbers!' A pause. 'Bum yesses!' And again. He turned back to Ian, clearly having run out of euphemisms. 'Look, let me spell it out, our kid.'

Ian hadn't been labelled a kid, except by girlfriends, for a good many years, but here, in the back of a van with cold metal sides and with the father-sized Frying Pan, it seemed apt. He was about to be told off and the back of his throat tightened and ached as it had in anticipation of childhood chastisement.

'We want you to do some work, at your work, for us, right. Now, we've got it written down here what we want you to do.' He handed Ian an off-white, self-sealing envelope with a large bump in it. 'When you've sorted it out, we'll give you your friend Archibald back, safe and sound. If not, you won't be seeing him again. All right?' It seemed fairly reasonable so far, so Ian nodded. He wasn't going to get beaten, robbed, gang raped, set alight or tortured, though Archie might. All in all it sounded an improvement on this morning's outlook. Maybe they would even let him go home. Frying Pan climbed out of the van and barked, 'Right, out the van, walk forward, don't look round, just straight ahead and face the hedge. Look round before we're gone and maybe we *will* make you munch a mattress or two.' Evidently pleased to have worked a euphemism into a threat, Frying Pan ushered him out of the van.

Ian walked towards the hedge, looking conspicuously at

the ground and away from the number plate, which was what he judged they didn't want him to see. The van reversed out of the country lane cul-de-sac, whining as it did so. Ian surveyed his trainers and the hedge in front of him until its diesel clatter escaped his ears. He turned round and began walking, struggling the envelope open as he did so. Inside was a wallet. He opened it. It was his wallet, with all cards, cash, receipts and useless bits of paper intact, as far as he could see. He looked inside the envelope and pulled out a small font paragraph printed on a folded A4 sheet. He read it with a growing sense of astonishment.

```
Account #478-4266-5911628. Transfer days single high-
est trade at close of day, Monday week. Suspend
protection code accordingly for max 10 secs whilst
transaction made. Run sub code intervening 10 secs.
Write distributor script to accnt 478-4266-5911628
first. Report sys failure.
```

Ian stopped walking and re-read it. It began to sink in. Jesus. For all he knew, it might be nonsense. Jesus fucking Christ, he repeated to himself. Sure, the thought had crossed his mind before, but seeing it on paper made it look almost possible.

Banks

'Don't tell me you've never thought about it?'

Archie looked up from his monitor. 'Don't tell me I've never thought about what?'

'Oh come on, surely you've sat there and thought about what we do and why and for who . . .'

'Whom.'

'. . . and how much money is involved.'

'No, I don't think I have.' Archie returned his scrutiny to the screen in front of him. 'And anyway, I'm not certain that it would be feasible.'

'So you have thought about it.'

'Well, not really in the terms that you have.'

'Well what terms then?'

'That nothing is secure. That theoretically everything could be hacked into if you know how.'

'Exactly,' Ian agreed, leaning back in his chair and interlocking his fingers behind his head. 'And the thing about banks is that they can't be watertight. If they were totally secure then traders wouldn't be able to trade, no money would be able to be shifted around between accounts and no money would be made for the investors. It has to have access built into the system, otherwise everything would just grind to a halt and it'd be useless.' He unlocked his hands and leant forward in his chair, dangerously close to the boundary of Archie's desk. 'I mean, has it never occurred to you why traders are people, barely people, I suspect, but people all the same?'

'People, as opposed to what?'

'Computers. Why not just let computers do all the trading?'

'Well, I suppose as long as you programmed them with past experience and gave them the capacity to make decisions based on the outcome of previous decisions, and you input future events into them, I'd say they'd be much better than human traders.' Archie looked up from his monitor again. 'But I'm sure you're about to tell me that's rubbish.'

'That's rubbish. Yes, they'd be better assessors, calculators, profit-making machines. But that's not what trading's all about.'

'No? Do tell me what you think it *is* all about.' Archie managed to muster a little sarcasm. He was in unfamiliar territory – Ian was firmly in charge.

'Trading's about gambling, about mistakes, about fallibility, about humanity, about one trader believing another has overestimated or underestimated or missed something that he has spotted. Two machines would simply freeze each other out because they wouldn't believe in the power of mistakes.'

'So?' Archie asked, obviously trying not to get drawn in.

'So, people do the trading, people have the access to the money to trade with, our money, and people make mistakes with our money. The system has to be open to abuse.'

'So you are saying that you could walk into a bank, electronically, of course . . .'

'. . . of course . . .'

'. . . and download millions of pounds into your account because the bank is like an open house with no doors?'

'No. For fuck's sake.'

'I've heard enough of this nonsense,' said Archie, getting out of his seat and leaving the office, picking up some papers as he did so as a transparent excuse to leave. Ian sat and thought. This was the first time he had put into words thoughts he had increasingly found wandering around his idle brain. Why he was telling Archie he wasn't entirely sure, but knew it must lie somewhere between the curiosity of discovering whether the same thoughts had occurred to him and the inclination to try by any means possible, theoretical or otherwise, to lead Archie astray. He tried to get his argument into a round, cogent form. He would have another go at him when he returned, which, given that he was virtually desk-bound, and therefore unlikely to be able to find anything else to do outside the office, couldn't be long.

'Look, Archie, the point is,' he said, as Archie sat down again, 'that banks have got to allow for millions of deals, trades, transactions and what have you, so they can't just bolt all the doors. I mean, look at the City. There are traders there picking faxes out of the fax bin, faxes which have come from us or other investment banks, authorizing our traders to invest X thousands in some dodgy sweat shop company in Thailand, and who are trading on our backs. And all because the system has to be open enough for all these deals to happen.'

Reluctantly, Archie was drawn in once again. 'So we go scavenging in wastepaper bins?'

'Metaphorically, yes.'

'What do you mean?'

'I don't know.' His argument was losing its roundness. 'But look, what's a bank's worst nightmare?'

'I don't know.' Archie was uncomfortable not knowing.

'Think.'

'People moving their money to building societies?'

'No.' Ian stood up.

'Everybody being overdrawn at the same time?'

'No. You're not following me.' He was, as was the usual course of events when he and Archie conversed, getting irritated, particularly when Archie quite obviously couldn't see beyond his pudding bowl fringe.

'A robbery?'

'No.'

'Well what is it then?'

Solitary words were forming ideas as he spoke them. 'Appearing to be unsafe.'

'What?'

'Appearing to its investors to be unsafe. Look, if a bank somehow gives the impression of being an unsafe place to house your finances, who's going to bank with them? No one. Because that's what a bank is all about. You get fuck all interest from them, they're rude to you, they rip you off, they charge you twenty pounds to tell you that you're overdrawn, which you knew anyway, and now you're twenty pounds worse off, they let direct debits go out of your account before money goes in, to enhance their chances of getting you overdrawn . . .'

'A bit cynical . . .'

'They only bother opening at times when you're at work so, instead of opening later, they offer you phone banking, which costs *you* money, and not them, and means that they can lay people off and employ twenty-four-hour-a-day computers to sort your finances out . . .'

'Yes but computers . . .'

'Shut up Archie, I'm on a roll here.' Ian paced around the office. 'They're the ultimate money-making machines. They're not there to do us any favours, we do them the favour by giving them our money to do what they want with and are then grateful when we check our accounts and see that it's all still there, safe and sound. That's the only decent function they fulfil. Locking our money up. And if it appears that they can't do that then they're fucked.'

'So?'

'So, it's not in their interest to appear to be unsafe. It's not in their interest to make it known that they've been robbed.'

'What about all the robberies you hear about on the news? They're not too worried about being seen to be unsafe then.'

'Yes but they're the violent ones, the ones with guns and knives and getaway cars. It doesn't do the banks much harm if people know that some nutter with a gun has walked into a bank and made off with five grand. They know it's not their five grand, and when it no doubt appears on Crime Watch or some other sad voyeuristic crime programme which makes the police look like some sort of fucking social services department, only nicer and fairer . . .'

'I happen to like Crime Watch, actually . . .'

'You surprise me.'

'And anyway, what's wrong with the police? I think they do a good . . .'

'Yeah, you would. Because I'll bet you've never had any real contact with them.'

'Well no, as a matter of fact, I haven't.'

Ian fell silent. He was losing his momentum. Something was nagging at him. He was gripped by an unwelcome feeling of dread. He sat down and tried to breathe calmly. Generally, anxiety made itself known to Ian before its reason became apparent. He would inhale abruptly and feel his stomach muscles contract, and only after a gap of maybe ten seconds would his brain design to tell him just what the fuck he was scared of. This time, however, the reason was clear enough.

Archie studied him over his monitor. He felt the tide change and decided to capitalize. 'So *you* have then?' he asked.

'Have what?' he muttered.

'Have had dealings with the police.'

Ian took a few seconds to reply. 'Mmm,' he said, as non-committally as possible.

'And what had you done?'

He tried to snap out of it, but it was never that easy. 'Nothing,' he replied flatly and morosely.

Archie was beginning to enjoy himself. 'But you were in some sort of trouble?'

'I suppose so.' Get back to the point. He felt his forehead become damp and cold. Get back to the point. Pick up the thread. Get back to the . . .

'And are you still?' Archie was enjoying this.

Ian mouthed an extended 'Yes'. The point. The fucking point. He wiped his forehead on the sleeve of his suit jacket and looked up at Archie, who seemed to have cheered up no end. 'Look, anyway, the point is . . .'

'And could they come and arrest you at any time?'

Ian closed his eyes. 'The point is,' he repeated, louder and firmer this time so that Archie wouldn't try to interrupt him, 'people only see small violent bank robberies as a comment on the state of the nation or some other such nonsense.'

'Is that what you did?' Archie asked gleefully. 'Robbed a bank?'

The fear was passing and Ian managed to ignore Archie and pick up the thread of his argument once more. 'But what I'm talking about is the crime that never makes it to Crime Watch or on to TV or into the papers.' Deep breath. 'What about when banks lose millions of pounds, money that just goes missing and that they can't account for?'

Distracted from the pleasure of Ian's discomfort, Archie asked, 'If it never makes the news, how can you be sure that it actually happens?'

'It must. It just must.' Ian thought for a second. He was back in control. 'I mean, it's got to be safer to go and buy a computer than a gun.'

'Yes, but then what?'

'I don't know. But look at this.' Ian dried his fingers on his trousers, opened his wallet and fished out a piece of well-worn and folded newspaper. He carefully restored it to its natural size and passed it to Archie, who read it out loud with as much disdain as he could manage.

'Superhighway Robbery. Carlos Carinos, head trader at the Argentinian firm Investment Capitol, picked up . . .'

'No, further down. Third paragraph, I think.'

Archie frowned, but continued. 'Will Barlow, a banking security consultant, put it into perspective: "The average bank robbery nets you eighteen hundred dollars, you get prosecuted seventy-two per cent of the time and you could get shot. With a computer you see one hundred and sixty thousand dollars and get prosecuted less than two per cent of the time . . ."'

'Two per cent. Think about it. That's one in fifty . . .'

'I know what two per cent is.'

'That's tossing a coin and getting six heads in a row – that's the chances of actually being caught – six consecutive heads.'

'I think I understand probability.'

'Look, I've got a coin. Now, I'll toss it six times and if it's heads every time I'll . . .'

'Ian, I don't want to talk about this any more.' Archie stood up, looked around the office, tried to think of something to do, couldn't, became a little flustered and then left the office again, this time with no papers, and they had never talked about it since. But Ian knew that he had touched a nerve.

Crime and Punishment

So, it had all been set up. He hadn't run into Frying Pan and Tattoo in a dangerous pub and at a low ebb by accident. They must have followed him, and the only way they could have followed him was to have known his address even before he left his wallet in the pub. And the only way they could have known his address must have been through Archie when he was arrested. Finally, Ian made the link. The fellow detainee who had shared a cell with Archie overnight and scared him witless was Frying Pan. There was no third psychopath with a vested interest in the contents of Ian's house, just the two, which was more than sufficient to be getting along with.

Ian read the note again, then folded it up and put it in his back pocket. It was money, digital money, that they were after. He would be an accomplice and this worried him. He knew from even the most minor of the petty misdemeanours he had perpetrated during an uneventful adolescence that he was the world's worst criminal. Just bending the law encouraged his ever-smouldering paranoia to feverish levels. His fear of the police was already at an all time high, and had been since the events of February. Anything which was illegal could bring the police closer to his door and this was to be avoided if at all possible. Added to that was the possession of Paul's dope plants. Were it not for the powerfully relaxing numbness held within their leaves, he would have paid dearly in sleeplessness and worry over their possession. As it was it seemed to balance out – it was, rarely, a criminal unease which came with its own remedy. Even breaking the speed limit made Ian uncomfortable, though not quite as uncomfortable as staying within it. All things considered, he knew that if it ever came down to it, he would make a terrible criminal.

Of course, Ian had studied the numbers. He was aware that, statistically, an unimpressive five to ten per cent of all crime is actually solved, fully solved, attributed to the right person, who is then punished accordingly, and that this meagre slice of all the crime committed includes crimes which are accidentally solved, and those solved by the diligence of the permanently suspicious public, and perpetrated by hopeless criminals who leave their name and address or their dog at the scene of the crime, and guilty souls who give themselves up and volunteer confessions for their crimes, and those eternally haunted souls who confess to other people's crimes. So, all in all, after committing a crime, the chances of it actually being detected, and of then being arrested, charged, found guilty and punished, were slim, at worst. And behind such statistics must, Ian reasoned, lie some fairly mediocre detective work. But he also knew that out there, in the sea of criminal activity, swimming with the useless schools of police mackerel, must be a small number of police sharks, who could sense your criminal blood from miles away and who would hunt you down remorselessly until they ensnared you in their trilayer of teeth. Characteristically, his paranoia allowed him to see only the sharks.

Despite his unease with all things illegal, and in common

with all sane people, Ian enjoyed breaking the law, up to a certain point. In the same way that fairground rides allow you to imagine that you are flirting with death, breaking the law thrills you by allowing you to imagine, momentarily at least, that you are free from the petty restraints that bind other men. Breaking the law is, therefore, an intoxicating blend of freedom and excitement. But for Ian it carried with it a debilitating hangover of paranoia and insomnia. The one detective who could actually detect, the one officer who could actually officiate and the one inspector capable of actually inspecting, these would be the people who would be assigned, in deference to the rank and file mediocrity, to Ian's case. So he tried not to break the law, conspicuously at least.

Ian walked back in what he imagined to be the vague direction of his house. He ignored the nearest bus stop and continued on foot. He needed to think. Something was bothering him but he couldn't focus on exactly what it was. Every time he got close to it he got too close, and it became blurred and eluded him. He realized for the first time that someone else must be involved – Frying Pan and Tattoo could barely speak, let alone type a list of instructions.

Two Wrongs

Although Ian had often thought it through, as a lazy daydream which fulfilled most of his get rich quick/beat the system/pull one over on your boss/retire to Mexico daydream criteria, it had always been more dream than cold light of day practicality. Maybe it was possible. Maybe someone had thought it through and had discovered that it could be done. But if it was possible, why risk roping two strangers in when you could do it yourself? That would surely only invite further problems. Unless the third person wasn't certain it could be done. Unless it could be easily detected and traced.

Ian began at first to suppress and eventually to concede to a rising nervous excitement, which bordered upon fear, but also held a tangible element of expectation. Police fear aside, he wasn't, all things considered, in too much of an unhealthy position. He was effectively being blackmailed into doing something illegal, which surely negated, or at least detracted from, the illegality. Two wrongs did sometimes make a right. It was the stuff of dreams. Acting illegally without the illegality. Everyone dreamt of being a bank robber, and here he

was with the chance to play cops and robbers, but with the
cops on his side. And that would make a change. Surely you
couldn't be arrested for trying to preserve the well-being, or
even life, of a very good and close friend. The more Ian
thought about it the further he journeyed into a scenario he
had long kept captive as a day-dream only.

Ian resisted the urge to go home and spent the afternoon
and part of the early evening in a large high street pub near
his house, mulling the situation over and alcoholically coaxing his pulse back to somewhere around its normal rate.
Three or four pints later (three in all honesty, four if he was
recounting his afternoon to a friend) he left the pub, and
ordered an Extra Value Meal in McDonalds which he tried to
pay for twice. At home, he passed unsteadily through his
front door and into the foreign territory of his hallway. There
was little in the way of post, one free and unwelcome newspaper, which was destined for the bin, and a couple of
messages from friends who had rung out of mild curiosity at
his recent scarcity. He entered the lounge and froze. They
had been here and he was instantly on edge again. It was a
mess. They had moved all the furniture to the outside of the
room and had torn the exposed carpet up. Floorboards gaped
through its large, square, jagged wound. Over the floorboards
the entire contents of a large tin of brilliant red paint was
starting to coagulate. The tin lay outside what was once the
centre of his living room on a remaining piece of untorn
carpet. The message was clear enough. He put his jacket back
on, left the house and got the bus to his office.

At work, he sat and stared at his computer. The Friday
rush had emptied the building and there was a calm about the
office which made Ian feel that he belonged elsewhere.
Although there had always been a menace about the proceedings of the last few days and he had felt frightened, it had
been a low, constant, dull fear which was becoming routine. It
had peaked at times and had even spilled over into terror,

but it had still seemed somehow external. That they had entered his house and ripped the heart out of his living-room sucked the fear inside him. He was shaking. They wanted him out of the house and programming. Sitting still became impossible. He was livid and violent and fidgety. He needed more alcohol, and a smoke wouldn't go amiss. 'Fuck it,' he shouted, getting up and leaving the office. His car was apparently unscathed in the car park where it had been since the day before yesterday. True to temperamental form, it started first time. He swore at it and drove to the nearest supermarket that sold beer, fairly confident that he was still well over the legal limit, but fairly confident that even in this state he was less of a liability than the myopic octogenarians that haunted the roads on Sundays and bank holidays. He bought a crate of strong beer and picked up a couple of tubs of instant noodles for sustenance. A smoke would be more difficult. He decided to try a friend. Martin opened the door evidently much the worse for wear. Things were looking up.

'Hi Ian, long time no . . .'

'Yeah, yeah,' Ian interrupted. 'You got any gear?'

'Might have. Just this once, like.'

'Any chance of a quick smoke? I'm gagging.'

Martin scrutinized his swollen scalp and fidgety demeanour. 'You all right?'

'Yeah. *Yeah*.' He wasn't all right – that much was obvious. He was anxious, irritable and impatient. 'Look, I'm in a bit of a rush.' Martin ushered him in and proceeded to scaffold a spliff together fairly, but not entirely, reluctantly. Ian sat on the edge of his seat palming off lazy questions and trying to make Martin's fingers move more quickly with his eyes. Finally, the white touch-paper was lit and Martin retreated twenty five metres into the sofa. Ian fidgeted and opened a can of export beer which was quite clearly never destined to leave the West Midlands, let alone the country. As an occasional smoker, these days, a spliff had to be handled with mild caution. A can of beer was the dock leaf to the stinging, mouth stripping, unfiltered smoke. Martin passed the spliff over, just in time for it to give up the ghost and for Ian to take a deep inhalation of rank unlit tobacco. He spat in the direction of the floor.

'Mind the floor, mate.' A chastisement from Martin was like hearty praise from the rest of the world.

'Sorry. The bugger's gone out.' He relit it and inhaled deeply and slowly several times, each draw punctuated with a first aid swig of beer. He felt his body clock return to idling speed, maybe slower, and his head become pleasantly heavy, as if someone had wedged a small brick on top of his brain to keep it from floating away. He returned the compliment to Martin and opened another can of strong beer.

'So, what y'been up to then?' Martin persevered.

'Not much. Been working on a new theory though.'

'Yeah?'

'It's to do with words and names.'

'Go on.'

'I reckon, right, it's possible to trace everyone's name back to a derivative word that explains that name.'

'You've lost me.'

'Right. Take Simon's girlfriend Cath. Now I think we'd both agree that she's a pain in the arse, yeah?'

'Granted.' Martin passed the spliff back.

'Cheers. So her name forms the derivation of several words.'

'Such as?'

'Well, there's Catholicism. Now that's all about pain and suffering. Cathartic. That means suffering, initially, at least.'

'Catheter. They're fucking painful to have inserted.'

'Yep. And cathedral – they can be painful places to be stuck on a Sunday morning.' Ian took a long drag which hit home with a delayed but pleasant anaesthesia. 'And there's the religious guilt and sin and suffering that goes along with them of course.'

'Fair enough, so far.' Martin reached over to his bookshelf, dragged out a dictionary and thumbed through till he reached a relevant page. 'What about cathode, then?'

Ian thought for a while, taking a couple more hefty and alternate inhalations and swigs, before passing what was left of the paper construction back to Martin. 'Cathode, that's the *negative* terminal of a battery, isn't it? Negative. Now tell me that isn't Cath.'

'OK, OK.' Martin conceded this point, at least. 'What about Sue, then?'

'Well, I'd only got as far as Cath with this particular theorem, but I'll give it a go. Give us the dictionary.' He leafed through it. 'Suede. Well, she liked suede. Suet. Yeah, she sometimes ate suet, you know, in puddings and stuff.'

'It's not exactly an all-encompassing theory, is it?'

'Hang on. Hang on.' Ian widened his search. 'Suffrance. Suffocate. Suggestible. Suicidal. Sulk. That's her! All of it! I rest my case.'

'Bollocks.' Martin remained unconvinced. 'All right, Sue and Cath, maybe. What about . . . Deborah?'

Ian opened the dictionary at a fresh page. 'Deb . . . Deb . . . Debauch. Debonair. Debrief. You see, all these words could have come from the way the bloke who invented them felt about his wife or girlfriend.'

'Mmm.' Despite the intoxicating weight of his cloudy brain, Martin still had his doubts.

'I mean, d'you remember that spate of jokes like "What do you call a swimmer with no legs or arms?"'

'Bob?'

'Yeah. But there were loads of them. Doug with a spade in his head, et cetera et cetera. The point is that names and words are inextricably linked. Think of all the names which are also words. Peter, Eddy, Hank, Nick, Sue, Matt, Mike, Rose, Adam . . .'

'. . . what?'

'. . . a dam . . .'

'Oh.'

'. . . Dick, Roger, Don, Ivy . . . I mean, what's to say that all of these words didn't originate from people who summed up, for whatever reason, a particular action or object that was previously unnamed?'

'What, so someone called Eddy, for instance, swirled round a lot in the old days and reminded people so much of whirlpool-like thingymajigs and whatd'youcall'ems and such like that they named them Eddys? I mean, is that really the nub of your gist?'

'Well, yes.'

'And a man called Roger went around shagging so many people that they had to invent a new verb around him?'

'Yeah, but . . .'

'And someone called Don kept putting clothes on?'

'Look I know it might sound a bit far-fetched . . .'

'A bit?'

'But it's got to be more than just coincidence.' Ian opened a fresh can. 'I mean, look at surnames.'

'What about them?'

'Well, Thatcher, Tailor, Smith, Carpenter – they're all names which have come from words, and that's perfectly acceptable to you?'

'Yeah, but they're all professions.'

'So?'

'Well, you can see how Bob the thatcher or Jeremy the tailor could have become Bob Thatcher or Jeremy Tailor. But Roger the rogerer?'

'I'm just saying it *might* have happened that way, that's all.'

'I'm afraid it all sounds a bit shit to me.' Ian, despite himself, had to agree. He made a mental note not to air any of his theories until he had thought them through, and, under such circumstances, not to do so unless he was in possession of an unclouded set of faculties.

The ritualistic spliff exchange continued until the last one receded to its cardboard shores, at which point Ian became instantly restless, in a tired, red-eyed sort of way.

'Gotta go, mate,' Ian said, fishing around for his car keys and standing up. 'Thanks for the doobie.'

'Oh yeah, right.' Martin looked up at him. 'You're not driving are you?'

'Yeah.'

'Hang on Ian, you're not really in any fit state . . .'

'You can talk . . .'

'Yeah, but you looked wrecked when you got here. And what've you done to your head?'

'Nothing.'

'Look, I'm not one to hassle anyone but, you know, you shouldn't . . .'

Ian headed for the door. 'Save the lecture, Martin, I'm off.'

'But . . .'

'Later.'

He left, slamming the door behind him, and started his car with the usual encouragement. He had had enough of people telling him what to do. He had to focus – he had a mission. He was going to get very wasted and then apply himself to the cause of programming. He headed back in the direction of work. Sobriety hadn't helped him so far, so he was going to try to do without it. Shit. Shit. Shit. Martin's brother's car crash. Shit. He'd been drinking. Shit. Ian pulled into a bus lay-by. Twelve weeks in hospital, still can't walk unaided. Shit. He should return and apologize. He looked into the rear-view mirror. His eyes were bloodshot. He looked terrible. *Drink driving ruins lives.* He tried to focus. *No excuses.* He badly needed a piss. *Leave the car at home.* He indicated. *The effects could last for ever.* He checked his mirrors. *One drink is all it takes.* Signal mirror manoeuvre. *Have none for the road.* He pulled out into the traffic again, dazzled momentarily by the oncoming lights. Fuck it. He was much too wasted to be bothered with etiquette. Besides, there was work to be done.

Back in the office, he filled the kettle. He was hungry. He opened one of the instant noodles he had bought, scanned the instructions and poured in some boiling water. He wiped a stained teaspoon on a scarf he found in one of Archie's drawers and stirred the expanding noodles in anticipation. It smelled good. He hadn't had instant noodles since his student days, but had been led to believe, largely by a TV advertising campaign, that these were the choice for a new generation. He gave it another half-hearted stir, waited two minutes, stirred it again and then put a teaspoon of its watery contents into his mouth. It was terrible. He remembered instantly why he didn't eat them any more. They were shit now and they always had been shit. He imagined a board meeting at the headquarters of Instant Noodle PLC.

'OK, gentlemen, it's time to be blunt. Our market research people tell us we've got a lousy product. The question before us is do we a) spend half a million pounds improving it or b) spend half a million pounds on better adverts? A show of hands? All in favour? Great. I'll get on to the ad agency.'

Ian opened another can of beer and emptied the contents of the tub into one of Archie's drawers.

Set a Thief

Four days passed. Ian began the task that had been set him. It was fairly straightforward and he drifted into a nocturnal routine of feverish programming and swearing through the night, returning home as the milk was delivered and sleeping as best he could through the day, aided by a can or two of breakfast beer. Beer at this time was super-potent. Even shandy could be mildly dangerous when drunk at six am. Ian had read up on body clocks once, in lieu of doing something constructive and followed his own descent into free-running arrhythmia with wry, detached interest, as if it was happening to someone he didn't particularly care about. He knew, for instance, that nearly all bodily processes are strictly timed, so that conflicting bodily events can be separated temporally rather than spatially, and that having this innate periodicity has some, almost forgotten, adaptive value. Pain thresholds, body temperature and alcohol tolerance cycle consistently through the day, so that at five am you will feel cold, be fairly susceptible to pain and will, if you're still drinking, be too inebriated to notice either of the first two conditions.

But, Ian was noticing with mild interest, all it took to strip the body clock of its hands was a little insomnia-inducing fear coupled with some social isolation. He was drifting out of sync with the world.

The need to work at night, away from his colleagues, was reminiscent of a period when he was unemployed. Having people around you all day seems to act as cohesive factor, as if everyone is continually synchronizing watches. Lose this cohesion and you drift into the trap of a nocturnal life where Jobfinder lurks and where you can't sleep because you haven't been to work because you don't have a job, so you don't get out of bed until lunchtime, which becomes your breakfast time, and all of a sudden your watch is running perpetually slower than everyone else's and even lunchtime begins to feel too early to get out of bed. Sometimes it seemed that work was really just there to tire you out so you would go to bed at a decent time, ready for the next day, so you wouldn't have time to stay up late and actually think about what you were doing with your life.

Ian had worked through Tuesday night and continued into the day. Time was running out – he had five days until Monday – and he wasn't making the kind of progress that was going to ensure Archie retained his full compliment of gangly limbs. Having taken the week off, people who saw him at work on Wednesday were surprised and slightly appalled at his dedication to duty. A low level of security was sufficient to protect the true nature of his task, aided as it was by the low level of enthusiasm that his colleagues had for each other's work. Munching the same flavour of sandwich he bought every day from the nearest sandwich shop, an idea suddenly came to Ian that made him stop chewing. He swallowed the dry bread and put the rest of his lunch in the bin. He was gripped by a fever of possibility. Of course, that was it. It wasn't set a thief to catch a thief at all. No thief is interested in catching other thieves. But set a thief to rob a thief, now that was a different proposition altogether. He returned to his office and sat and stared at the script he had been working on. It was useless, irrelevant, he could see that now. He selected large chunks of the code and cut it. Was he sure he wanted to delete the selection? He typed 'y' in confirmation and pressed return. This called for a completely different strategy. For a couple of hours, he burned with possibility and began again, this time from a different starting point.

A programming impasse loomed later in the afternoon which couldn't be traversed by lateral thought. Fairly undeterred, Ian returned to his house, still gripped, just as the phone ceased ringing and launched into its recorded greeting. He got to the receiver and interrupted Elvis in full flight. 'Hello?'

'Monday's five days.' It was Frying Pan.

'Fuck that. What about my fucking living-room?'

'What about it?'

'It's fucking ruined, that's what.'

'So?' Frying Pan's barely suppressed, rattling diesel laughter shook him. He had enjoyed cutting Ian's head open. He had enjoyed ripping his carpet up. He was enjoying holding Archie captive. He was enjoying the barely detectable but still painfully apparent tremor in Ian's voice. He was enjoying every second of the intimidation.

'Look, I need to talk to Archie.' Ian tried to cloak the tremor in short quick words.

Frying Pan's mirth subsided, reluctantly. 'I'll ask. Mind you, anything to stop the fucker talking to me.' The phone was deadened by his palm. Presumably he was asking if it would be OK. Frying Pan's voice returned.

'What do you want to say to him?'

'I need to talk to him about some programming.'

'What about it?'

'Look, I have to see him.'

'Well you can't.'

'I have to – I'm stuck.' The receiver was again obscured by Frying Pan's hand, this time for a longer duration.

'We'll be round in half an hour. Don't fucking go any-where.'

'Right.'

'Bye.'

'Bye.'

It seemed a little incongruous to hang up with such rela-tive pleasantries, given that the man he was talking to was holding his workmate (in the broadest sense of the word) captive, albeit, by the sound of things, to his own detriment, but it was involuntary, and to hang up without saying any-thing, no matter how popular in films, would have felt more awkward than not to. Ian dialled 1-4-7-1. No number was stored. Though by no means ruthlessly efficient, they were efficient, and, by the look of things so far, fairly ruthless.

Around two hours later a horn sounded in the street out-side his house. He went to the window and looked for the van through the gap where his curtains didn't quite meet. There was no van, just a shabby Ford Orion taxi. Frying Pan sat in the front and Archie in the back. Frying Pan looked weary, while Archie appeared remarkably at ease. He left the house and got into the taxi wondering, as he often did, whether Archie was really alive. Obviously Archie displayed some of the vital signs of life, but little more. It was the non-essential signs that he lacked – passion, excitement, fervour, error, loathing, fallibility, desire, apathy – signs which are essential if life is to be lived fully. What additional luggage he carried in excess of the bare minimum required to get by comprised inertia, intractability, obstinacy, mediocrity and inflexibility, combined, somewhat fatally, with a dogged self-belief. This made arguing with Archie a simultaneously tortuous and unsuccessful pastime. Still, it beat working. But there was a thin line between fearlessness and death. If you weren't alive on the inside, and he suspected that Archie wasn't, there were no knots to tie, nowhere for butterflies to settle, and no neurones to be tormented by adrenaline. He did, after all, look remarkably at ease in the company of the ever-threatening Frying Pan. The other option, which Ian at once found unthinkable and yet couldn't help thinking about, was that he had misjudged Archie. Maybe he wasn't as soft as shit. Maybe Archie was made of sterner stuff. He shuddered.

The taxi driver turned to Frying Pan and asked, 'Where to?' with a weariness that suggested the beginning of another long night mopping up the results of the city's good times.

'Just drive,' instructed the equally weary Frying Pan.

'Yeah, but where to?' the driver asked again.

'Anywhere, for Christ's sake.'

'Look, I've got to tell base where I'm dropping you,' he said, picking up his radio mike, 'so they can arrange a pick-up there.'

'God, I dunno, go into town, to the train station, I don't care.' The driver indicated and pulled off begrudgingly in what felt like at least second or third gear. Frying Pan snarled without turning round, 'Right, I'm fed up of this. Ask 'im what you need to ask 'im and maybe I can get home and put my fucking feet up.'

There was nothing that Ian wanted to ask Archie, at least not in Frying Pan's presence. He would have to hope that his discussion with Archie would be inaudible from the front seat, where the taxi's radio provided crackly bursts of cover. The driver announced his destination, then turned his radio down. Ian cursed under his breath.

'Drives me fucking mad all night,' the driver explained, to no one in particular.

Under the circumstances, he thought he'd better make some sort of effort at a technical conversation. 'You know the distribution bridge,' he asked Archie, 'is there any way of reprogramming it?' Ian knew of at least two easy ways of doing it.

'Of course there is,' Archie began. 'You know you really should read your manuals more thoroughly.' Ian looked out of the window and sighed through clenched teeth, watching the window cloud with the condensation of his breath.

'Well, how?'

'Log in via Telnet. Take the D.B. Change Config File over to Sys Repair. Drop the Edit code. Choose Edit Options. Tab F12 then save as a dot PCR file. Easy, if you know how.'

Ian strung the conversation out for several more minutes. As they approached New Street station, and Ian approached suicide, Frying Pan unexpectedly told the taxi driver to stop. 'I've gotta get some tobacco.' He turned his head round to face Ian and Archie between the front seats, a difficult task given that his head seemed to bypass any thought of a neck and be simply an extension of his torso. 'Now, if either of you talk about anything while I'm gone, *anything*, I'll break your fucking jaws, all right?' Ian and Archie nodded. He heaved himself out of the car and disappeared into a Late Nite shop. The taxi driver flicked the central locking button. Frying Pan had made his first mistake. Ian fumbled rapidly through his pockets and found a twenty-pound note and thrust it between the front seats towards the driver.

'Sorry pal, you're not getting out of the taxi.'

'No, take this, and if he asks you if we were talking, just say no.'

The driver hesitated. 'Only if someone tells me what this sodding goose-chase is all about.' Ian remained silent. 'Well?' He pushed the note towards him, conscious that they were wasting time. 'Oh what the fuck. I'm only the driver. Here, give me that.' He took the note. Ian turned to Archie.

'Now, we've only got a couple of minutes. How would I set up an account?'

'Why would you want to set up an account?'

'Look, I don't know how much they've told you . . .'

'Not very much at all.'

'But they've got an investment account, right, and they want me to hack into the distribution bridge, so that instead of getting spread around all of the thousands of accounts we handle, the day's single highest trade from the City goes straight into their account.'

'Oh,' said Archie.

'So they're going to rake it in. But the point is this. If I can set up a ghost account, somehow, a fake one, then I can channel all of that money away from their account and into one of my . . . one of our own.' Ian looked out of the window. There wasn't much time. Frying Pan was second or third in the queue and was glancing over every few seconds. 'So how would I set up an account?'

'You would have to see your financial adviser and instruct him to deposit two hundred and fifty thousand pounds with . . .'

'Yes, yes, but what if I didn't have the money to be an investor?'

'Well then you couldn't . . .'

'No, I mean, what I'm saying Archie is that I want to set up a ghost account, without having the minimum quarter of a million stake. Do you know of a way of doing that?'

'I don't think it would be feasible.'

'Why not? I mean, people instruct accounts, right? If there's a way of instigating an account there must be a way of falsely instigating one.'

'I hardly need remind you that accounts aren't instructed by us, they're instructed by financial investment houses. Patching into their systems would be virtually impossible,' Archie looked at Ian, 'even if *I* was doing it.' Thirty seconds of Archie's patronage and Ian was ready to kill him if it wasn't for the burning idea which had been consuming him since lunchtime.

'I'm not talking about hacking, just intercepting and rerouting.'

'I'm not sure I quite follow what you are *trying* to say.'

'Look, what I'm *trying* to say is that, no matter where it comes from or where it goes, at some point, that information has to pass through our system.'

'So?'

'Well, if it comes through our system, there must be some way of getting hold of the data and altering it or rerouting it or something.'

'And how would you propose to do that?'

'I don't know.' Ian glanced out of the window. 'That's why I'm asking you – you're the expert – you think of a way. Now.' Through the window of the shop Frying Pan was pointing at what was probably a shelf of cigarettes. 'Now, Archie, now, for Christ's sake.'

'Let me think.' Archie thought for a moment. Ian savaged his nails. 'Oh well, much against my better judgement, because I can't see just how this is going to help our . . .'

'Archie!' Ian almost screamed. The taxi driver looked round. Frying Pan was receiving his change. Archie came up with the goods.

'OK. I think you'll need two workstations in parallel, with a serial lead. Import the data into station A, then crash the whole system. While it's down, copy it across to B. Wait for the sys' to reboot but as it's doing so, drop it again.'

'Why two stations?'

'It won't reboot if any data is missing or altered.' Frying Pan was approaching. 'Anyway, that should give you about two minutes to edit the data on B, unplug the serial cable, take A's network cable and put it into B . . .' Frying Pan opened the passenger door.

'What the fuck are you two talking about? I said I'd fucking kill you. What were you saying? Come on, I saw you, you specky twat. What the fuck were you talking about?'

Archie remained calm, or dead, one of the two and answered, 'Nothing.' Frying Pan glared at Ian, who held his eye and then looked at the driver, who shook his head in silent affirmation.

'Well you'd better not have been.' He was outnumbered, and knew it. He turned his anger to the driver. 'Right, tell your fucking boss we're going back to Kings Heath to drop this fucker off,' he said, thumbing vaguely in Ian's direction, 'that's if the useless cunt can remember where he lives.'

'No, drop me at work,' Ian said, 'I've found out what I need to know.'

Licence to Steal

Work was deserted but brightly lit, as if trying to beckon the workers back from their homes. Ian, too, was on fire. Two workstations – he would need to liberate one from someone. He took his boss's. This was James Bond stuff – licence to steal, and all in the cause of hostage protection. Ian began to wonder what other illegal acts he could get away with under this umbrella. Commandeering a car, a real one, with more than one point one litres of lethargy sulking under the bonnet, for instance. 'So, Mr Gillick, you were forced by the sluggish nature of your own Peugeot 205 to take possession of a seven-litre Jensen Interceptor with fuel injection and twin turbo chargers, in the interest of protecting your close colleague and friend, Mr Archibald Wilson? The court finds this act entirely understandable, and further, commends your choice of . . .' Two computers. And a serial lead. By 11.30 pm, Ian had assembled the hardware he supposed he would need – two workstations and all the right cables. He began to install the code that had survived the afternoon's savage editing, together with the script that he had been working on frantically for most of the rest of the day. Little by little his fever began to subside, dulled as it was by the medicine of reality. He had no idea whether the codes would work – he was by no means an expert programmer – and wasn't enough of a pedant ever to be. He swore, fidgeted, scratched, stretched, yawned and generally cursed the programmes into life throughout another sleepless night.

It was roughly 4.40 am. Ian watched the second hand of his watch stutter around from 0 to 30 and back again, falling between each second markation as it did so, so that it was difficult to tell whether it was 22 or 23, or 23 or 24 seconds past the minute. He looked more closely. The minute hand missed its mark as well. He pulled the winder out and the second hand stopped dead. If it couldn't be arsed to actually tell the time properly it wasn't going to do it at all. It was like paying a taxi driver to do the one thing nearly all taxi drivers were incapable of doing properly – driving. He looked at the watch again and it felt strange that time was passing despite his watch, that seconds were ticking without being counted by its hands. He put the winder back in and the second hand juddered back into action.

In the empty hours before dawn, Ian found himself once again thinking of Sue. Sex had always been good, better than good in fact, but then things had gone wrong. She had, at first with silent, then with physical and, finally, spoken indications, intimated that the sexual part of their relationship wasn't all it might be. Ian had been gutted. In common with most men, he feigned sexual ineptitude at every opportunity, particularly with his male friends.

'What the fuck's a clitoris?'

Or: 'Thirty seconds, and that was shagging her twice.'

Or: 'What do you mean, "Did she enjoy it?" – *I* came didn't I?'

But if he had believed for one second that he couldn't

find a clitoris in a haystack, that he couldn't on a good night and after a couple of beers, admittedly, last half an hour, and that she didn't really enjoy sex any more, he would have been distraught. Which is more or less what happened. She suggested that they buy a book, one with lots of ideas for . . . for what Ian didn't know – in fact, had he been asked a week or so earlier, he would have sworn he could have written such a book, if he'd wanted to. He became obsessed with finding out just what it was that he didn't know about sex.

One rainy Saturday morning, they found themselves browsing self-consciously through the euphemistic Adult Health section of Waterstones. Was there a Child Health section for paedophiles, Ian wondered, but this was very secondary – tertiary, quaternary, even – to the deep feelings of insecurity and resentment which were building up inside him.

'I think someone recommended this book,' she said, picking up *The Art of Sexual and Spiritual Effectiveness*.

Once again, Ian was mortified.

'You mean you've been discussing this with someone?'

'Not this little problem specifically, just, you know, what if someone I knew . . .'

'Oh fucking great, like no one's going to see through that one.'

The phrase 'little problem' struck home with delayed impact and started to undermine what was left of his fast-evaporating confidence. Was she referring to his cock, he wondered. He hadn't had any complaints before, but, on the other hand, not too many glowing recommendations either. He had gone from a man with an all-protecting, reflecting sunglass aura of confidence, a computer game character who had found the cheat code for invincibility, to a whimpering cub scout who had suddenly forgotten how to tie knots and was having trouble with his woggle. As usual when something penetrated his skin, he welcomed it deeper inside himself and sulked around it.

'We'll take this one then, if you're OK with it,' she said.

'Mmm,' he grunted, with a lack of enthusiasm which belied his interest in some of the pictures it contained, and which he made a mental note to study later and alone.

In the intervening time between buying the book, Ian overcoming his insecurity, a parental visit and actually getting round to giving it a go, he had started to see the idea's attraction. He realized it was an opportunity to persuade Sue to try things which had hitherto been firmly off the menu – dishes you heard of being served, but only in the exotic restaurants of other people's girlfriends. At the very least, it would be sexual blackmail – how can you complain that *I'm* boring in bed if *you* won't try new things?

A moment at last presented itself and the time was deemed right by mutual consent (with one abstention), so the book method was begun. Sue read aloud.

'Thank you for buying *The Art of Sexual and Spiritual Effectiveness*. From time to time in everyone's loving, fulfilling relationship, there arrives a point where . . . hang on, no, yes, here we are . . . chapter one. Spiritual Awareness – Making Your Loved One Feel Loved. Undress and face each other, seated on cushions, in the middle of any room except the bedroom. Light candles, and, if you wish, burn fragrant oils.'

Ian begun to have doubts. The undressing part was fine, but the candles would prove a bit more fiddly. He remembered having some somewhere, maybe in the toolbox, but they didn't have anything which could be remotely described as a candle holder.

'We could melt some wax in a saucer.' he suggested.

'What?'

'To hold the candle.'

'Why don't we just put the main light out and turn the small lamp on?'

The necessary lighting changes were made, and Sue continued.

'Present your partner with a love gift – something which tells your partner "I love you, I value you, I have gathered this love gift for you."'

'Jesus, what is this? I have to buy you a present every time I want to fuck you?'

'Look, are you going to take this seriously?'

'I'm trying, but I'm stuck in Marks and Spencer's underwear section desperately trying to buy you a fucking love gift.'

Sue continued.

'Thank your partner and present him with a love gift, with the words "I accept your love gift as my spirit accepts your spirit".'

It began to dawn on Ian who had recommended the book, and whom Sue had, hypothetically, told intimate and crushing details of their love life. Sue's friend Liz was a sucker for any sort of spiritual nonsense. Ian had never been sure whether her open acceptance of eclectic philosophies reflected a deeper understanding of spiritual teachings, or just a deep vacuity. After all, eclecticism is often confused with a lack of direction, and openness with a lack of critical faculty. He wondered whether Sue had bought a book about the spiritual side of lovemaking (whatever that might be) because it was not a physical problem *per se*. If it was a spiritual thing, then Ian was out of his depth and he knew it. He decided to ask, tentatively.

'This spiritual stuff sounds like it could be pretty fulfilling, you know, if you got into it.'

'Sounds like a load of old shite to me,' Sue declared. 'There doesn't seem to be anything about actually getting round to shagging in it.'

Momentarily relieved it wasn't a spiritual matter, he began to panic again, affirmed in the knowledge that it was indeed a physical problem. He didn't know which was worse. In fact, he did – no one would deride you if your girlfriend stood up in the pub and announced that the spiritual side of your love-making needed further honing. But if she broadcast your ineptitude in the basics of shagging, well, he started to shudder.

The book idea was, however, a disaster and was quickly abandoned. Ian began to try harder, which achieved Sue's original aim. The book, on the other hand, became a symbol of their inability to communicate, moving from the book case to under the bed in the spare room if visitors came to stay, where it remained long after they left.

He looked back at the screen and tried to focus his thoughts. He had reached another impasse. Archie's instructions weren't working. They were at least partly right, but something was missing or conflicting. Ian sat back in his chair and attempted to balance it on two legs, using his feet as counter weights. He managed three or four seconds on his first couple of attempts, but then almost fell off and decided to give it up before he broke his neck. He stared into his dimly lit monitor. He had thought and unthought, read and scribbled, cussed and whistled, had even dreamt of solutions, but nothing worked. Progress had slowed almost to the point of stagnation. Although his life had recently been rearranged, he had managed none the less to establish a new pattern of actions over the last five or six, he couldn't be sure, six probably, nights. An idea. Try it out. It works, partially, or not at all. An impasse. The fever subsides. Think of another route. The fever burns again. Try it out. Partial success. Think. Swear. Scratch. Yawn. Stand up. Stretch. Sit down. Think. Swear. Read. Scribble. Think of another way. Try it. Edge forwards, crab-like. Change a parameter. Start again. Reach another impasse.

Now, as he looked at the screen, he realized he had again

gone as far as he could on his own. Suddenly, he gave out an unrestrained, diaphragm-stretching laugh which echoed around the empty office. He had caught Archie out. At last, after months and months of didactic one-way traffic, he had him. Purer than pure, duller than dull Archie had been thinking this through. Maybe Ian had planted the idea there, but Archie, for all his denials, had been working on this very scheme himself. He had given him the answer, or part of it, in an instant in the back of the taxi and Ian knew that, by their very definition, plodders are incapable of spontaneity. But Archie didn't have the complete answer. In essence it seemed right, but essence and programming are contradictory notions. He needed Archie again. The concept made him shudder. Great ideas, though, often come not from one genius but from two mediocritics, simply because two people have different thoughts and therefore cover more ground. He needed Archie because the task needed feeling and reason. Archie largely represented reason. Ian would supply the feeling, whatever that entailed. The only consolation was that another meeting with Archie would, at least, be some sort of human contact.

Dawn was approaching and that meant that the early birds would soon be breezing into work. Ian made one last attempt to balance his chair on its hind legs, achieving a respectable, though quickly counted, five seconds, then returned his boss's computer and made his way to the car park.

Being Alone

Since this farce had begun, he had hardly seen or spoken to anybody. He had taken the week off work and slept as much of the day as the traffic and dogs would allow, arriving at work only when he was sure that everyone had returned to their dismal husbands and wives on their dismal detached estates. For Ian, solitary confinement of this nature was a disaster. He needed people he knew to surround him like clothes and disguise his nakedness. He had already discovered that being alone with himself was a catastrophe, because he had experimented with it once before on holiday. It hadn't been through choice, it had just happened that way. The fantasy of the golden words 'abroad' and 'alone' had always been there, for as long as he could remember. As it was though, he and Sue took the standard British two weeks of foreign sun, and were grateful enough for that, though they were shackled together in their isolation abroad, and Sue was shackled to the sun. She saw only the warmth of the blueness that surrounded them, while he saw only its cold, blue frown. She didn't merely worship the sun, she embraced it, kissed its sandy toes and let it stroke her upturned stomach, while he hid in the corners of the church that even the sun couldn't find. Her troubles evaporated as beads of perspiration, while his collected in his knotted brow, forming tributaries of torment. Ian longed to be alone, to explore, to roam, to cruise around and, if he was honest with himself, to meet new, adventurous girls in each town. Then, one summer, it happened. He and Mark, who also longed to travel alone, booked a holiday together. Alone to them wasn't compromised by their friendship, for two men together are often alone. After all, together is just a matter of geography, not necessarily of minds. Mark rang him up a week before departure.

'Work won't let me go.'

'Won't let you? What do you mean "Won't let you"?'

'The other bloke that does my job, his wife has just had a miscarriage.'

'So they won't let you go?'

'Well, I suppose they would, but come on.' Ian was being selfish, not for his self, but in the general cause of panic. A holiday alone. Alone alone, not just alone with a male friend alone. 'I mean, it's a bit of a pisser all round, but what can I do? Look, if it's the money, try and cancel it and get what you can off the travel company, and I'll see if I can't make up the difference.'

'No, it's all right.' Ian thought for a second, then paused for dramatic effect. 'I think I might go anyway.'

'What, alone? Like alone alone?' Mark sounded horrified.

'Yeah, I'll manage. I mean, it'd have been more fun with you there . . .'

'Cheaper, you mean.'

'Yeah, but it'll be OK I suppose.'

And it was OK, for a little while at least. California. Californ-I-A. Two weeks and a car, a proper one with a real engine and electrical things. But the first week declined from splendid isolation to just, well, isolation, with progressively

more time each day spent in the womb of the car. As a diver-
sion from himself he visited Alcatraz. This had always been
a dream. An island, close to mainland San Fransisco, which
housed the country's most notorious and popular criminals,
in mocking proximity to the many and various thrills of the
city. Prowling the prison corridors with a Walkman guide
focused the isolation of the holiday. The penitentiary was
instilled with an eerie calm as other tourists shuffled in time
with the headphoned voices of ex-prisoners.

'The thang 'bout sol'tary ain' the lack o' light, or soun' or
people, even, i's been alone with yo'self. Tha's the worse
thang 'bout sol'tary – i's what you got in yo mind.'

So that was it. In one blinding moment, on a rock, on an
island, Ian realized that the only thing worse than being surrounded by people you didn't like was to be surrounded by
yourself. Just where that left you on your own list of popularity he didn't know, but it couldn't be that high. He saw that
the other people on the planet are merely distractions to keep
you from yourself, and that Archie, the antithesis of all that
was Ian, at least gave him someone to hate, other than himself. Surely Ian should stick together, for his own sake. But it
wasn't that simple. If you were alone, you thought about
yourself, and there were two problems with self-perception.
First, you probably weren't exactly the sort of person you
thought you were. No matter how hard you self-analysed,
how honest you were with yourself, how objective, humble or
detached, you would still be unlikely to judge yourself as a
cross-section of people would judge you. Second, and the
shadow cast by the first point, was that people didn't see you
as you really were. They would judge you, categorize you,
place you under a series of headings which were in themselves meaningless, like generous, mean, deep, shallow,
selfish, selfless, and all this based upon superficial signals, so
that different people might put you in different categories, or
worse, the same person might put you in opposing categories

on different days or under different circumstances. Such judgements would be compounded by the times when you were, as ever, fulfilling some sort of role to suit someone else. So who you really were was fairly impossible to sum up without putting bits of yourself into often contradictory boxes. You didn't really know you, and nor did anyone else, and no one, particularly you, was really in any position to judge. So Ian decided to try to suit only himself in matters of personality. This in itself proved to be unsatisfactory in that it still felt as if he was playing a role, even though that role was just to be himself, but, to play himself, he had to know himself, and this was the point at which he had come in. He wondered whether it really was possible to be yourself and act naturally any more. It would, he reasoned, be much easier to be someone else and act out their personality. Or, better still, to put yourself into a category and wear it unashamedly and unquestioningly, and use it as an armour against self-doubt and uncertainty, which is exactly what bigots, socialists or evangelical Christians do.

He left the island as quickly as the San Francisco fog would allow and headed downtown in an attempt to shop himself happy. Just to talk to shop assistants would do. He was in luck. A pretty sales assistant in a clothes shop offered to nurture him out of his solitary confinement.

'Can I help you?'

(Yes. Yes. Oh yes. Please yes).

'I'm, um, looking for a jacket.' He wasn't, but he could hardly say, 'I have no friends and I'm driving myself mad with my own company.'

'Yeah?' She drawled 'Yeah' in the most inviting way Ian had ever heard it drawled, which, admittedly, hadn't been that often.

'I'm not looking for anything too expensive, I mean, I'm on holiday, by myself, and, you know, running out of money a bit, I mean, it's so expensive by yourself, compared with going with your girlfriend or whatever and you split the car hire and motel rooms and petrol . . . er, gas . . . and stuff.' She was beautiful and Ian was rambling. Amazingly, she listened. '. . . And I've just been to Alcatraz . . .'

'Yeah?' There it was again.

'Yes, and there was this ex-prisoner saying how, if you're in solitary confinement then what drives you mad is just being exposed to all your own thoughts.'

'Yeah, I bet some of those prisoners were preddy screwed up, right?'

'Yes, but I reckon it would happen to anyone, no matter how sane. I mean, I'm on holiday by myself and I'm starting to get on my nerves after only a week. And it's not like you can have an argument with yourself, sulk for a bit and then make up and have sex with yourself.' He glanced at her as she looked momentarily away. She was amazing. 'Well, I suppose the last bit's possible (A smile, a good sign). Anyway, look at Robinson Crusoe.'

'Who's that?'

'You know – the book by Daniel Defoe – Robinson Crusoe was perfectly sane before he was ship-wrecked on a desert island. Then he met this native he called Man Friday and went to all the trouble of teaching Man Friday to speak English just so he could have someone to talk to.'

'Well, I guess I could be your Friday.'

'Um . . .' This was unfamiliar territory. He had been by himself for almost eight days now. Luckily, innate reason took over and allowed him to panic. 'Um . . . I'll just try this one on.' Cursing himself, he tried on an ill-fitting jacket. He was useless, anyone could see that. His Girl Friday got called away to the phone and he lingered in the shop long enough to feel awkward before making a tactical retreat. His solitary continued, while he tried to recall the golden pleasure of holidaying with his girlfriend.

The Other Voice

Frying Pan wasn't at all pleased.

'What d'y'mean you want to see him again? I thought you were a programmer.'

'I am.'

'Well fuckin' programme then.'

'I can't.'

'Trust us to pick a useless cunt. It should be you here and not that other irritating twat.'

'Look, I'm stuck again.'

'Well I'll be buggered if I'm coming all the way over there again.' For the first time, Ian heard a voice in the background, and it didn't belong to Archie or Tattoo. The line went quiet under the weight of Frying Pan's palm. He returned after a minute or so. 'Look, can't you just speak to 'im on the phone?' This was a dilemma. Clearly there was someone else in the room and whether he talked directly to Archie or through the interpretations of Frying Pan, he would run the risk of the third person realizing that Ian wanted more information from Archie than the scheme strictly required. And, at a guess, it was likely that the third person was involved, and at a further guess was even the instigator, which implied that any audible deviation from the planned programming would be detected and in no small measure frowned upon. Ian decided to insist upon another meeting and to rely upon the ignorance of Frying Pan for cover.

'No, I have to see him.' The phone disappeared into Frying Pan's hand.

'Right. No pissing about. We'll be round.' No 'Bye' this time – formalities had officially been dropped. No idea of when was given, so Ian sat down and thought. He predicted the Other Voice wouldn't show up with them. His shyness was understandable – no point in exposing yourself to unnecessary risk – but maybe there was more. It probably wasn't someone they worked with, as Archie would now know who it was. If the Other Voice was quite happy to expose himself to Archie, and this would be an unpleasant experience in any conceivable context, it was likely that Archie didn't know him. If he was willing to encounter Archie but not Ian, maybe it was someone that Ian knew, but not through work. Ian racked his brains, which were in no fit state for a good racking, and came up with nothing. He tried to sit still and think things through but sitting still was impossible. There had been a time when it had been possible, he believed, but had no idea when it was or how long it had lasted – it was like an event from childhood which you had a photograph of and couldn't quite discern whether it was the event itself or just the photograph that you remembered. A car horn announced the re-run of the taxi fiasco. This time, the dress rehearsal had served them well and things ran smoothly. The Other Voice wasn't present. The four of them set off for the train station.

'Right, ask 'im what you want to ask 'im.' This should be easier. Archie has been primed, no need to explain the premiss.

'Thursday night. For fuck's sake,' Frying Pan grumbled from the front seat.

Ian gambled, and it was a fairly safe bet, that Frying Pan wouldn't understand the context of their conversation. 'Archie, I'm having problems instigating the secondary account.'

'What sort of problems, specifically?'

'Well, I've sorted out a lot of the code that's going to adjust the distribution of the money into the first account, but setting the ghost up, and then getting the cash into our secondary one, well, it's not particularly straightforward. I'm stuck.'

Archie seemed weary and a little uncomfortable, but otherwise OK. He proceeded to monotone Ian what he needed to do and what he had done wrong. Ian sat silently and cursed his own incompetence. Frying Pan didn't leave the car, and as soon as Ian was happy with what he had been told he once again asked to be dropped at work before he forgot it. And so another night began.

Ian was once again gripped by a fever. It was occasionally abated by incompetence and lack of knowledge, but it was there nonetheless, growing and multiplying, and waiting to feed on Archie's insight. It was a fever that eschewed food and comfort and sleep, to burn brightly through the night until it could burn no more. Archie decided that Ian had been too thorough, too stringent in his calculations. Progress often means simply taking short cuts – discovering what you can get away with not doing. Things become quicker, processes more efficient, systems more robust, not through the things you put into them, but through the things you learn they can live without. Progress is a lean, wiry and restless man. Status quo, by comparison, is flabby and contented. Ian's programmes needed to lose a few pounds of non-essential code before they would run. So he set about editing out the cautious junk he had burdened the programmes with and pairing them down to their fundamentals. In the spider's web of a programme, to remove lines of code is to threaten the well-being of all interconnected threads while still protecting the integrity of the whole mesh and is more precarious than spinning a web from scratch. It was irritating and tiresome and subject to many problems, but, a couple of hours after dawn, he was fairly sure that everything would work.

It didn't. There was little time to find out why though, as his colleagues would be shaving and washing and showering and wondering why they had woken up on the sofa with the TV on and eating their cereal with added bran, and generally preparing themselves, one way or another, for another artificially lit day at Intron. Ian worked quickly. Instead of looking for fundamental conflicts or omissions, he did something that programmers are, by their very nature, loath to do. He used his intuition. He saved all his previous versions under new names (there was no reason, at this stage, to rule superstition out of the equation) and set about ripping out any script he simply didn't like the look of, or that irritated him, or didn't somehow seem 'natural' or was too Archie. He replaced them with code which 'felt right'. This was feeling over reason, superstition over logic, man over machine. Half an hour later and he had torn its logical heart out. He looked out of the window. There were a couple of cars already in the car park. He could hear a security guard unlocking doors. The odd light flickered into action on the other side of the building. The inevitable misery was about to begin again in vain. He had minutes, at the most. It was do or die. He ran the code and then accessed the list of Intron accounts, scanning through for his account number. 'Come on, come on.' It wasn't there. 'Where are you?' He checked again. It was nowhere. 'Bollocks.' Then he had an idea. He closed his current window and instead accessed the new accounts listing and scanned through them. 'Come on, come on.' He clenched his pen between his teeth. 'Please. Please, you fucker, please.'

Then he saw it. He checked it and then checked it again. It was there, as clear as day. It had worked. He was a quarter-millionaire. He now had a ghost account.

Even as a quarter-millionaire, his finances were still a mess and he wouldn't be buying any Ferraris or helicopters. He couldn't do anything with the money and never would be able to. It had no actual fiscal value. What it did represent was a passport into potential proper money of the spending rather than digital variety. It was a carrier bag that could be filled with cash at some later juncture. All he had to do now was work out how to fill it. He disconnected the workstations he had been using and returned one of them to his boss's desk. As he headed for the circular bus the fever was still alight, glowing rather than burning, but well aware that it was time for action.

'Seventy-five, please.' The bus was empty, but Ian still hesitated in choosing a seat. This was a luxury. The standard single deck Number 11 bus characteristic of the Circular Route had been replaced this morning by a double decker. Ian climbed the stairs and treated himself to the front seat, where he had played at driving the bus as a child and adolescent, and, admittedly, when the coast was clear, as an adult. From the top deck the bus seemed to take turns impossibly wide and appeared to be destined to mount each kerb and hit every sign post. Ian drove the bus home, lulled by the detachment of the top deck.

Rush Hour

Ian slept fitfully, as was becoming the norm. How did shift workers manage it? Dogs, car alarms, children, car doors, whistling workmen, radios, car engines, the permanently cheerful and the permanently noisy. Fuckers, fuckers, fuckers. In between fits, he schemed schemes of undetectable murder, disguised homicide and secret bloodshed. He fantasized about dispatching anyone or anything that tainted the silence with the dirt of their noise. He poisoned dogs, firebombed cars, had the mouths of whistlers stitched shut, inflicted beatings, detonated radios, slaughtered children, but, mostly, machine-gunned anyone who breached the exclusion zone of his street. Murder, however, seldom compliments sleep, so he broke several social taboos by drinking beer in bed and masturbating, as a means to overcoming his scheming insomnia. Nature's way, with some unnatural assistance, came up trumps again, and Ian dozed off into a deep anaesthetised sleep.

Ian awoke as the light began to fade. It was time to put it all to the test. He dragged his hand down from his temples, across his nose and off his chin, then repeated it in reverse, on the advice of a former girlfriend who had told him that dragging his hand down over his face would make his face sag. He didn't believe it, but then again there was no point in taking the risk. Logically, he should just stop rubbing his face, but he kept forgetting, so had to redress the potential damage each time by a reverse sweep. It was seven o'clock and time to go to work. Rush hour had subsided, not that the volume of traffic had decreased significantly. It seemed permanently to be Rush Hour. There was no Slow Hour or Lag Hour or Gradual Hour. There was still the same amount of traffic, but instead of a grinding population of workers fleeing work, it was now a population of people 'doing things'. What things were arbitrary – they were getting out of their homes to do something other than work and that was the main point. Ian caught the bus to work as the people he worked with were finishing their evening meals and settling down to Big Break, Play Your Cards Right, Pet Rescue or some other such Friday night nonsense. Given the general state of affairs, he decided to take the circular bus, but in the wrong direction. It was certainly longer that way, but served as a summary of recent events. Brierly Hill, the Jug of Ale, the blood, the cash-point machine where he discovered that he had lost his wallet. He touched his scalp. It felt swollen and still a little sore, but it was healing. If ever there was a bad come-down from drugs, this was it. Probably the worst ever. Perhaps it could be used in some sort of anti-drugs campaign. Drugs. The effects can last quite a few days and could involve extortion, head wounds, social withdrawal, computer programming and wrecked living-rooms. Or something.

Work was deserted. Some prevarication was needed. When faced with an important task, trivia always becomes something of the utmost necessity. It is a symptom of performance anxiety, a way of avoiding, or at least postponing, the failure which might follow the terror of having your actions judged.

It was like making endless cups of tea when preparing for exams, just to avoid revising and thereby finding out how little you actually know. For once, however, Ian was too nervous and too excited to be occupied for very long by trivia. He set up the two workstations and the serial cables.

'Right, data from A to B. Simple. Ghost account's OK. Account number 478-thingy's OK.' He looked again at a hard copy of the script he had written. 'Code seems OK. Edited distributor code's all right. Set a Thief code's installed on A. Bridge, yes. Fuck it. No . . . yes, that's all right . . .'

Ian tried to curse it into life but it was having none of it. The code was OK, he knew that much – separately, all the programmes had shown some semblance of a pulse. He'd even managed to set the ghost account up pretty successfully. That in itself was an achievement, though a slightly anti-climactic one, as breaching the bank's security had been disappointingly straightforward. Crashing the system would be relatively easy when the time came. He had written just five lines of code which he called Yes Yes and Thrice Yes, which would grind the system to a crashing halt in seconds. When installed on workstations C and D, Yes Yes and Thrice Yes would request confirmation from computer D, in triplicate, that it was on speaking terms with computer C, and vice versa, with each message of correspondence including all previous messages of correspondence and each confirmation of correspondence initiating a counter correspondence. It was beautiful. Within twenty seconds, three point five billion messages would each have to be answered in triplicate, and everything would seize up with an unrescuable inevitability.

'Are you there?'

'Yes. Yes. Yes. Are *you* there? *Are* you there? Are you *there*?'

'Yes. Yes. Yes. Yes. Yes. Yes. Yes. Yes. Yes. Yes. Yes. Yes. Are you there? Are you . . .' et cetera et cetera. It was hardly Pinter, but it would do the job.

Oyster Perpetual Date

Slowly, programmes and systems and workstations began to co-operate with each other through the night. He looked at his watch. It was three-thirty. Normal people with normal lives would be getting out of taxis and stumbling through their front doors, the sweat on their backs cold now, making straight for their kitchens to wash away the lingering taste of cold-filtered beer and unfiltered cigarettes with lukewarm tap water. Again, he watched the second hand counting the night away, and thought of a fake Rolex he once owned. He knew it was a fake because he paid a fake price for it in a fake border town in Mexico. On the unlikely chance that it wasn't a fake he asked a friend for a second opinion.

'I'll tell you how you tell whether a Rolex is a genuine Rolex,' teased Chris

'How?'

'Perpetual motion.'

Ian checked his watch again. Apart from a couple of occasions, or so, the second hand had turned perpetually since he bought it. It was, by this criterion, fairly Rolex.

'Well, the second hand's turned fairly perpetually since I got it.'

'What do you mean "fairly perpetually"?'

'It's stopped a couple of times,' he said, watching the second hand stutter round, 'or so.'

'What do you mean "or so"?' Chris asked.

'OK, about four. Or five.'

'Not perpetual in the strictest sense of perpetual then.'

'Not really.'

'Let's have a look at it.' Ian took his beloved possession off and surrendered it. 'This isn't perpetual – look.'

'What?'

'It ticks.'

'I thought that was the basic point.'

'No, I mean it's not moving perpetually.'

'You've broken it!'

'Christ,' Chris sighed through evaporating patience. 'Look, when I say it's not moving perpetually, that it's ticking, that's a bad thing Rolex-wise. The second hand should sweep round in a continuous, non-ticking sort of way.'

'Oh. Bugger.' Ian thought for a moment. 'There is one perpetual thing I've noticed about it.'

'Yeah? What?'

'You know it says Oyster Perpetual Date?'

'Yeah.'

'Well, I've noticed that it's perpetually been the third of August since I bought it.'

'Yeah?'

'Yeah, the hands are glued on.'

Looking now at his watch, all its hands appeared to be glued on. Even when you become accustomed to nocturnal living, time still passes disturbingly slower in the early hours. He looked back at his screen. It was time to crash the system. Ian pressed Enter on the keyboard in front of him and Yes Yes and Thrice Yes initiated the inevitable discourse between

workstations C and D. Ian glanced at the wires which net-
worked the computers and imagined pulse after pulse of
futile information passing almost instantaneously back and
forth between the two machines. He thought also of Archie,
and the pulse after pulse of dull pointless information passing
between his lips and the ears of his captors. Probably, in his
stifling presence, they felt no more or less captive than
Archie.

Morning Call

The telephone woke him. His head was on his desk on top of various bits of paper and opened manuals. He held the receiver to his ear, or thereabouts. His eyes tried their hardest to close again of their own accord.

'Have you done?' Ian vaguely remembered the voice from somewhere, but he might still be dreaming, it was hard to tell.

'What?' he yawned.

'Have you done what we asked?' He started to come round a bit.

'Er . . .' Recognition slowly filtered through his semi-consciousness. It was a voice he had had in his head for several days now. 'What did you ask me to do?'

'You know exactly what we asked you to do. Don't fuck me around.'

'Er . . .' His eyes opened. It was the Other Voice.

'Well, have you?'

'Yes.'

'Has it worked?' There was excitement, menace and a little disbelief in the Other Voice.

'I think so.'

'What do you mean you think so?'

'I mean, it looks to me pretty much like it all worked.' Ian stretched. 'Fuck knows how though.'

'Good.' The voice switched quickly back to menace. 'You will, no doubt, be eager to be reunited with your friend.' Archie. He'd almost become secondary. In fact he *had* become secondary, and that was pushing it.

'Erm . . . yeah.'

'You will find what you need at home.' The line was cut, giving the continuous tone an intensive-care machine emits when all is lost. 'You will find what you need at home'. What a joke. It was like the end of *The Wizard of Oz*, except Dorothy's house didn't have a fucking great hole in the middle of the living-room. He looked at his watch. It was eight o'clock on Saturday morning.

There was no way, of course, that it should have worked. The fact of the matter was that computer systems just weren't that simple or straightforward. Even anoraks, some of the most straightforward-thinking semi-humans this planet has ever seen, had the sense to engineer random, illogical, devious, haphazard, promiscuous and downright unfathomable commands into their systems to deter would-be hackers.

But, incredibly, it had worked, on paper at least. And, as he stared at the screen, focusing beyond it as if it was a partition concealing the real folding money stored behind it, he understood that the reason it had worked was that his thoughts were, by their very nature, random, illogical, devious, haphazard, promiscuous and unfathomable. He was human and, as such, made mistakes, took unlikely gambles, was intuitive, underestimated, overestimated, missed obvious things, saw things which weren't there, and was, in short, fallible. He had found his way out of the maze, not by memorizing the route and relying upon rationality, but by making mistakes and trusting to intuition. It was a triumph of feeling over reason, of intuition over logic, of man over machine. And the best thing was that he had fucked over Frying Pan, Tattoo and the Other Voice on his way out. He returned his office to near normality and decided to treat himself by ringing a taxi to take him home. The Circular Route would have to go about its circular business without him today.

The Home Stretch

Archie wasn't there. He was half expecting him to be standing outside his house, maybe noting car registrations or tying and re-tying his shoelaces, but there was no sign of him. Ian wasn't overly disappointed. He entered his house. It had crossed his mind that Archie might have actually come to some harm and might be strung up in his living-room. He wasn't. Maybe they would drop Archie off later. Surely they would have to check that he had done what he said he had done. He began to panic. It would only take a phone call to check. They wouldn't be able to touch the money for at least seven days, but they would know today as soon as the investment houses opened that they were rich. Ian was relying on their impatience. If they were calm, everything could go badly wrong. He should have been more cautious.

He tried to relax. He lay down on his repositioned sofa and, with his eyes closed, attempted to shut out the violence of his living-room, but it seeped in through his barely closed lids like smoke under a door. He got up and put on some music which under other circumstances would have been

soothing and relaxing. But it was no good. He started dis-
sembling the music into its constituent noises until each noise
became a mere distraction from the calm. He turned the
music off, sat in silence and let his mind go wherever it felt
like going. It shut itself down and went to sleep.

A couple of hours later, the phone rang and woke him up
instantly. He had slept and his neck was taut. He picked the
phone up after three rings. It was Frying Pan and he was
angry.

'Right, you little cunt. Fucking listen to me and listen fucking well. Don't fuck with us. Don't even think of fucking with
us.' Frying Pan was very angry. Fuck. They were on to him.
'I'll be coming round for you in the night, any fucking night I
choose, and I'll break your fucking neck. Don't fuck with us,
you pathetic twat.' The very real threat in Frying Pan's voice
came as a shock. Frying Pan was deadly serious now. He could
almost feel the violence charging down the phone line and
escaping into the room as an all-encompassing blackness. 'You
don't know who the fuck we are, or where we fucking live, or
what we fucking look like or anything, right? Right?'

'Right.'

'And you cunts stay well away from the cops, right?'

Ian hardly needed warning. 'Right.'

'If I think you've even walked past a fucking cop shop, I'll
be coming for you and that sad wanker pal of yours. Got
that, you useless piece of shit?' They weren't on to him. It
was goodbye with a liberal dose of humiliation and threat.

'Yes.'

'Yeah?'

'*Yes.*'

'Right, that wanker'll be round yours later. Remember
what I said. Don't make me come round and rip your throat
out.'

The line went dead. Ian replaced the receiver and half
smiled.

Pretending to Sleep

February 9th 1997

Where the fuck is he? Where is he? What's he been doing all
this time? He said he might go to a club but this is taking the
piss. 3.30 am and still no sign. I can't sleep without him here.
Too used to him snoring. Think I'll read, something unin-
spiring. If he's off with some tart there'll be hell to pay,
birthday or no birthday. Try to sleep. Try. Don't try. As soon
as you start trying . . . Sod it, put the light on. This is no
good. Why can't I sleep without him? That's him. At last!
Where the hell has he been? This will have to be good. Turn
the light out, pretend to be asleep. What's he knocking for?
Drunken bastard must have lost his keys. It'll be that football
lot, spiking his drinks, no doubt. If he thinks I'm getting out
of bed on a freezing night like this to let him in . . . You can
knock all you like, sunshine. OK, OK, you'll have the whole
street up. I'm coming. Yes, yes, heard you the first time. Neil?
Is that you? Louise? Is that Louise Elland? Yes. This is WPC
Walker. What's wrong? Can I come in? It's Neil, isn't it?
What's he done? Louise, can I come in please?

Re·union

Ian and Archie sat in silence in Ian's raped living-room. They had sat and drunk cups of tea sweetened with sugar that had seen whiter days, and had described their respective ordeals in quiet, tired words. They had tried to reassemble the peaks and troughs of their last ten days so that they meshed into one cogent period of time. Ian hadn't been entirely honest though. He was saving the best for last. He had left out the details of his extra curricular activities with Set a Thief. He was terrible with secrets. Holding on to one was sweet torture combining the power of knowledge with the torment of itching powder. He had held it as it wriggled in his throat over the last two hours or so since Archie was released, and it had always been on the brink of escaping. Their shared experience, though not particularly shared, made Ian feel closer to Archie. It was still by no means a close*ness,* just clos*er.* He had thought it through again and again. He had tossed coins, thrown screwed up balls of paper at the waste basket and generally bestowed any routine action he could with the responsibility of making the decision for him. He had prevaricated beyond almost all previous prevarications, and still couldn't decide whether to tell Archie about his scheme. Of course he realized that Archie knew he had at least tried it, but that was all he knew. To tell him about it would cost him money, and a lot of money. It would be painful, but they would have to split Ian's earnings if there was to be any sense of fairness about the situation. Archie would probably find out eventually, and maybe in a way that involved broken legs and Frying Pan. To share the secret would give Archie the chance to make up his own mind. But it would cost an awful lot of money. Fuck it, he couldn't hold on to it any longer.

Ian broke the silence. 'Archie, you know that stuff you told me in the back of the taxi, about ghost accounts, I've got . . .'

'Don't tell me you actually tried it,' Archie interrupted impatiently. 'You must have known that there was no chance of it working.'

'But I thought you said that . . . but you gave me instructions on how to do it.'

'They wouldn't have worked though.' No wonder he'd had so much trouble with it. Archie had never meant it to work.

'Why not?'

'Why are you so interested? What difference does it make?' Archie was now standing in front of Ian and staring intently into his eyes. There was an uncharacteristic intensity and anger in his face that reflected his recent captivity. Ian changed his mind. He had no idea why Archie had been less than helpful but he had no idea about a lot of the last ten days. The ball of paper rattled around the rim of the bin and fell on to the floor. He would tell him some other time.

'You know, just interested. Kept me occupied, gave me some hope when I dropped DBs. It was fucking boring doing all that programming you know. Something to keep my spirits up.' Archie continued eye contact. Ian changed the subject. 'So, what do we do now? Personally, I'd rather we left the police out of it.'

'Yes.' Archie looked away. 'I suppose we just go back to work and pretend nothing happened.' He turned to face him. 'Look, Ian, I don't know what your reasons are but I'm scared of going to the police. After all, that's where I met Godzilla . . .'

'Who?'

'Look, it's not as if he actually told me his name. The huge man who's been keeping me captive and ruining your front room.'

'Oh, right, Frying Pan.'

'Who?'

'Never mind.'

'But, anyway, he told me not to approach the police. The trouble is I don't know who I'm more frightened of. And then there's Cyberman.'

'Who?'

'You know, the other man with the . . .'

'Tattoo.'

'Well, tattoos actually. '

'Yes, I meant, oh, it doesn't matter.' There were still a couple of things that troubled Ian. 'Archie, who was the other person? There was someone else, wasn't there?' So far, Archie had skirted around the Other Voice. 'I heard him in the background when I was on the phone once and thought I'd heard his voice before, and then he rang me this morning. I couldn't think who it was though.'

'I have no idea who it was,' Archie replied flatly.

'Well what did he look like? Is he someone that I might know?'

'How should I know who you do and don't know?'

'But what did he look like? Maybe I could . . .'

'I didn't see him Ian.'

'What do you mean you didn't see him?'

'I was,' Archie looked weary, 'I was blindfolded.'

'What, all the time?'

'Yes. Please don't make me go through it all again. Look Ian, I've had a rough time of it and I want to go home. I need to get some sleep.' He was retreating into his anorak shell as quickly as he had emerged from it.

'Well what are we going to do?'

'Nothing. We'll talk about it at work.' Archie turned and walked out of the living-room and opened the front door.

'Hang on, I'll give you a lift.'

'No, I'm fine Ian, I'll see you at work. Goodbye.'

Archie shut the front door and walked up the street. Ian walked back into his front room and sat down, deflated and alone. You couldn't share anything with Archie, not even an experience. He would shrug you off even before you got within hand-shaking range. It had probably been a fairly normal ten days for the isolated twat. His life was fairly confined as it was, and subject to a good deal of animosity. He . . . Ian realized at last and with a start where he had heard the voice. It had plagued him and plagued him. It wasn't a particularly distinctive voice. It wasn't particularly regional, it wasn't burdened with an impediment, it wasn't coarse or quiet, harsh or soft and it wasn't overly deep or shrill. It was educated, though, and a little nasal, and these are things which telephones hunt out and expose. The telephone at work had mis-redialed. He had spoken to, or rather, insulted, someone on their mobile phone. Someone that Archie had doubtless been speaking to on the office phone before Ian used it. Jesus. It was the Other Voice. Ian jumped up, grabbed his keys and ran out of the house. Archie turned the corner at the end of the street. Ian shouted after him and increased his pace, then slowed as he approached the corner and rounded it. Archie was nowhere to be seen. A car pulled off fifty yards away.

Gardening

Ian realized that he mustn't do anything out of the ordinary, at least not in public. The was no way that anyone could be aware of any hint of illegality for another seven days until Set a Thief sprang into electronic life, and even then, discovery was unlikely. There was no need, therefore, to panic yet. But Ian's omnipresent police fear pleaded with him for an enforced caution of behaviour, and so he decided to be as normal as he could endure being, maybe more so, just for now. There would come a point when it would no longer be worth the risk of remaining at work but he would go to work on Monday, do as little as he could manage and pack his belongings up at night, just to be on the safe side.

Although there was no reason to think that Set a Thief *would* necessarily draw any attention to his illicit programming, there was also no reason to hang around and find out. After all, the real trouble for Ian wouldn't be detection at work, but detection by a more ruthless and immediate organization. At work it might be months before anything appeared amiss, when the banks and investment houses carried out their biannual audits, and even then it was drop in the ocean stuff. But banks and investment houses didn't break your legs. Your heart and soul maybe, but not your legs. No, the real problem would be apparent in eight or nine days or so, or whenever Frying Pan et al checked their bank balances after Set a Thief had done its simple and ruthless business. At the moment, Set a Thief was dormant, but in the early hours of next Monday morning it would, he hoped, germinate, for a matter of seconds, milliseconds even, and spread its new green shoots out across the system, transferring the majority of the cash languishing in account 478-4266-5911628 into Ian's newly set up ghost account, before quietly withering away to nothing. It was beautiful. It lived and died and left no remains. It was a mayfly that lived only for the minute it fucked and passed on its genes. Its whole reason was just to donate its DNA, and to donate it all to Ian.

At work on Monday morning, little had changed. He hadn't expected it to, but it's always a surprise when you have been away from normality to find it quite so normal on your return. He thanked God for the contractual nature of his work. There would be no month's notice to serve. A week would probably do it. In fact he could just decide upon a day and then quit. He would be asked why. He would tell them a better offer had come along. There was no allegiance, no honour, no commitment, no compassion, no faithfulness. No one would ask any questions. This was the late nineties. More money was offered so you quit. The company was so fragmented that you had no friends to lose. You were admired for it. You were ruthless, aggressive, you went out there and you got the best for yourself and fuck the rest. Fuck solidarity, fuck the corporation, fuck the people you worked with, fuck retirement speeches, fuck pride, fuck promotion, fuck *everybody*, but yourself. They would offer you more money and ask you to stay because it was cheaper than recruiting a new contractor. Someone would quit their job and take yours.

You would take someone else's job, someone who had quit theirs for more money elsewhere. The whole thing was a rotten, piss-stinking elevator and, at this moment, Ian loved it. It was his getaway car.

Archie was not at work, the office was quiet and Ian was glad. He took the opportunity to manoeuvre his desk apart from Archie's, making infringement of his own desk possible by only the furthest spanning of Archie's junk. This completed to his satisfaction, with a new gap of five and a half inches recorded with Archie's ruler, Ian continued his one-man strike action. This was going to be a new record. He looked over at Archie's wall calendar. He had managed six working days before the lunacy started, eight days during it, making today the fifteenth. And still no one had noticed that he had singularly failed to do anything constructive in all that time. After lunch, Archie reappeared. He was obviously well rested and was almost genuinely pleased to see Ian. Ian wasn't at all pleased to see him and had, to some extent, been dreading it. He was glad that there was now a little distance between their desks.

'How're you feeling?' he asked Archie.

'Oh, not so bad now that I've rested,' he said, sitting down opposite him. He surveyed the gap and looked up at Ian. 'I've been offered a new job.'

'Yeah?'

'Yes. There was a message on my answer machine when I got home yesterday from Spartech who are looking for a DBA.' This was news. Not unexpected news, but news all the same. What was surprising was the rapidity with which Archie had acted.

'When do you start?'

'Next week.' Archie turned his workstation on.

'Where did you say it was?'

'Spartech, London.

'So you'll be moving?'

'Er, no, I don't think so.' He rummaged through his drawers and pulled out an old scarf, which he held up to the light. It seemed to be covered in what looked like noodles of some sort and was soaking wet. Ian ducked down behind his screen. 'I think I'll stay there in the week and come back to Birmingham at the weekends,' he muttered half-heartedly, continuing to puzzle over a couple of reconstituted peas and some flecks of meat, or perhaps vegetable matter, he couldn't be sure, which adorned the back of his scarf.

'So you won't be selling your house then?' Ian asked, desperately trying not to laugh.

'No.' He sniffed the scarf. It definitely seemed to be food of some sort.

From the cover of his monitor, and between suppressed bouts of giggles, he asked, 'When're you handing your notice in?'

'I don't know. Today or tomorrow I suppose. I'm owed a lot of holiday. Think I'll spend some time on the garden over the next few days. I'm afraid it's starting to look a little unkempt.' Archie began to tell Ian about his garden. Ian pretended to listen. His giggles quickly subsided.

Archie enjoyed gardening. It was his hobby and he was going to inflict it on Ian. Ian hated gardening. It was a misconception. Gardening isn't about gardens – it is about gardeners. You construct your own world around you. You decide what flora and fauna you have in your fenced, pivoted, hedged, enclosed world. It isn't a love of nature, of the cycle of seed to plant to fruit to seed. Nature is *out there*, beyond the barbed-wire-topped fence or broken bottle-encrusted wall. Nature is anywhere that man has no say. No, this isn't about the beauty of the plant world, this is about the insecurity of the gardener. This is about reclaiming the autonomy the gardener has systematically been stripped of in the world outside his hedged boundaries. This is about controlling life, not loving it.

It was the same for children. Ian hated people with a blind love of children and put gardeners and kiddie lovers in the same loathsome, sinking, rotten-timbered boat. Ian didn't mind children. He didn't mind the thought of one day owning some, or whatever the relevant phrase was. He didn't particularly mind other people's children. What he couldn't tolerate were those people who actively went out of their way to like children. They were usually female, and if not devoted housewives or mothers, worked as primary school teachers or nursery assistants, and would dote on their children, their friends' children, children they met, children on TV, in books and in magazines, children they didn't meet but heard about and children who hadn't even been born yet. At first, Ian had thought that this was a good thing. The world was miserable, any adult could see that, and humanity was hopeless. And these child-addicts loved the hope that children represented, the unbankrupted innocence, in a word, the future. It was charming to see people taking genuine enjoyment from the very origin of the cyclical process of humanity. But then Ian reconsidered. Was this really worship of the joy of human perpetuation? Wasn't worship of the innocent, by implication, a denial of the ugliness of the adult world? Weren't these people desperately trying to submerge themselves in an ocean of rejection of the disfigurement that was the grown-up world? A thin line. He took a coin out of his pocket and tossed it. Tails. Denial it was then. Archie looked at him.

'What was that for?'

'Nothing.' He put the coin back in his pocket. Archie continued to talk and Ian to think.

Deliverance

There were no two ways about it. He would have to kill one of them. They just stood there and looked helplessly at him, unable to move or shout or protect themselves. He looked away. It wouldn't be pleasant, and the repercussions and recriminations would be difficult, at best, but he couldn't take both of them with him. That it had come to this. Two weeks ago he wouldn't have contemplated ever having to make such a decision. He would kill one and dismember what remained, and take the other, still alive, to Martin's house. Let him take care of the disposal. But which one? And what to use? He had a hunt around the house for objects which could be considered fairly lethal. He came up with a long, solid kitchen knife and a serrated bread knife. It was not a task to be undertaken lightly. Which one? Martin hadn't been too pleased to hear from him and was unaware of the surprise that was on its way round to him. He hadn't been able to be specific on the phone, for fear that someone might be listening in. Think clearly, coldly. Smaller remains, easier disposal. Don't think. Just do it. Don't look at them. Just do it.

He looked up and down the street until he was sure the coast was clear. It was dark but there were still people around. No one was on the pavement on his side of the road and there were no cars approaching. He stepped quickly back inside his front door. He was sick with worry. This was not a sane thing to do, by any standards, but he had little choice. Circumstance had forced his hand. If anyone was guilty it was circumstance. To get caught now would ruin everything. The load was surprisingly heavy and awkward. Hopefully the journey wouldn't be fatal. If it was, there would be nothing to do but leave the country. He had wrapped it as best he could in a couple of spare sheets, tied them tightly round the middle and taped them shut at each end to prevent escape. He dragged it, like an over-sized roll of carpet, out of his front door, turned it around and shoved it into the open hatch of his hatchback. It was almost farcical. After a degree of struggling, he managed to force it far enough in past the folded-down rear partition so that it rested heavily against the back of the front passenger seat and protruded only six or so inches out of the boot. Such visibility worried him. He decided to rely on more blankets for camouflage and tied the hatch down so that it rested gently against the protrusion. He drove carefully and attentively.

Martin wasn't at all pleased to see him.

'Look, I'm sorry about last time I was round,' Ian said, as he stood on Martin's doorstep, 'but I had a lot on my plate.'

'You were in no state to drive.'

'Yeah, I'm sorry. I was going to come back and apologize . . .'

'What's this all about, anyway?' Martin interrupted him.

'You'll see.'

'OK. You coming in?'

'No, I need a hand. I've got something for you,' Ian motioned towards his car.

'Yeah?'

'Yeah. It's in the boot.' They marched it in through Martin's front door and into the rear downstairs room, leaning it in a corner of the room, where it sloped menacingly.

'Jesus, what a *huge* fucker.'

'Yeah, it's been a right struggle.'

'Must be, what, six-and-a-half foot, easy.'

'I'm just loaning it, you understand. Take off the new buds but nothing else. Keep it warm. Don't over-water it. Don't let it die. And for fuck's sake don't smoke the whole lot. Paul's expecting some semblance of a plant left for him when he gets back.'

'How come you don't want it any more?'

'I'm going away for a bit,' Ian said, slumping on the settee, sweating lightly.

'What've you done with the other one?'

'I cut it up and stuffed it in my compost heap. I figured you wouldn't have room to keep two on the go.'

'What a fucking waste.' Martin sat down opposite him. 'Where're you going anyway?'

'I don't know yet. Look, I've saved some money up and I'm going off, you know, travelling for a bit. Work's getting on my tits.' He surveyed the ashtray which was full of burnt out roaches. 'I suppose I just fancy a change.'

'D'you fancy a quick one for old time's sake?' Martin asked.

'No, I've got to go,' he said, standing up. 'And you know me, sobriety when I'm driving.'

'Yeah. Well, you know . . . good luck and stuff. And thanks for the plant.'

Resignation

As Ian's strike action was the most unofficial in the history of unofficial strike action, in that no one had noticed he was on strike, he decided to turn himself in. It was Tuesday and he had managed, to the best of his knowledge, seventeen days. He had planned to see a few more days of work out, but on a whim, and the first constructive thing he had done for as long as he could remember, he went to his supervisor's office and told her that he was quitting.

'Do you not feel comfortable here, Ian?' she asked in a Scottish tone several shades softer than her usual woman-who-has-made-it-in-business growl.

'It's not that exactly, it's just that I've been offered another contract.'

'How much're they offering?'

'A couple of grand more.'

'We'll give you two and a half to stay.' Ian felt obliged to at least look like he was considering it.

'Look, Kate,' a rare piece of honesty was struggling, uncomfortably, to the surface, 'it's not as if I really actually do anything here.'

'So it's challenge you're after?'

'No, I just mean, you know, nothing I do actually seems to matter to anybody.'

'We're all small cogs in a big institution, Ian, it's natural to feel like that from time to time.'

Ian looked out of the window and tried to spot his car in the further of the Intron car parks. 'Look, Kate, tell me what I actually do here.'

'What do you mean?'

He located it, a red, rusty speck in the middle distance. 'Just tell me, in your words, what you think I do.'

'Well, you . . . you check code for mistakes, omissions, conflicts . . .'

'And?'

'Well . . . you . . .'

'OK, let's say the code is always fine, then what? Then what do I actually do? I check something that doesn't need to be checked. So, I get paid a lot of money to do nothing.'

'I don't think it's quite that bad, is it Ian?'

Looking again, he realized that it was probably a bit too red to be his car. 'I dunno, sometimes I just feel . . .'

'Well, it's a bit of a bugger you wanting to leave. Archie's just jumped on to a contract and Jamie   '

'A contract?'

'Yes. Finally made the grade it seems. Never thought he would, but there you go, another Permie bites the dust.' Kate looked out of the window, trying to follow Ian's line of vision. Seeing nothing more interesting than the car park, she glanced back at him and added, 'Handed his notice in a couple of weeks ago.'

Ian was about to say something, paused and then said, largely to himself, 'I never realized it was a Tractor post.'

'Oh yes. And Jamie's moved on as well. Look Ian, we're very understaffed – won't you reconsider?'

'Two weeks ago?' Ian was having difficulty keeping up.

'What?'

'You said Archie handed his notice in two weeks ago.'

'Yes I think so. I'd have to check with human resources to get the exact date.'

Ian turned round to face Kate. 'And Jamie? Where did he go?'

'Oh I don't know, you know how it is. Just got a job, the City, I think, and buggered off.'

Ian returned to his office, empty and a little confused, and began to collect up items which were worth salvaging. He would see the week out, and call it a day on Friday.

One Man Short

They held an inquest, just a small one, largely at Louise's insistence. All of the football team went, except Ian. Just couldn't face her, just couldn't look her in the eye. The last one to see him alive, in the pub car park. The only one who could have stopped him. A sham of an inquest. Accidental death. Ian was called as a witness. He couldn't face her. Why didn't he stop him, call him a cab, walk him home, anything? she had asked him at the funeral. Screamed at him. Couldn't face her again. Called as a witness but didn't show up. He didn't know whether it was a criminal offence or a civil one. He'd received three letters from the West Midlands Constabulary but had binned them all. The police had called on the day of the inquest, his neighbour had informed him, with the expectancy of someone who has had half a story read to them. Ian went to visit his parents, where he said nothing at all for the two days he was there. But the inquest reached a verdict without him so he didn't see how his opinion could possibly have a bearing upon anything. He might be in some sort of trouble, but to open the letters that arrived

after the hearing would have been to open up the guilt he had
enveloped with the unthinking routines of his life. Probably,
the police would come round some time and he would be
charged with something vague and unimportant, like
obstructing justice. But he couldn't bear to think about it.
The charge itself was meaningless. It was the police he could-
n't think about. The police meant death, the death of a
friend, something that he could have prevented. The police
meant blame. The police meant Louise. The police meant
knowing that the last words Neil had said were 'Louise . . .
Louise . . . Louise . . .' The police meant facing Louise's
hollow eyes. The police meant everything that Ian could no
longer think about.

None of the football team blamed him, particularly. No
one mentioned it any more. There was a tangible communal
remorse, but no one said anything. The teams picked up
where they had left off, one team one man short.

'You coming then?'
   Neil looked long and unsteadily into his face. 'No.'
   'Right. You'll find your way home OK?'
   Another long, unsteady look. 'Yeah.'
   'See you later then.'

Over and over, again and again.

Stickleback

The thing to do was to reduce life to its bare, sun-bleached bones. Do only the things that need doing and do them without thought. Swim through life like a stickleback. Do nothing but swim and mate. Cause no ripples or turbulence or friction. Do what is expected of you and no more. Move where the current moves you. Move where the others go when it suits. Go where you want to go when it's quicker and easier. Every action to achieve an aim. No actions which achieve no aims. All behaviour innate. All you need to know how to do you already know how to do. Do only what needs to be done and no more. Reduce life to a series of routines. This was Ian's life.

To take this life abroad with him he had to think carefully. Having handed in his notice he ambled through the week and began to get organized in the evenings. Take one suitcase and fill it with one life. No baggage, just essentials. Take only those things you rely upon. No wants, just needs. Reduce life to a suitcase. Everything functional, everything fulfilling a need. He had bought the largest suitcase he could find, just in case his life was bigger than he thought, and was surveying a number of items which he had placed on the floor beside it. He was sure, despite the capaciousness of the suitcase, which had wheels and a complicated pull-out handle for towing purposes, and which should have come fitted with its own baggage handler, that they wouldn't all fit in. He had even made a list, or rather a series of lists, ranking items in order of necessity. Items which survived the first list were promoted to the second list and so on, until the play-offs. This was life or death, this was where the real decisions were made. Faced again with losing his possessions Ian discovered that they were all indispensable. Fewer socks maybe, he mused, his pen hovering over the entry 'Socks, ten pairs'. There were two quick knocks at the door, and then one wood-splitting crash. He put his left hand on the outside of the back pocket of his jeans to check he had his wallet, and his right on the outside of his front right pocket to check for his keys, and grabbing his passport dashed through his living room and kitchen and out of the back door. There was shouting in his living room. He locked the back door behind him. Another crashing blow. The Victorian terraces were clustered in huddles of six and were further bisected by an alleyway which ran from the front to the rear under the extra bedroom of each third house. He gambled that they would still be inside and dashed through the passageway out on to the road at the front of his house. Frying Pan came flying out through the front door followed by someone Ian recognized, not wholly consciously, but just enough for him to be aware that he had seen him before. He didn't have time for details. This was a re-run of the pub incident. Suddenly he was sprinting and Frying Pan and the partially recognized man were flailing after him, screaming. No time to think where. Just run. They are close. A vehicle behind him and to his right. Doesn't seem to be going past. He swings his head round. It is the silver diesel van. Archie is driving. They are on the pavement and are two, maybe three, seconds behind. Just keep running, anywhere. The van is noisier, closer. Approaching the end of the road. Speed diagonally across it. The van is suddenly very close. Across the road, nearly. The van accelerates, a rattling, consuming, grey blur. Lunge for the pavement. The van is everywhere. Make the pavement. The van's side-mirror smashes into his left arm. He keeps running. Turn right on to the main road. People, surely there must be people about. There are a few, most of them uninterested. The van skids to a stop at the junction. A door slams. They are twenty, twenty-five, thirty yards back. The van jumps across the junction. Ian is barely breathing, not through fitness, but through panic. The traffic is a good deal heavier on the main road. He looks back again. The van is just about stationary. It is trying to pass on the wrong side of the road and is causing a fury of horned chaos. The doors open and they jump out again but he has fifty or so yards on them. Thank God for traffic. He keeps sprinting. He can taste blood at the back of his throat. His lungs are pleading for air. He approaches the high street and its adornment of shops and spots a pub. It is a large pub on a corner with a back door which leads on to a side street. He runs in and dashes past a sparse population of seasoned all-day drinkers already stationed for a Saturday marathon. They look up from their pints. He reaches the back door but changes his mind. He sees the entrance to the ladies toilet. He opens the flimsy door and walks through, shutting it gently behind him. He hears nothing but the complaints of his starved respiratory system for twenty seconds, then the unmistakable boom of Frying Pan and another quieter, terser voice. There is a short-of-breath discussion. A door opens and is gradually shut by its rusting springs. Ian opens the door to the ladies a fraction and can see no one. They have taken the bait and are chasing him down the side road. He walks back the way he came, warily, and without confidence in his assumption. The all-day drinkers glance up at him again. He looks out through the heavy, brewery logo-ed glass front door and still can't see them. Sweat begins to desert every pore simultaneously forming instant patches of uncomfortable wetness. His arm hurts. He edges out into the daylight. There are people in the street but he feels vulnerable and conspicuous. He enters the nearest, brightest and busiest shop to the high street bus stop. It is a newsagent, which seems to exist on the meagre trade afforded by people who need change for the bus and who feel obliged by the 'We do *not* give change' notice to buy cheap items of confectionery to amass the required coinage. With merciful and uncharacteristic promptness, a bus shows up. He looks again up and down the high street, runs out on to the street and boards the Number 11. He has one more task to complete.

Password

Ian sat by himself at the back of the bus and looked out of the rear window as it crawled its way between the bus stops of the Kings Heath high street. They hadn't seen him board the bus, so he was safe, for a while at least. Despite this, his heart was reluctant to give up the ghost of the chase and continued to surge relentlessly. Archie. Dull fucking Archie. He was trembling slightly and sweating profusely. How did they know? He leant his head forward and cradled it in his hands, watching droplets of sweat fall with alarming frequency on to the floor of the bus, where they momentarily enlivened the dull, grey-brown surface, before being consumed by the all pervasive dirt. There was no way they could have known anything for at least three or four days. Archie. Jesus. Ian continued to perspire. Many things were puzzling him. His heart rate refused to ease its frenetic pace and droplets of sweat formed with renewed vigour. His T-shirt was sodden, and was stuck to his back, with the areas of heaviest activity highlighted in darker tones of grey. It was Saturday. There was simply no way they could have known, not until Monday.

He looked closely at his left forearm. It was tender and bruised, but not broken. He wiped the sweat away from his face with the back of his right hand, and wiped the back of his hand to little effect on the impervious rough upholstery of the seat beside him. How the fuck did they know?

The bus moved unhurriedly on with its faltering journey. Ian tried to link the day's events to what he already knew. Everything had been OK, everything had made sense, until half an hour ago. He had even made the link between the Other Voice and Archie, via the misdialled phone number, and had realized that Archie might not have been the entirely innocent party he had purported to be. But things were still relatively simple only half an hour ago. Now there was someone new, someone who was familiar. He swallowed and as he did so tasted blood in his mouth. Who the fuck was it? His chest felt heavy and tight, as if it was filled with a dense liquid rather than a light gas.

The bus deposited him within a few hundred yards of Intron UK and Ian walked cautiously through the tarmac fringes of the Tindle Industrial estate towards the main entrance of the building. He keyed in the four digit security code on the touch pad of the door and entered. Inside, the building was empty under the scowl of its strip lights. Ian had never seen the place dark. He made his way down the first floor corridor that bisected the Intron headquarters, towards his office. As he did so, he experienced a sudden, gripping *déjà vu*. Frying Pan was lungeing towards him with all the momentum his bulk could muster. Ian's muscles tightened involuntarily. He began sweating again. Tattoo was flailing alongside him, screaming, his features contorted with fury, his facial tattoos twisted, his Birmingham City football shirt a blur of royal blue. Ian stopped and wiped the sweat away from his face with his T-shirt. Jesus. He realized with a jolt who was with Frying Pan this morning. Shit. He tried to dismiss the idea, but it wouldn't leave him. He surveyed the dark-grey damp patch in the centre of his shirt. How could he be so blind? It was Tattoo. But now he didn't have any tattoos and his crew cut had lost most of its cut since he had last encountered him in the corridor. He had even been wearing relatively smart clothes. Christ. So much for his powers of observation. It was the permanency of tattoos that had deceived him. He had taken it for granted that tattoos last for ever. But who the fuck was Tattoo now if he no longer had any tattoos? He started walking again.

The office hadn't changed, particularly. Some of Ian's possessions remained, ones that he hadn't cared enough about to take home with him when he cleared his desk. There was the radio cassette that played tapes at perplexingly different speeds and then chewed and erased them for good measure, a couple of manuals for out-dated software, a pen holder which had never held any pens and the spider plant which had long since run out of enthusiasm for office life. In contrast, Archie had been thorough and had purged the room of just about everything but his wall calendar. Their desks had, in his short absence, been reunited. Ian sat down at his old workstation and logged on. He was going to find out what had gone wrong. He searched his main directory for Set a Thief but couldn't find it. He checked and re-checked. It was nowhere. He checked his list of recently deleted files. Nothing. He checked the list of recent logins on his account. They had all been made by him. No one had been into his files. Then he cursed himself, remembering that he had set the programme to run from Archie's terminal, just in case anything backfired. It hadn't seemed fair at the time, but he had figured out Archie's eight letter password, and there was no way he was going to run it from his own terminal. In retrospect, though, it was more than fair. He walked round to Archie's desk, turned his workstation on and waited for the host presenter to prompt him for a username and password.

Around the time that he installed Set a Thief on Archie's

computer, he tried one morning to initiate a coffee break conversation on the subject of computer security, hoping to coax a password or two out of his colleagues so that he could run any risky code through other people's accounts. In this way, he had hoped to avoid tarnishing his and Archie's computers with the fingerprints of his hacking.

'Fuck off, Ian, no chance.'

'Look, I'll show you mine . . .'

'No way.' Simon was having none of it.

'Why not? All I'm saying, right, is that your password says a lot about you.' He tried a new tack. 'I mean, your password's nothing to be embarrassed about or anything, is it?'

'No.'

'Well, what is it then?'

'Look, Gillick, I'm not ashamed of *mine*, but there's no way I'd share it with you, either.' Jamie joined the omnipresent anorak paranoia.

'Why not? What the fuck do you think I'm going to do with it?'

'I don't know, but you're not having it.'

'OK, no need to be so touchy. All I'm saying is that people choose passwords that sum up a certain part of their life – girlfriend's name, favourite band, someone you fancy, favourite TV programme, the year they last had sex,' he looked at Simon, who blushed, 'et cetera et cetera, because it's like having your own little secret from the world.'

'So?'

'Well I reckon from what I know about you and Simon I can guess your passwords.'

'No chance,' countered Simon.

'No, let him have a go. Come on, what do you think mine is, Gillick?' Jamie seemed a little too confident. 'Because I reckon the real truth is that your guessing'll say more about what you think of me and Si than our passwords could ever say about us.'

Jamie was right, and obnoxious with it. 'Maybe. But you'll have to let me know if I guess right.'

'All right.'

'Right. Simon. Let me think.' He looked at Simon, who looked away after attempting a half-hearted smile – a standard programmer response to personal contact. This was going to be easy. Simon had very little personality to hinder him in his choice of password. Eight letters. Eight straightforward, obvious letters. Something undisguised. Something logical. Something lacking imagination. 'Got it. Password,' he said. 'That's it, isn't it?'

Simon blushed again and thought about a denial, but Jamie's words had sunk in, and he realized that he had, somehow, just been insulted.

'What about mine, then?' tempted Jamie.

Ian could think of a few choice words that described Jamie, but none of them were eight letters long. His bluff was being called. Jamie took a pen and a folded envelope out of his suit jacket, wrote a word on the back of the envelope and handed it to Simon, who looked at him and then at Ian and laughed.

'What?' Ian asked.

'You tell me, smart boy.'

Ian gave up and left the coffee room.

The Host Presenter prompted him for Archie's password and he typed 's-t-a-r-t-r-e-k'. As people went, Archie was unimaginative to the point of negligence when it came to secrecy, and some months ago Ian had deduced through trial and error that this was indeed Archie's password. He pressed return. Invalid password. He had mis-typed. He tried again. It was having none of it. He tried capitals. You have exceeded the maximum number of permitted password entries. Please log in again. Bugger. The wanker had changed his password. He must have done it before he left. The selfish cunt. Think. Think. Eight letters. Think. He tried again. 's-t-a-r-w-a-r-s'. No. 't-h-e-t-h-i-n-g'. Fat chance. Last chance. Please. Please. You transparent twat, please. OK, here we go. 'c-a-p-t-k-i-r-k'. You have exceeded the maximum number of permitted password entries on 2 occasions. Contact mainframe support for assistance with your password. Bollocks. Bollocks. Bollocks. Ian stared at the screen. Outwitted by Archie, again. As a reflex action, Ian picked up the phone to dial Mainframe Support. He stared at the key pad of the phone, not quite sure what he was doing. Something wasn't right. He tried to think of the number. Shit. It was Saturday, there would be no one there. He cursed his stupidity, and replaced the receiver. Then, as he looked at the phone and back at the screen, something occurred to him. The telephone, of course. The wrongly re-dialling phone. That was the link, not just between Archie and the Other Voice, but between Ian and the Other Voice. The phone had woken him after he had worked all night to initiate the ghost account and he had talked to the Other Voice for a second time. There had been something familiar about his voice, but not just from the re-dial fiasco. It was something familiar from somewhere else, somewhere more buried, somewhere face to face. At the time he hadn't given it any further consideration, in his relief at having finally finished the required programming. He closed his eyes and pressed his thumbs into his eyelids. He had seen the Other Voice, maybe recently. Where? Someone who sounded like the Other Voice. Someone he had met in the last few weeks. He struggled to put the voice to a face. Irrelevant and distracting images appeared to him. Half-formed faces came and went, unrecognized. He pushed his thumbs further into his eyelids. The night club. The amiable Cockney. Archie. Passengers on buses. Chewing gum floors. Jamie. A soulless sixties estate. The ageing thirty-year-old bar man. Dismal concrete pub. The Jug of Ale. The yellow walls and glass-scratched floor. The frequently missed dart board. The Jug of Ale. Where he first met Tattoo and Frying Pan. The threat. The Tattooed skinhead. 'Are you a student?' 'No.' 'Well, you're still a cunt.' Look somewhere, anywhere. 'I said you're still a cunt.' A threat without a Birmingham accent. A heavily tattooed man without a regional accent. Fucking hell. Something was shaping. Images formed as he opened his eyes and stared through the screen of his monitor. He closed his eyes again, and the voices and faces suddenly came together. The telephone voice and the threat voice. He opened his eyes. That was it. It was the same voice. The pub threat remained vivid in every detail and the more he thought about it, the more nasal and educated, and less regional, Tattoo's voice became, until Tattoo's voice became the Other Voice.

The Instigator

This put things in a very different light. Clearly Tattoo wasn't the hired thug Ian had believed him to be. Ian had been taken for a mug, and would have been distraught if he hadn't returned the favour by writing Set a Thief. Tattoo may even have been the instigator of the scam, not that it particularly mattered now. But Ian felt conned. He had been targeted as an unwitting accomplice, and all it had taken for him to fall for it was a phone call from Archie saying that he was being mildly threatened. His life had fallen apart for two long weeks and might never be the same again. But, as Ian sat at Archie's desk gently shaking his head and biting his lower lip, largely in disbelief, he began to understand that what really mattered to him was who had instigated the plan. It was a matter of pride. If he had been duped by a serious criminal mind, then a degree of dignity could be rescued from the situation. Even the dupee can feel a little admiration for the scheme of an intelligent con man. After all, people gladly pay money to be deceived by magicians.

Clearly, someone had to have a plan, an idea, a beginning.

He hoped to God that it was Tattoo. As he stared at his own desk from Archie's chair, he realized that to be duped by Archie would be, at best, unbearable. Ian stretched back in the chair and looked up at the ceiling. He had finally stopped sweating and was getting a little cold. He would probably never know the absolute truth, but it wouldn't hurt to speculate a little. Whoever had got the ball rolling had done it with some style. As plans went, this one had it all. All, that was, except the happy ending. Ian had done the leg work, Archie had the alibi and Tattoo had the disguise. Clearly, Frying Pan, for all his strength, would have been the most vulnerable of the trio had things gone wrong. But Ian's plan, he congratulated himself, had been the most effective.

Ian couldn't help wondering about Tattoo. Maybe Archie had actively sought out criminal experience in the form of Tattoo. Obviously Archie couldn't carry the plan off by himself. And he would have needed financing. There was no way of setting up an account in the first place without the ready funds. A ghost account was possible, as Ian had found out, but only on the back of a real account with real money. So if the instigator was Archie, he would have needed some hefty investment in his scheme. But why had they been on to him so soon? As far as they were concerned, the scam had worked and they were wealthy. What had changed?

Vodka and Magnets

As Ian sat in Archie's chair and looked across his now empty desk he tried to see the world through Archie's myopic eyes. Directly in his line of vision was the back of his own monitor, perched on an untidy desk housing scattered pens and an empty pen holder. The desk also supported a plant that was obviously in its death throes, and which just sat there getting browner and browner from the tips inwards. And beyond the plant and a host of semi-discarded pieces of paper which served as his in-tray, would be the bowed top of Ian's head. That was Archie's view, from morning till evening, day after day. Ian's view was much the same, admittedly, but maybe didn't involve quite as much animosity. It was difficult, but having tried to see as Archie saw, Ian now tried to think as Archie thought. There must have been a turning point, perhaps when he finally realized that Ian's disdain was actually concealing unadulterated hatred. He would have been well aware of indifference, from fairly early on, but not, until this point, of anything more active. Rudeness had crept into Ian's tone, somehow, and the longer his semi-permanent contract had dragged on, the more aggressive he had become. Somewhere during a damp April Ian had reached a point where he was intent on little more than invoking running battles of conversation when in Archie's presence. And through his terse exchanges a more tangible loathing began to dominate which must have become obvious. Ian had tried to conceal it at first, with sentences that started out viciously and ended in a more placatory tone, but it must have been apparent that Ian had eventually stopped censoring himself. Conversations exceeded mere provocation and finally bordered upon bullying. Archie, to his credit, had reacted by doing his level best to irritate Ian whenever possible, and this at times had been more than effective given that Ian seemed to have a head start on most people as far as irritability went. So Archie had just cause to feel aggrieved.

Ian rocked back slightly in Archie's chair, folded his arms and continued to shake his head gently. He surveyed Archie's desk and then looked down at the locked drawer. He tugged it, but it held fast. Why would his drawer still be locked when he had clearly quit? He gave it a firmer tug to no success. A use suddenly occurred to Ian for the paper clips in Archie's unlocked drawers. He unfurled one into a straight, if periodically kinked, piece of wire and stabbed it optimistically into the drawer lock. A couple more waggles and it would jump open, if films were to be believed. Not for the first time in Ian's life, they weren't. Ian continued to stab and waggle, and as he did so, he wondered how Archie had tried to rationalize his conspicuous antipathy. He probably had no idea why Ian didn't like him. He may even have tried to think it through from Ian's perspective, which would have proved difficult to the point of futility for the one-dimensional nylon man. Unable to move on from one problem to the next until he had solved the first, no matter how inaccurately, Archie would doubtless have come up with a nonsensical reason, like envy or something. Ian stabbed a second paper clip into the aperture but the lock refused to budge. He stood up. This would take some thought. He looked down at the knee-height wooden drawer, then turned round and kicked it smartly with his heel, and once more for luck, before kneeling down in front of it to examine his handiwork. The whole facia came off in his hand as he pulled the handle to open the drawer, signifying a job well done. He peered inside. There were two objects – a horizontal bottle of Vodka, which was nearly empty, and a matchbox. The label of the bottle was decorated with a small sticker, which had 'Plant Food' written on it in neat biro-ed letters. Ian stared at it for a couple of seconds, before opening the matchbox. Inside were four or five small magnets clustered together. Alcohol and magnets. It wasn't a particularly appetising mix. Plant food. He opened the screw-top bottle and sniffed and was rewarded with a faint odour of alcohol. Plant food. Ian looked over to his own desk and at the only plant in the room, his limp, browning spider plant. He stood up. 'The cunt!' he shouted, rushing round to the other side of the room. He lifted the lacklustre leaves out of the way and sniffed, but was unable to detect anything more pungent than the soil itself. Colourless and virtually odourless Vodka. The devious sod. So that was why the fucker was on its last legs. Archie had been treating it to a regular dose of Vodka when he wasn't around. The devious bastard. It was difficult to imagine Archie capable of expressing such, for want of a better word, personality. But this was the very point. Ian would never have imagined Archie having the potential for such behaviour if he hadn't experienced the insanity of the last few weeks. Archie was dull, as dull as ditch water, or so he had believed. But maybe that wasn't very accurate any more.

Ian returned to Archie's desk and shook the box of magnets distractedly. The worse thing about it all was that Ian had probably comprised the bulk of Archie's personal interaction, and he alone had made it bitter. Ian had made what was quite probably the only human contact Archie experienced on a daily basis a miserable affair. Archie's working days had become a silent agony. He woke up alone, breakfasted alone, travelled to work alone, and save for lunchtime, when Ian risked the canteen and Archie ate his sandwiches in the office, Ian had been his primary contact with humanity. And, to make matters worse, Archie shared most of his free time with aliens. Magnets. He scratched his head. So that was it then. Revenge. That was as good a motive as any. Ian had made Archie's life a misery, and Archie had returned the favour. And fantastic revenge it was too. Ian puffed his cheeks out and let the air escape through pursed lips. Archie had pulled him apart at the seams. Ian had been forced to face his vilest demons. He had been made, with his obvious fear of the police, to act illegally. He had had his carefully nurtured, routine existence shattered. He had been forced, as a lucratively paid Tractor, to make a large sum of money for an underpaid Permie. And, worst of all, Archie had forced Ian to show feeling, compassion and emotion towards him. And he had even arranged for him to be beaten up for good measure.

Archie had very probably been the instigator. Day by day, he had rooted out Ian's weaknesses by vexing him as thoroughly as possible, and bit by bit, and in moments of unguarded frustration, Ian's failings had appeared like gaps in the clouds. The icing on the cake, however, was that Archie had dreamt up a way of exploiting all of Ian's weaknesses simultaneously. Aside from the issue of lost pride, Ian felt a sense of admiration for Archie that had never been called upon before. If Archie was the instigator, he had shaken free from his dogged adherence to propriety, common sense and reason, and Ian felt pleased about this in that he believed, whatever the motive, that he had been responsible for Archie's transformation.

But none of this explained why they had been on to him.

Doom

Ian drummed his fingertips on his teeth and switched Archie's workstation off and then on again, to reset it. Maybe he had misprogrammed. He listed the files on Archie's hard drive. It was virtually empty. One directory which remained unscathed, and which Ian hadn't come across before, was called Doom 2. Ian opened it up. It was an alien shoot 'em up on demo. He had never noticed Archie playing it, and guessed that it was a recent acquisition. Archie had more than likely installed it to kill some time while he served out his notice. He started the game up and was greeted with the message, `Preview version, release date 3rd October 1997:` Ian stopped. An awful thought occurred to him. He closed the game down and brought up the internal clock. `13:04, Wednesday, 8th October 1997.` But it was Saturday, Saturday 4th of October. He opened up the directory again. `Preview version, release date 3rd October 1997.` The fucker! The petty fucking wanker. Archie had brought the clock of his computer forward sometime last week to load a game which wouldn't normally be accessible until the 3rd of October. And for the sake of playing a game four days before its official release, he had fucked Ian's timing up completely. Set a Thief had kicked in early and then deleted itself. No wonder they were on to him. It was time to get the hell out of the building.

There was no way he could go home, and to hang around here would only invite disaster. He needed a bank. He had his wallet and his passport. He looked at his watch to check that Archie's computer at least had the right time. Fuck. He had missed Saturday opening at the bank. Fucking banks. Useless, closed, brainless, inaccessible fucking banks. This made things difficult. Wary of staying too long at work, he turned on his computer and typed a rapid letter.

On his way out of the office, probably for the last time, he walked over to Archie's wall calendar. September had all but disappeared under a succession of identical, top left to bottom right biro lines, one per day, three on Fridays, to include Saturday and Sunday. There was, however, a large gap in the month, which represented the days that Archie hadn't been at work. Ian had watched Archie perform his ritual almost every evening for ten months now, and it riled him. It was a grateful deletion of each day, a celebration that one more day had been lived and would never have to be lived again. In this way, Archie hadn't so much been marking time as counting out his misery in day-sized boxes. Ian snatched the calendar from its wall fixing, tore it in half and threw it in Archie's bin. As he left the office, the useless cassette player caught his eye. He picked it up and was about to achieve a long overdue ambition by smashing it violently on to the floor when an unpleasant idea occurred to him. He put the tape machine down on his desk, and using the rounded end of a still-folded paper clip, loosened the two cumbersome screws at the back which held the wretched thing together. Ian removed the back panel, peered inside and then swore. This really was taking the piss. Trying to ruin his life was one thing, but putting magnets inside his cassette player was quite another. No wonder the fucking thing played tapes erratically and then rendered them unplayable. And he was willing to bet that from time to time Archie varied the number of magnets just to keep him guessing. Ian fulfilled his original ambition and as the machine hit the floor it died with a hollow and unconvincing thud. Ian finally left the office and headed down the interminable corridor towards the exit, and, while he was in the business of tidying up loose ends, he walked into Jamie's office and turned his computer on. It prompted him for a password. Ian typed 'p-a-s-s-w-o-r-d'. The workstation booted into action.

'Obvious wanker,' he sighed, turning it off and leaving the office.

Shedding a Skin

At the airport, Ian relaxed. He was about to shed a skin. He had virtually no possessions and the lack of weight made him dizzy. He had an unencumbered hour and wandered around the kiosks that populated the space where useful shops might have been if common sense had ever prevailed upon airport design. There was virtually no point in spending an hour purchasing nick-nacks. Besides, from now on, he would be living in style. He was the least prepared traveller in the history of travel, but what he did have he had in abundance. He had cleared his two bank accounts out first thing and had a healthy wad of three thousand pounds or so in his pocket. It felt good through his jeans. But this was nothing compared with what was to come.

He bought a cup of tea which had never seen a tea plant, diluted it with some milk that had never seen a cow and sweetened it with some sweetener which had never seen the outside of a laboratory. Two nights at the Hilton, Heathrow, a mad dash into London to his bank and several travel agents, the letter had been posted and everything was ready.

The letter instructed the investment house to transfer eight-and-a-half thousand pounds from his account to his bank on the first of every month. One hundred thousand pounds a year and he might still only be spending the interest. In the rush of his departure he had no way of knowing exactly how much money he was worth. He had assumed that he would have the time to do things properly. Set a Thief would have transferred everything but the initial quarter-of-a-million pound stake from Frying Pan et al's account into his own ghost account, so that he would be living off the profits maybe of a single trade in the City on a single Monday a week ago. Ian was not naïve enough to believe this would be a small amount. A tiny margin of profit was sufficient enough when traders traded with hundreds of millions of pounds. At the very minimum he had several hundred thousand pounds to his name. And the great thing was that he had erased all record of his actions. All that remained in account 478-4266-5911628 was the original quarter-of-a-million pounds.

Ian had decided not to touch this for two reasons. First, account 478-4266-5911628 was a genuine account set up with genuine money, money that someone had put up for the scheme, someone who would be eager to have it returned to them. To have taken this would only increase the urgency with which he would be pursued once his scheme became apparent. Second, was Archie, who would be forced to return to his old job, where he would doubtless spend weeks or months torturing himself trying to retrieve the money. It was also a firm bet that Frying Pan and the Other Voice would encourage Archie as much as they could in his endeavours. Maybe he would get caught. Ian's account was almost certainly untraceable, just a number, with nothing to link it to him or anybody else. Computers were like that. You didn't have to see any real people any more and this was the beauty of it. No bank manager, bank tellers, financial advisors or

investment consultants to identify you – no people, just numbers, cash-point machines, faxes, emails and remote banking
(press 1 to check your account, 2 to order a statement, 3 to
authorize bill payment . . .).

Bus Lane

He didn't want to kiss her. He was looking at her from the other side of the abyss and she was looking back. Between them lay a gulf of time, change and other partners. Before, he had imagined it would be all he could do *not* to kiss her if he ever saw her again.

Their bodies made a pact the first time they were alone and naked together which their minds hadn't been party to, and which had kept them together for the months at the end of the relationship, when their minds refused to concur. During this time, their bodies continued to meet in secret. It would have been easy to call it shallow, to say that they had long since left each other emotionally and all that kept them together in the end was the joining of their hips, but no, their physical love for one another was deeper and wider than any spiritual love could ever have been. Their physical love had no arguments, no conflicts, no external issues. It was opening, accepting, enveloping and satiating. It had just one aim. It was like lying two ice-creams one on top of the other and watching them melt into each other, until there was no other.

So Ian was surprised that he didn't want to kiss her, with her face here, in front of his, talking and smiling and frowning and telling him how much money she had saved him on the ticket. She stopped talking, leant her head towards his and kissed him.

He had been trawling the travel agents in Euston. A car slowed, stopped and then beeped. London, noisy, messy, bloody London. He looked at the car. It was her. Another horn, from a taxi. And another. She was beckoning, almost frantically. He walked over, his legs trembling a little. She leant across and wound the passenger window down.

'Get in.' He got in. 'I'm in a bus lane,' she explained, pulling smartly away and rejoining the traffic in the outer lane. He said nothing. She seemed to be driving largely by the rear-view mirror, but he realized after a few seconds that she was looking at her hair and surreptitiously adjusting it when she thought he wasn't looking.

'Where're you heading?' she asked.

'I don't know,' he replied, which, however honest, appeared evasive.

'Oh.' She frowned. 'Well, have you got time for a coffee?'

'S'pose so, if you make it a tea.'

'Oh, I forgot . . .'

They sat down at one of the vacant pavement tables in front of a café. It was getting cold and they fidgeted in the cool, early October afternoon air. She told him that she hadn't intended to move to London but her sister had offered to put her up when she moved out and here she still was and she'd started seeing someone here who thought that Birmingham was somewhere near Manchester and she had a job now and it wasn't that bad once you got used to it and what does he do? he's a scientist, an academic, and they were thinking of, you know, looking for somewhere.

'So, what about you?'

'Oh, you know, nothing much really.'

'Come on Ian, you must have done *something* since I . . . since we split up.'

'No, not really.' Ian looked past her. 'Same stuff in the same order, day in day out.'

'Same breakfast?'

'Same breakfast.'

'Football every Wednesday?'

'Every Wednesday.'

'Sainsbury's once a week?'

'Yeah. Well . . .' It irked him that he was being ridiculed for the very things he had built his life around, the very things that had been denied him for around three weeks now. He looked at her. '. . . actually, you might find this hard to believe, but no, I haven't played football on a Wednesday evening, haven't had a decent breakfast, been shopping, or done anything I've wanted to do for weeks now.'

'Why not?'

'Oh, I dunno.' He wanted to tell her everything – how his life had switched back to its stickleback existence when she left, how he had lost faith in almost everything, how he still couldn't think about Neil, how two psychopaths had disrupted his carefully programmed world, how he was now a man of considerable but undetermined wealth – but he couldn't face going through it all again. And the fewer people that knew, the better.

Sue gazed at him inquisitively. 'Something *has* happened to you, hasn't it?'

'Not really,' he lied. 'I've just decided to quit my job and go travelling.'

'Yeah?'

'Yeah.'

'Why?'

'Oh, you know . . .'

'No. I don't know.'

'Since you left, I . . . you know . . . it's just . . . I've not really . . .' Ian was trying to express a genuine feeling, but the feeling was having none of it. He swallowed it, which was much easier. 'I just fancy a change, that's all.'

She had insisted on bringing the ticket to him at his hotel. She had a friend who worked as a travel agent and could get him a cheap ticket. He wanted to tell her that the money didn't matter now, but said nothing.

She kissed him again. The first kiss had taken him by surprise, the second more so, since he had failed to reciprocate the first.

'What about your scientist?'

'Shut up. I want you to kiss me goodbye.'

He kissed her. And again. He felt her press herself tightly against him. She tried to tug his shirt off over his head but his hands got stuck as the cuffs were pulled inside out.

'You'll have to undo the buttons on the cuffs,' he instructed.

'No. I don't think I do,' she said, smiling.

She took one step back from him and began to undress, slowly, teasingly. Ian was stranded. He tried to pull his hands out of the cuffs. Sue undressed to her underwear and then led him over to the bed. She laid him diagonally across it and took his shoes, socks and trousers off. She took the inside-out body of his shirt and looped it over the nearest bed post.

'Now, if you try to free your arms, there'll be trouble,' she warned. He didn't struggle.

His flight was called. During Saturday and Sunday at the Hilton, he had entertained himself with the question of where. Clearly, he had to go somewhere. He had two years on the ticket that Sue had got him, and a choice of starting destinations. Spain. No, too underworld, and full of Cockneys. Brazil. No, too Great Train Robbery. Australia. Too far. America. Would need a work permit to stay for any length of

time. Round the World. Hard work. On the move. No chance
to establish any routines. Fuck it, round the world. That was
the point. In the first travel agents he visited he had suddenly
realized that that *was* the point. Go round the world, leave
yourself behind, at home, with your friends and parents.
Take the you that you never really see, the you that you hide
behind day to day life, the you that you shield with actions
and routines, the you that you drown in beer, the you that you
try desperately to lose in someone else when you are in love,
the you that you go to work to avoid, the you that torments
you on Sunday mornings, the you that you try not to think
about, in short, the conscious, spontaneous, instant you.

In the morning, he wanted to ask Sue to come with him.
They had hardly slept and he had the kind of dazed, happy,
morning numbness that he remembered from the first few
weeks that he had known her, when they would fuck and talk
all night. He tried to ask her but she covered his mouth with
her palm. He knew as he was struggling with the awkward,
cumbersome words which describe simple feelings that it
would be futile, but he wanted to ask anyway. She answered
with her hand.

As he finished his tea he realized that it was as if they
hadn't been apart at all. They had still managed to have a
mild argument over something trivial, and yet had had fantastic, perfect, complete sex. It was almost automatic.

In the end, he chose Nice. It was certainly nice there, and
he wouldn't feel too conspicuous given its popularity with
British holiday makers. It wasn't much of a dent in the overall journey, admittedly, but it was a start. Besides, it was good
policy not to wander too far until he knew the money was
safe.

The final call. This was it. He prepared to shed his skin. A
new start. He reached for his ticket. Inside was a note.

'0171 280 2801, when you find somewhere . . .'

Nice, Seven Months Later

Ian established a new breakfast routine. He removed the second *pain au chocolat* from the boulangerie bag and sipped from his glass of orange juice. The kettle switched itself off and he poured some water on top of a tea bag of English breakfast tea. He still didn't like coffee and he still hadn't called Sue.